8 95

This Bygone

Ron Berry

First Impression—June 1996

ISBN 1 85902 321 5

© Ron Berry

All rights reserved. No part of this book may be reproduced, stored in a retrieval system, or transmitted in any form or by any means, electronic, electrostatic, magnetic tape, mechanical, photocopying, recording or otherwise, without permission in writing from the Publishers, Gomer Press, Llandysul, Ceredigion.

This book is published with the support of the Arts Council of Wales.

*Printed in Wales at
Gomer Press, Llandysul, Ceredigion.*

I

The stooped official jerked his thumb. 'Down the Four Deep with Irfon Tŷ-isaf.'

'My butty gone bad then?'

'Llew copped a bump yesterday.'

'Much?'

The overman jetted mucus: left nostril, right nostril. 'Fishplate flew out from a pair of fourteens, clouted him across the *gwddog*.'

'Al'right is he?'

'Should be in a few days. Get on now, Dewi, do as I said.'

Dewi Joshua had the self contained style of youthful dream, feline eyes upslanted inside blunt cheekbones, his wedgy jaw pitted with a chin dimple. Dream dwelt in the light-flecked Tartar eyes.

He tramped Pencaer main to a double-parting where men and boys were resting.

'Irfon Tŷ-isaf!' he shouted.

'What's up, kid?'

He squatted beside the collier. 'I'm with you, Irfon, because my butty took a bump.'

'So I heard.' Irfon squirted Ringer's juice. 'Any 'bacco?'

'Nuh, myself I don't bother.'

Irfon into chuckling, 'What you got in your box?'

'Sardine sandwiches, piece of *teisen lap*.'

Irfon gave him a friendly nudge. 'Mine's a crib of a place. No allowance either.'

'We had a two foot roll in our heading few months back.'

'Ne'mind about Llew Kitchener, man's a bloody *trych*. Seven shifts a week, the fucken grab.'

Dewi grinned. 'Aye, every Sunday Llew's on that big holt out on the main.'

'There's a few *trychs* in this pit, some on the Lodge even.'

'Pencaer's not a bad pit though,' he said.

'You eighteen yet?'

'Next September.'

'Keep your eyes open, boy. Nasty scaling peeling off of clay joints in my stall.'

'We never set eyes on those in Llew's place.'

'Bugger Llew Kitch,' said Irfon.

Dewi shrugged unspoken loyalty to Llew.

'Tell you straight, fella, agenst the time we fill three and pack that top hole, pair of us'll be like dishrags.'

'I'll do my whack, Ive.'

'No doubt.'

They walked down the Four Deep, men and collier boys trailing away into headings below another double-parting. Irfon went into the second heading, turned left again into the fifth stall.

'Dry as a bone down here,' he said.

Irfon bellowed like a cheer leader, '*Y Pencaer ew y gora, y gora, y gora, y go-o-ora!*'

'New one on me, Ive.'

'Not much humour in you.'

He said, 'I can take a joke.'

'Better had. This do for a wardrobe?'

Dewi hung his jacket and pullover on slivers of wood jammed into the gob wall.

'Righto, sonny-boy, scrounge both sides so's we'll have enough for our first dram. I must lay a pair of yard pieces before Joby comes.'

Kneeling in the face, he hewed and shovelled small heaps of coal back to the top of the road. Irfon cleared shot-fired roof muck, forcing his round-nosed shovel into the debris. Squatly built, long armed, thick nimble legs, Irfon had quick dark eyes and the round lumpy face of a sharp-natured battler.

Dewi sounded the coal with the head of a patent mandrel. Undercutting the seam, he said, 'Hard as the bloody hobs.'

'Mind that scaling over the top coal.'

'Hey, what's your real last name, Ive?'

'Francis.'

'Funny, I didn't know that.'

Irfon paced his grunts, hacking furrows in the debris. He cramp-nailed yard-long pieces of rail to the end sleeper.

Flaky shale rustled soft, shining, floating down. Dewi crabbed back from the seam. 'Listen.'
'Dribbling. Go careful.'
'Where's your regular butty, Irfon?'
'Bad in bed.'
'Oh aye.'
'Real bad.'
'Is he?'
'Spot on his lung. 'Flu to start off, then bronchitis, now he's fucken TB more'n likely.'
'By the Christ,' he said, clambering down over the top hole muck. 'I'll stick a post up,' then, 'Joby's coming.'
'Another backslider from Sinkers' Huts.'
'There's a lot like Joby. Big thing years ago, religion.'
Irfon said, 'Leave it there. Help Joby with our empty.'
Joby unshackled the pony. He trilled soft tuneless whistling. The pony pissed. 'Get your arse by here, boy.'
They heaved together, tumbling the empty tram in a layby.
Joby shackled his pony to the full tram. 'Your turn'll be hour from now. Manage?'
'Aye.' Irfon looked up into the face. 'Fetch me two flats, Joby.'
'We could use some four'n half Norways,' said Dewi.
'Norways an' all. My new butty's full of himself.'
Joby to Irfon, 'Remember this boy's old man?'
'Theo Joshua, worked hard headings up Cwmffrwd North.'
Irfon lightly butted Dewi's shoulder. 'Theo laid out a few blaggards in his day.'
'Too fucken right,' vowed Joby.
'I was just a kid,' he said.
The haulier cracked falsetto, 'Course you was!'
'Still in Infants' School when he died.'
'The dust'll beat any man,' said Joby. He rode out, crouched, one foot on the gun, the other on the hitching plate.
Irfon went, 'Zsstuh,' spurting brown juice. 'Level bed will do us.'
'I'll stick a post up first.'
'Leave it to me, boy.'
He flung coal, a full-armed throw over the debris into the

tram. Rankled by allegiance, he said, 'Llew and me, we used to clear every top hole before we started filling.'

'That *trych* never had a rough place in Pencaer. You can kick it out in Llew's heading.'

'Good face slips, aye, not like this stall.'

Irfon roared shallow rancour, 'Grow up, kiddo! Llew's Elsie, she's flashing her fanny in the Con or the Legion Club every weekend.'

'Rumours, I thought.'

'Don't be so bloody daft.'

'Naah, it's town rumours.'

'Some men'll poke anything. Tell you, boy, whooring, backhanders, y'know *trumps*, and a cushy place on the coal, they go together in Pencaer.'

'Now you're talking. That's Llew, big trumps.'

'Ossie the checkweigher and Dai Greg, they take turns with Elsie Kitchener.'

'Street corner bullshit, Ive,' he said.

Hooting derision, 'She's like the whoor of Babylon!'

'Blokes get jealous of Llew.'

Irfon laughed, shovelling like fury. 'We'll be holing away, cutting under the stank for hours, lucky if we pull enough for three drams all told.'

'It's hard al'right, Ive.'

Their tram was barely filled when Joby came. He rode out as before.

Irfon cleared roof muck. He laid a pair of two yard rails, 'Take the right hand rib, Dewi. I'll work up from the other side.'

Lying down at full stretch, they undercut the seam. He hacked mindlessly, gobbets of coal spurting from the point of his mandrel.

Eleven o'clock came, Irfon saying, 'Give Wyndham Mabon a shout.'

He crawled up the face. 'Wyndham! Ready for grub?'

Wyndham Rhys and his nineteen year old son, Ellis, came down to Irfon's stall.

Comfortably handsome, Ellis said, '*Shwmae*, Dewi.'

'*Shwmae*, Ellis, how's things?'

Said Wyndham, 'He's stinking of last night's beer. Say, what's the word on Llew Kitchener?'

'By what I've been told, Llew'll be out for a few days.'

'Fool to himself, Llew is. Once he breaks he'll go like a shadow.'

They went back in the road. Dewi sat by Ellis. Respite, restfulness accumulating until Dewi said, 'Try one of these, Irfon. Sardines.'

'Swop you for a paste. Honest, you'd swear my Missis was brought up on the fucken parish.'

Wyndham complained informally, 'Roll on knocking off time.' He drank water from a beer flagon. 'Boring tomorrow, Irfon?'

'Sure to. What's wanted, a few pops in the coal, give us chance to fill the turn.'

'Dai Greg wouldn't give you the skin off a grape.' Wyndham called, 'Catch,' lobbing half an apple to his son. 'There's a pile of us on the min down here in the Four Deep.'

Casually from Ellis, 'It'll spew out once we knock through.'

He said, 'Knock through?'

'Should do,' grinned Irfon, and, 'Ta,' to Dewi for a piece of *teisen lap*. 'There's a cross heading from Farley's district. Three shifts on it.'

Said Ellis, 'They're marking twenty-five, twenty-six drams a week, raced up, not level bed like ours.'

Wyndham clicked open his brass-cased pocket watch. 'Aye, near enough another twenty yards on.'

'We'll be in gravy,' crowed Irfon. 'I'll buy the Missis a quart of paraffin from my first good pay. We've been using candles for weeks.'

'Don't know why you're staying in that Tŷ-isaf cottage,' said Wyndham.

'Family! Been there since my Grancha came down on tramp. *Rhonc* old Cardi with a bible in his pack.'

They watched a cap lamp jouncing in from the mouth of the stall. 'Dai Mighty on his rounds,' said Ellis.

The forty-two year old bachelor fireman hunkered in the roadway. He was undersized, caliban-browed under wide-set eyes and a white ridged nose. 'Finished ripping, Irfon?'

'Packed in the gob, all of it, but there's not a bloody slip in my face.'

The fireman jigged around on his heels. 'Look, policy comes straight from the office. They won't let nobody blow coal in this Four Deep. I don't make the rules.' Dai spoke to Dewi, 'Al'right, boy?'

He pitched down from juvenile, 'Yeh-yeh,' to firm, 'I'm al'right, Dai.'

Irfon balled newspaper wrapping off his sandwiches. He punched it aside. 'How's Elsie Kitch these days, Daio?'

Dai huffed umbrage. 'Know what, your mouth's bigger than a gorilla's. Let me tell you this, my name'll still be good when you're six feet under in Brynrhedyn cemetery.'

Irfon appealed, 'For Christ's sake, get the dirty water off your chest, Daio.'

'Lay off then, just you leave it.'

Irfon carolled, '*Home, home on the range, where the dee-ar and the antelope play, where seldom is heard a discouraging word, and the skies are not cloudy all day* . . . you'd make a smart cowboy, you would, Dai.'

'Dull bugger,' said the fireman. 'More sense in a bottle of pop.'

'Husht, ma-an, there's ears listening.'

Dai Greg sniggered quittance. He ape-walked into the face, sounded the coal with his safety stick, sounded the roof, briefly sat cross-legged and crawled up to Wyndham's stent.

Irfon shook crumbs from his tommy boy. 'See Dai's performance? Never worked on the coal in all his born days.'

Wyndham added, 'Drove haulage, coffee-pot up Cwmffrwd West. Chasing after Mrs. Kitchener, is he?'

'She's Dai's whist partner. Clever ooman, Elsie. Used to be Elsie Evans. She's deep, tongue like a whip.'

'I've seen Mrs. Kitchener in the Legion,' said Ellis. '*Duw*, the shape on her, she makes Mae West look half starved.'

'Hey,' said Irfon, 'Elsie passed every exam in Dewinton Grammar.'

'Matric?'

'For definite.'

Winking at his father, 'I should have stayed in Dewinton,' said Ellis.

Wyndham shouted, 'Innit a bit bloody late!'

Said Irfon, 'There's those who stick to books and those who can't.'

'Won't, you mean,' argued Dewi. 'I didn't like school. I wanted some *dwsh* in my pocket.'

'So this boy is sent to work with Llew Kitch, worst barefaced *trych* in Pencaer,' said Irfon to Wyndham.

Dewi persisted, 'Queer, teachers are, not like other men.'

Ellis flung harsh mockery, 'Women teachers and all! Treat you like dogshit they do.'

Wyndham set off back to his stall. 'C'mon, Bow-wow.'

★ ★ ★ ★

Dewi chalked their second tram at 1 o'clock. Irfon was lining up a top-of-the-road post. Dewi threw another 4½ foot Norway into the face. They hacked shallow indents for the butts of the posts, balanced a steel flat across, Irfon scurrying with a sledgehammer, banging the timbers upright.

'You're pretty good with a hatchet, Dewi-boy.'

Spreading his hand, he said, 'Eight inches from there to there. Llew showed me. Eighteen inches from there to there'—elbow to fingertips. 'And I can notch a pair of timbers, make a measuring gauge for laying rails . . .'

Irfon jeered, 'Pair of wedges you need.'

'Aye, thin.'

He went behind the tram, chopped twelve inches off a Norway and shaped two smooth sided wedges. Irfon raked his arms against the post while Dewi hammered the fox wedges above the flat. Sighting for alignment, Irfon approved, 'Nice and tight, sonny-boy.' He sliced a plug of Ringers. 'Feel safer now 'til our next top hole. Must remember to take the patents out. Pick 'em up in the morning.'

'Righto, Ive, that's my job.'

'Listen, kiddo, there won't be any trumps off me come week next Friday.'

'Few shifts then I'll be back with Llew, I expect.'

They half filled their third tram, Ellis coming down the face, bawling, 'Quarter past two! Tools on the bar!'

Irfon straightened his back in the roadway. 'Knock the patents out, boy.'

He slackened the steel wedges, releasing the slender pick-heads. Pulling into his jacket, he confided to Ellis, '*Iesu*, real graft. Every capful counts in this face.'

They walked out. Confidently strong, innocently brave, Ellis said, 'How'd you get on?'

'Okay.'

'Christ-aye, there's others worse than Irfon Tŷ-isaf in Pencaer.'

'He'll have to ask Ginty the manager to make up his money.'

'My old man's the same most weeks. Fucken mad, sweat your bollocks off for two pounds 'leven and six before stoppages. Just the bare in my docket: one pound sixteen.'

'Lodge should fight the case,' he said.

'No committee-men down the Four Deep, notice that?'

Blinking in summer daylight at quarter to three, they by-passed white-faced afternoon shift men gossiping to the pit shaft from the lamproom. He chalked Irfon's number on the pick-heads, the blacksmith saying, 'They rushed Llew Kitchener into Moel Ward this morning.'

'What for now?'

'Collapsed indoors. Christ Almighty, she was *scraching* for the doctor, Llew's missis.'

He plodded dirt lanes to 9, Dinmel Terrace, his widowed mother hostile against fate: 'Llew Kitchener had a stroke. Finished he is. She'll be in a pickle. God knows how she'll take this, sick man on her hands.'

'What's a stroke, Mam?'

'Hem'rage inside the head, blood vessels go burst up here.'

'Only yesterday a fishplate smacked Llew across the throat.'

'Nothing make sense under the Ystrad and Talbot Company.'

She washed his back and shoulders over the half-cask tub on the kitchen lino. While he soaped and swilled his lower body, Zena Joshua snatched off spent rose blossoms, her sprawling bushes tied in carnival extravagance to the chickenwire fence.

Towel around his waist, he went up to his bedroom. Shine gleamed the knees and seat of his navy blue serge trousers. Darnings thickened the heels of his black woollen socks. His starched white shirt looked new, tingling the skin of his muscled chest.

Zena called up the stairwell, 'When you're ready!'

Corned beef pie and mashed potatoes. Brown gravy curdled like lava to the rim of his plate. Zena drank strong tea with cheese on toast and a triangle of *teisen lap*.

'Well?'

'Tastes great,' he said.

'Some day we might be able to afford a big chunk of silverside.'

'There you go. Myself, I don't feel poor.'

'Like your father, high minded with holes in his shoes.'

'Mam, don't say it. He went through a lot of pain.'

'Yes he did, and I can't forgive myself.'

'To be honest, that's what gets me. Blaming yourself.'

'Theo Joshua died in my arms,' she said vindictively.

'I know, I know.'

Her bitterness squalled raucous, 'There's no such thing as God.'

'Beyond me, you are, Mam. Once you've got the dust, that's the finish.'

'Eat your dinner,' she said.

★   ★   ★   ★

Late afternoon heatwave held Moel Exchange. Zena wore a trimmed cabbage leaf on her head, beneath a corner-knotted square of muslin. She weeded among pansies, bluebells, marigolds, stock and seeding primroses, occasionally spearing slugs under lank daffodil leaves with a broken kitchen fork. At 43 she looked spent without grace, moving slipshod to the backgarden wall, throwing weeds from a cardboard box onto Nantglas bankside. Two newly shorn ewes pecked, sure-footed, across the droughted, black-enamel brook. 'Shoosh,' she peeved, ignored by the ewes.

Lying on the couch with the *Daily Herald*, he felt drowse

closing his eyes. The newspaper lowered to his chin, his breathing steadied into expected oblivion.

He awoke to his mother's, 'Dewi, it's Mrs. Kitchener.'

'Sorry about Llew,' he said.

'Awful shock, boy, terrible, but look, I promised him to give you these.' Elsie Kitchener placed three half-crowns on the table. 'Llew can't talk properly. He said, "Give my butty seven-and-six trumps for next Friday, in case I'm not there." Llew knew *then*, understand? Knew he wouldn't be right to start back in Pencaer. It wasn't the bump though, Zena. What happened, there was no signs at all! No signs of the stroke! Well, I've done what he asked me to do.' Elsie wiggled her ballooning figure, round breasts, belly and buttocks, but her hands and feet were tiny, immaculate, the symmetry of fairyland. She wiped her mouth. 'Poor Llew, he never deserved this. Of course he wasn't *in* with lots of chaps down the pit, but I did my best, looked after him no matter what rubbish they gabbed behind his back. That's Moel Exchange for you. In their eyes a man's supposed to listen to the Fed., keep his mouth shut instead of trying to better himself. Llew Kitchener wouldn't create a fuss. Never a petty word. Always minded his own business. Always, same as yours truly. They go to Ebenezer or Carmel or Horeb or Calvaria or Bethany every Sunday with their bibles, then they want to run Moel Exchange. It's not on, Zena, they won't get away with it. Dewi, I'll bring the rest of your pay next Friday. Who are you working with now?'

'Irfon Tŷ-isaf.'

Elsie pursued amiable luke-warmth, 'Oh, he's al'right, Irfon is. Bright pair, him and Hetty Francis. There's such a thing as not knowing any better. Agreed, Zena? I mean, you've been through it, left all on your own since Theo passed away. Those who help themselves are best off in the long run. Lord above, look at the time! It's all rush.' She splayed three letters from her handbag. 'Must post these. Llew's Uncle Ivor in Australia—shan't see him again. His cousin in Hemel Hempstead—funny old devil, that one. And this is for Llew's sister, Sallyanne who went to Birmingham. Never got married, wouldn't let a fella touch her, no fear. Ta-ta, Zena.' She brimmed a warm smile at Dewi.

'Thanks for coming,' said Zena.

'Promised him, didn't I?'

He pocketed the half-crowns before his mother returned from the front door. Resignation overwhelmed her malice, 'Like stone, Elsie, yet I don't envy her.'

Side by side drinking tea at the table, they gazed out through the kitchen window. Upstream from south-east, a dry weather breeze whiffled roses blazing on the garden fence.

'Think I'll stroll to the Institute for a game of billiards,' he said.

'Same as most nights.'

'Nowhere else is there?'

'Until you start drinking.'

'Suppose so.'

'Or courting. What about Greta Picton?'

'She's off to service in London.'

'Gone already?'

'Yeh, West Ealing. Doubt she'll ever come back to Victoria Street.'

★   ★   ★   ★

He booked a table with Jesse Watts, a top pit labourer from Sinkers' Huts across the G.W.R. lines, eleven back to back wooden shacks felted and tarred before Queen Victoria went into mourning.

Ellis Mabon shoulder-armed him towards the Institute tuck-shop. 'Watch that bloody rodney. Don't trust him.'

'I can beat Jesse,' he said.

'Not safe, man, he's shitten.'

'Only a game of billiards.'

He shared a penny bar of Cadbury's with Ellis, who said, 'I'm going to the Club.'

Jesse came to the tuck-shop counter. 'Lend us tuppence, ah?'

'Bugger off, Jesse.'

'For a packet of Woodbines. Pay you back tomorrow night.'

'What a bloody cadger.'

'Honest, pay you full.'

A clock pinged in the billiard hall. 'Our game,' he said.

Jesse slouched forward, 'Loser dibs out the fourpence.'

Dewi grinned. 'Take you on.'

Jesse taunted him throughout the half hour, threatened to boot him up the arse and clip him across the earhole. The elbow-locked caretaker marched to and fro, tutting for order.

He felt supreme, winning with a 14 break before the bell ended the game.'

'Pay, and no more chops,' he said.

'C'mon, lend us tuppence.'

'Fuck off, Jesse.'

'I'm tuppence short. Give it you back tomorrow.'

He racked his cue. 'So-long, Jesse.'

'Mingy bastard. I'll see you outside.'

'Righto, if that's the way you want it.'

He watched Jesse wrangling with Mal the caretaker, who took Jesse's empty wallet, pledge for the two pennies.

Thumbs hooked in his belt, he leaned against the gate pillar. Straight left, right cross, he thought, but Jesse Watts rushed crouching, throwing round-arm punches.

He backed off. 'What you say?'

'Up and down,' Jesse snarl-faced, lunging, kicking, fists flailing.

Spectators ringed the fight, all ages, crocked pensioners to collier-boys fresh from school. Dewi leapt away, avoiding a kick in the groin, and his head tilted into a right-hander. Numbness ached his skull. The instinctive straight left hit Jesse's mouth. Jesse's lower lip doubled on blood.

'Fight fair, Wattsie,' they were saying.

And, 'Dig him, kid, knock the daylights out of the waster.'

Straight left, right cross, straight left, straight left, straight . . . RIGHT. The punch jolted back to his shoulder. Jesse's face shook to gargoyle, turned blank, unseeing as he buckled. The back of his head went *crack* on a flagstone; only his feet twitched.

'Serve him right,' they were saying.

'Watts asked for it.'

'Sling a bucket of water over him.'

Held slack in his trouser pocket, he cherished warmth throbbing his right hand. He examined his left hand. Two cuts from Jesse's teeth. Well, he won't bother me no more. Settled once and for all, the dirty bastard.

He went back into Pencaer Institute, bought a small bottle of dandelion and burdock and another chocolate. Until ten o'clock he chatted with mates and watched billiards. Men came from the Reading Room, saying, 'You're a good un.'

'There, you've put him in his place.'

'Your Dad should have seen what you did to Jesse Watts.'

Ten to seven next morning, more of the same on the double-parting above Four Deep. Irfon Tŷ-isaf stressed for all to hear, 'I can vouch this butty of mine don't chuck his weight about. Anybody who says different, he's a fucken liar.'

They were on grub back in the road when Dai Greg arrived. As usual, hunkered between them, 'Men, word came down the pit. Young Watts from the Huts, he's not right in the head. Memory gone. Amnesia they call it.' He jigged around to face Dewi. 'You might be in trouble.'

Irfon raged temper, 'Hey, Dai Bad-news, leave the boy alone! Who the fuck d'you think you are? Fucken betsi, g'wan fuck off! Mind your own fucken business for a change!'

Dai sighed a laggard truce. 'Loudmouth they ought to call you, Tŷ-isaf. Me, I got no grudge against any man.' He said to Dewi, 'Don't fret, you fought fair. All reports say the dirty stuff came from Jesse Watts.'

'Jessie'd thieve the shirt off your back,' said Ellis.

Wyndham Mabon reflected, 'Old man Watts went down Cox's Farm years ago. The long strike. He kill't fourteen sheep. Mutton in every one of the Huts.'

'Faaque me pink,' muttered Dai Greg. 'Firing tonight, Irfon? Six pills?'

'Do me, six.'

Dai wrote, *Irfon Francis. 6 pills. 1 det.* Then, 'Posts?'

'Pair of six'n halves, eight four'n half Norways, one flat.'

Dai booked the timber and the steel flat. 'All the best, men. Two months from now on we should be knocking through.'

'*Happy day,*' sang Irfon, '*happy day, when Jesus washed my sins away.*'

Wyndham said, 'Bloody Rechabites used to sing *Happy day.* Most miserable buggers under the sun. Dribs and drabs of Moel Exchange they are.'

17

Holing under the stank again, Dewi speculated about amnesia. Now and again he sounded the tight grained coal. They had to undercut a foot before the seam sagged, and then the graft of hacking out lump coal.

They lost a tram while drilling a six foot hole in the roof. Slow, slow toil, swinging the boring machine handle.

'*I'm an old cow-hand,*' sang Irfon quietly, grunting, spraying Ringer's juice from between his teeth, retrieving the lyric, grunting, concluding as ironic statement, '*Yippee yi okyi fucken ay.*'

'Heard about Llew Kitchener, Ive?'

'I heard, aye.'

'Bloody shame.'

'Like Wyndham said, always been the same, Llew. Fool to himself, no give and take in the sod.'

'Want a change, Ive?'

'In a minute, not yet.'

He sounded the roof. 'We kept that scaling up al'right.'

'Sometimes she'll run to a wafer, other times she drops down like a ball of mine.'

He said, 'Christ, no warning.'

'Keep your eyes open, kiddo.'

Irfon holed under the stank.

Dewi swung his weight on the cranked handle, fine rills of dark grey rock spinning down from the hole.

By one o'clock they were filling coal.

★ ★ ★ ★

Walking out on the main, Ellis said, 'Come to the Legion Club tonight. Let me sign you in.'

'I'm under age.'

'Heap of poop that.'

'Okay. What time?'

'Ha'-past eight. See you there.'

'I got a few bob.'

Ellis swaggered brawny shoulders, wet red lips and white teeth venting above his black, pudding basin chin. 'Sixpence ha'penny a pint, Clyne Strong, cheapest beer there is. We'll get slewed.'

At the dinner table, Zena side-squinting, more curious than vexed.

He dipped mincemeat rissoles in H.P. sauce. 'Mam, any news about Llew today?'

'Tch tch, we-ell, begging with his eyes according to her next door. Big row between Elsie and some doctor from Cardiff. Oh, she called him rotten. But there's no change. Llew might improve, but one side of him never will be much good. Nobody wants to die.'

'Llew's hard as a lump of *avar*. Later on I'll call in Moel Ward to see my old butty.'

Shrilling disgust, 'Dewi *dwl*! The man's critical. No visitors.'

'Do me a favour then. Take Llew some Gold Flake with a bottle of stout. Money's in my drawer upstairs.'

'I'd best see Elsie first. Now listen a minute. Why's it others come telling me about this row outside the 'Stute last night? Answer me that.'

'Bit of a scrap. Jesse Watts's idea, not mine. I don't pick fights.'

'He's serious. Can't remember a thing, can't stand straight on his feet. Mrs. Watts, she'd feeding him sop like a baby. They've kept the police out of it.'

'Jesse fell down bang on the pavement. They all saw it. Jesse was putting the boot in.'

Zena Joshua crimped her mouth. 'Well and good. A man's entitled to stand up for himself.' She smiled bereft disbelief. 'You are more and more like your father.'

'Bound to in a way. Look, Mam, I'm having a few pints with Ellis Mabon tonight.'

'Don't land a summons for under age.'

'Who's to know?'

She said, 'You might get shopped.'

★   ★   ★   ★

He saw their fuzzed heads wavering behind frosted glass.

'Old bags, regulars in the *cwtch* behind the lobby,' said Ellis.

'Locals?'

'Just local.'

He said, 'What's on upstairs?'
'Whist drive night.'
'Mrs. Kitchener up there?'
'I'd say yes. Fancy a dekko?'

He followed Ellis. Rows of small tables in the Concert Room, and Llew's wife sitting opposite Dai Greg, the fireman's pale sandy hair thinly layered across his head.

Ellis sniggered, 'Who'd have thought the fucker was bald? Let's see who's in the Side Lounge.'

'Hullo, boy,' they said. 'Your mother al'right up in Dinmel Terrace?'

'Pretty good, thanks.'
'With Irfon Tŷ-isaf these days then?'
'Aye.'
'Met Hetty his wife in Tonio's *bracchi* shop. She was telling us.'
'Same looks on him as Theophilus Joshua,' they said.
'For definite! One of the best, Theo was.'

He turned to Ellis. 'I wanted to ask Mrs. Kitchener about Llew.'

'Later if I was you. Wait 'til round about ten o'clock.'
'Not bothered much, is she?'
'Christ, course she isn't. What you think of this Clyne Strong?'
'I could do with a slash.'

Ellis pointed, 'Through there, first right. Anybody ask, say you're with me.'

Later he experienced double vision. Two Elsie Kitcheners refused to merge. He stopped, stared down at his feet, felt his eyes wobble when he tried to fast flick-flick to clear his sight.

Dainty in glace court shoes despite her bulk, she came over to him in the Concert Room. 'Dewi Joshua, what a surprise.'

'Howdo, Mrs. Kitchener. Meant to ask you about Llew. Any better, is he?'

'Long job, the specialist said, but I don't trust him at all. Smarmy, too damned *naice*. Llew's trying, he's trying. Dear God, awful to see him struggling. I want him home with me so's I can tend to him. It all depends on the damage. These doctors are tight as misers. They won't come out with anything direct to your face. Ah, here's David Greg. David, d'you know Dewi Joshua, used to be Llew's butty?'

Dai handed Elsie a gin and tonic. 'This boy's in my district now.'

He said, 'I came with Ellis Mabon.'

'Huh, he'll drink you under the table.'

Elsie airily clicked finger and thumb under Dai's thin-boned nose. 'We're all very sociable in the Legion Club. Very friendly atmosphere. Never any fights, are there, David?'

The small-bodied fireman preened his cuffs. 'Uncalled for altogether.'

'Tram home?' she inquired brightly.

'We walked, Mrs. Kitchener.'

'Why don't you catch a tram with us? Ten-fifteen by Sampson's Corner. Nice company for you. David gets off at the bottom of Uplands Road, you at Empire Crossing.'

He felt slow tongued. 'What about Ellis?'

Dudgeon snapped from Dai Greg, 'Chapel Street! Two spits and a *cam* from this Club. Anyhow, we're on our way in a few minutes.' He gestured *drink up* to Elsie.

'Ten-fifteen, Sampson's Corner,' she said. 'Don't rush me, David!'

Downstairs in the Side Lounge, Ellis Mabon was depicting a backhand rugger pass, because he enjoyed pantomiming sporting skills. 'Righto, Dewi, see you on the double-parting.'

In the tramcar he sat behind Mrs. Kitchener and Dai. They were slanging each other, muttering, her shiny black curls shiggling. Dai's dissent jerked against the rake of his pearl grey slouch hat.

Dewi felt drum-tight as a cockbird.

Dai soft-soaped as he left, '*Nos da*, Elsie.' To Dewi, 'So long, boy.'

'Sit by me,' she said.

'I'm off next stop, Missis.'

'I insist. Sit by me.' And then, 'Oh no, really!' her small finger-nails like scarlet beetles on his wrist as the tramcar squealed to standstill at Empire Crossing. 'It's early yet. I'll make you something for supper. You don't want Zena to smell beer on your breath.'

He said, 'Okay, Missis.'

She unlocked the front door. 'When I was your age I was the best looker in Dewinton Grammar. Come inside, Dewi Joshua, and make yourself comfy. Shan't be long.'

Hush in Parc Villa. Posh gramophone cabinet taller than the window board. Wireless on a three legged table. Glass bowl of fruit on the sideboard. He went sniffing pears and Victoria plums. Luscious. Strange woman, Mrs. Kitchener. Brownish photograph of Llew. He'd be in his twenties. Poker face on him, centre parting, wing collar under his chin like a deacon. Old heading man Llew. Photos of her. Countryside snaps in fretwork frames. Huge studio portrait on the wall. Before she put on weight. Long black hair waved to her shoulders. More Spanish than Welsh, shiny curls plastered across her forehead, all smiles, bunch of flowers on her left arm.

He smothered burping. Four pints of Clyne Strong. I'm not used to booze. Few swigs Christmas Eve, sharing a flagon on the q.t. in the *gwli* behind Dinmel. Where's she gone to? Indoor lavs in these Villas.

'For God's sake don't look so shocked'—Elsie Kitchener wearing pink silk shimmering down to pink pom-pom slippers. 'Do you like coffee?'

'*Camp* coffee, aye.'

'Percolated actually, and omelette with ham on a *cwlff* of fried bread. Two eggs for a growing fella.'

She played records while he ate supper, a ringing tenor singing *Your tiny hand is frozen* and some deep contralto's *Can't help loving that man of mine*, which frizzled his nape hairs.

Little finger cocked, Elsie was eating crackers smeared with honey. Her thoughts were direct: Now-or-never—a confluence of past and present. Wildness in his eyes; tame manners as if he's waiting. Night-time eyes. Been-here-before-eyes. Jungle eyes in this Moel Exchange menagerie. Cradle snatcher they'll call me. Names. Duchess when I managed Moel Emporium. Elsie Evans Trousers after I married Llew. Names since I threw away my gymslip and blouse. Their tongues will catch fire. This boy, he's a quiet *cythral* . . . I want him.

He forked a balance of omelette and ham. 'What a voice. *Duw,* she's the best in the world.'

'Mm, we're all the best in the world at certain things.'

Aromas of ham, coffee and honey pulled his senses.

Elsie strolled, swayed, paused behind him, fingertips stroking his temples.

'I'll fall to sleep, Missis.'

'Call me Elsie,' leaning over his shoulder, her lips brushing, tickling the side of his neck.

'But there's Llew, isn't there, laid up in Moel Ward.'

'He won't mind in the least.'

'I'd better go home now, Missis.'

'Elsie!' his head held firm, rolled, jammed at her breasts.

'Oh Christ . . .'

'Enjoy!' from outcry to pleading, 'Enjoy-enjoy-enjoy,' hauling him down to the hearth rug.

At first deluge of wonder, blinding wonder, Dewi Joshua losing Dewi Joshua. Lost and found. Safely couth and rioting his heart out unbeknown to himself between her heaving thighs. Herself forever and ever.

Deed and sequel bared him.

'Lord above, *cariad,* that was awful strong of you,' her small hands palming over his ribs, his belly, his loins. Mysterious as sky, her dark brown eyes staring. 'Feel nice now?'

'Great.'

'Our secret.'

'Right.'

She cuddled him. 'Lovely boy you are, my lovely boy.' A nipple squashed at his eye. 'Ever so good.'

He mumbled, 'I won't tell nobody.'

Sharp tingling delight then she breathed, 'Cross your heart.'

Struggling with the obeisance, 'Promise.'

Elsie bounced his head off her bosom before lunging free. She reached two napkins from the sideboard drawer. 'Wipe yourself.'

Watching her, thinking, she's white as milk, she's big, she's huge, two times huger than Greta Picton who wouldn't let me. Pee tee Greta. No doubt she'll try a Cockney bloke. Any road, best of luck.

Her curly black head surfaced. 'Mustn't tell a soul,' she repeated, the pink gown slurring down to her feet as if alive.

'Elsie, mind if I ask you something?'

'Now now, lovely. I may answer lies so as not to cause offence.'

'Worst anybody can do, tell lies. Aah, thanks for the supper.'

'My pleasure, *cariad*,' hugging him, swaying on tiptoes.

'Elsie, let's make a date for Saturday night.'

She gently kneed his crotch. 'Too risky. Just leave things be as they are.'

'Please, Elsie.'

Softly low-pitched plaint as she swung to and fro, 'Leave well alone.' Then swiftly flashed arrogance, 'Out the back way.' She switched off the light. 'Hurry.'

Under hazed starlight they smudged kisses on each other's faces.

'Goodnight.'

'G'night, Elsie.'

'Take care, boy.'

'Aye, know what you mean.'

★   ★   ★   ★

Monday morning, the cage grounded like velvet at pit bottom, Irfon saying, 'That Jesse Watt's starting back, saw him coming over the gantry. Fuck all the matter with Jesse, only short on guts.'

He said, 'Word came to my old lady about Jesse being ready for work.'

'Right bloody set across there in the Huts.'

'Llew Kitchener's on the mend,' he said.

'He is, fair play. The man's contrary 'cause he's losing time. Llew's beat though, won't pull coal agen in this pit. You wait, Llew'll mooch around town 'til he's ready for his box. Awkward bastard he is.' Irfon shrugged. 'They might shove him in the lamproom.'

'Hope they do,' he said. 'If Llew's idle he'll go mad.'

Shoulder to shoulder they tramped Pencaer main, Irfon confiding, 'It's work to rule, butty, until we knock through into North

Main. Me and Wyndham have agreed. From now on it's work to rule, and Dai Greg can go and piss into the wind.'

He said, 'Take better men than us to fill three a shift down there.'

So they carefully timbered the face, kept their stalls safe, gob walls neat, packed to the roof. They intended filling two trams a shift and driving on three yards a week instead of four or five.

'Men, I'm with you,' conceded Dai Greg, their work to rule like a splinter in his fireman's conscience, 'but it's you'll have to take your case to the office. Understood?'

'We'll bring in Ernie Spiller the Lodge chairman,' they said.

Dai rapped his safety stick on his boot. 'No chance at all. Like red rag to a bull, Bolshie Spiller to Ginty the manager. What Sid Ginty'll do, he'll dump you lot on company work by afternoon, then sign a fresh batch of men on a promise. They'll take the cream after we knock through.' Dai rapped his boot again. 'Let me tell you the plan. Keep this confidential—you, Irfon, you, Wyndham. You two boys. Righto. Brand new electric cutter, four foot six jib on her. She'll run nonstop, every stall from this district back to the supply road. Get that? Easy coal. It'll fall out. Forget about under-cutting the stank. You'll fill five, six a shift. Faaque me, in no time you'll be traipsing 'round Moel Exchange like bookies in plus fours.'

Said Ellis, 'Dai, how much a ton is cutter coal?'

'As far as I know, near one-an'-tenpence. Down here you can pile drams up to one-ton-six or seven. There's height enough up the Four Deep.'

'What you think, Irfon?' inquired Wyndham.

'Can't work out the bloody figures! I need pencil and paper.'

Dai was dogmatic, 'Remember the extra yardage. Stands to reason you'll clear more yardage.'

Ellis said, 'Twenty-five drams comes to two pounds fifteen, counting level bed as a ton.'

Hands on his knees, Dai pushed himself upright. 'Collier and his boy should fill thirty-five drams, that's well over forty-five tons a week. Once we've cut some *pwcins* here and there, they'll go up the Four Deep, no bother.' Sincerely urgent, he said, 'Look, I'll put your case to the manager as regards a few pops up the rib sides. Make things easier for you for the time being. Fair offer?'

'It's taken you a fucken long time,' said Irfon.

They went into the face with the fireman, Dai pleading, 'Listen, Ginty wants us to knock through, quicker the better for the new cutter. Therefore, see,' (sounding the hard coal), 'I can supply facts to Ginty about these conditions.'

Irfon thrust forward, grinning under the glare of Dai's cap lamp. 'They'll tell me Sid Ginty fancies himself, he's a proper ram on the quiet. Tell Siddo Mrs. Kitchener's on the batter.'

Stifling giggles through his nose, Dai Greg went up the face.

Dewi gripped himself against shivers.

Irfon bellowed after Dai, '*In the sweet by and by, we shall meet on that beautiful shore.*'

'*In the sweet, in the sweet by and by,*' sang Wyndham and Ellis, crawling behind Dai Greg.

★   ★   ★   ★

He saw Llew Kitchener in the Reading Room, gawkily motionless as a heron at the newspaper rack, his once gaunt face fleshed podgy, feeble right hand hidden in his jacket pocket, his mouth corner-tucked, a grey-blue droop in the outer nook of his right eye.

'*Shwmae,* Llew'—offering a Cadbury chocolate. 'Know what, Ellis Mabon joined the army. Mates see, me and Ellis, next stall to us down the Four Deep until they put him behind the cutter. How you feeling, Llew?'

Llew's head lowered, peak of his cap hovering. 'I've seen um, Dewi. Men been abroad, men done twelve years, soldiers since they were boys with the Borderers or the Guards. First thing, new working boots, new round-nosed shovel. Buy shovels their-selves. No Company tools. Then sent nights in the muckhole or filling out muck for repairers. No chance of a place on the coal. I've seen um, aye, stripes on their arms, medals for this and that, but there's damn all else for um in the pit.'

'Husht, please. You, Dewi Joshua, husht please,' ordered the lock-elbowed caretaker.

'Sorry, Mal,' he said.

The Institute caretaker accused Llew. 'Rewles! Rewles plain as day struck on that door.'

Llew muttered, 'Fussy bugger.'

They walked home together, the hotchpotch streets transformed by moonglow. Exchange Manor ruins where the town began were a ragged silhouette with nearby hills rolling for all time ever in 1936, tumped below and beyond two horizons with slagtips, odd-sized pyramids still accumulating, landmarks of mining over 180 years. Truck buffers clanked in Pencaer sidings. Ragamuffin kids maypoled on orange box ropes tied to lamp-posts. Sheep slept against the side walls of chapels. Rapt audiences in five cinemas gawped at American epics and classic illusions from Home Counties studios.

'Llew, come to our house for a cuppa tea. Put your feet up. Only my old lady indoors.'

Dour contempt from Llew. 'Don't you start pitying me. Look our for yourself, nobody else will.'

'I'm not bloody pitying you, man.'

Llew's left hand plucked the sleeve of his jacket. 'Boy, enough said.' Carefully slow, he flagged his right arm up and down, up and down. 'Think I'll go to Birmingham for a spell. Been offered by my sister. Smart girl years ago. Cook Sallyanne is now. Do me good to get away.'

'Nothing to lose,' he said. 'Never been on holiday myself. Outings to Aberselsig, Barry once, Porthcawl once.'

'Time drags, boy.'

'Best collier in Pencaer you was, Llew.'

'I might like it up there.'

'Best trumper and all.'

Llew Kitchener turned to face the moon.

'As I for one know personally,' he said.

But Llew was talking to himself, 'Don't take much to put a man down on his arse-end,' then a rare digression, 'Lovely night tonight.'

'Come and have a cup of tea.'

'Trouble is, so quiet in my house, just slop from the bloody wireless. Elsie's always out on the trot.'

At the pitfall of guilt, Dewi said, 'Ah, well . . .'

'I don't want any pity.'

'*Iesu*, Llew, give over.'

'Earned my salt since I was twelve.' Llew joggled himself into striding. 'Never cadged off nobody.' Rage blurted thick. 'There's not much left.'

'Much what?'

'Off work, for fuck's sake! Insurance since July eighteenth.' Llew blundered aside, distanced himself, kept his pace. 'She says, "Being idle, it's affecting your mind. Go on up to Sallyanne Kitchener, stay with Sallyanne 'til you feel more normal."' Slowly pistoning his right arm. 'Guh, until this I went my own road like a good un. No fucker'd best Llew Kitchener in Pencaer.'

Dewi rubbed his hands close to Llew's face. 'C'mon, butty, rhubarb tart and custard, then a cuppa tea better than any *bracchi* shop.'

'Righto, boy.'

Cautious Zena Joshua, warm near the fire with a library Romance, rose to greet them. 'Glad to see you out and about, Llew. Here, sit over by here. Son, fetch Mr. Kitchener a cushion for his back. Put some weight on, Llew? Yes, I can see. Feeling al'right in yourself?'

Llew gazed at his shoes. 'I won't be going down the pit agen.'

'Light job on the Council would suit you.'

He said, 'Mam, let's have some tart and custard.'

Zena thought, he's about the same age as my Theo. Look at the state he's in. Poor man, lost all hope. 'Never mind, Llew,' she said. 'Pointless worrying.'

Llew spooned up the tart and custard, drank a mug of tea, declared like a foreign visitor, 'Thank you, Mrs. Joshua. Goodnight, both.'

'I'll walk with you over to the Villas.'

Llew shook his head. 'Boy, you got to get up for work.'

'Be seeing you then.'

'Unlikely. I'll be raising a ticket to Brum. Thirty years since me and Sallyanne set eyes on each other.'

'That's the idea,' he said.

His mother tushed regret. 'Another one left to moulder. Always the same once they leave the pit.'

Feeling wretched, he clubbed his fist on the table, 'Llew put his guts into Pencaer. Why can't they find him a job in the lamp-room?'

Zena cried outrage, 'There's ignorant for the son of Theo Joshua!'

Then came her mood at breakfast. 'Listen to me, half of Dinmel Terrace are stuck on the parish. Bread and scrape-it for starving kids. After Theo died I went begging outside of Liptons shop. You was reared on charity.' She sniffed misery. 'Jesus God, I'm sick and tired.'

He picked up his tommy box. 'So-long.'

'Go on, pig headed like your father.'

'Only in your mind,' he said.

In the cage he pushed alongside Irfon, who unwrapped a Toffee Rex with his teeth. 'You are, butty, shove this in your chops. Cutter broke down last night. We're back on hand-cut.'

He chewed, saying, 'We'll make our number up by Saturday.'

'Better had. Me and the wife and kids, we're moving to Heol Cerrig, number seventeen. Three bedrooms. Electric light throughout! Hot water for Chrissake, hot water on tap! God's pocket for us, after Tŷ-isaf.' Irfon slurped toffee juice. 'Nigh twice the bloody rent.'

Wyndham shouted down the face, 'How many today?'

'What d'you say?' returned Irfon.

'Four with any luck. Pity to spoil the week.'

Said Irfon, 'We'll give it a go.'

But they toiled and sweated filling their fourth tram. Irfon hung his tools on the bar. 'That's me done in. I'm supposed to start clearing our backyard after dinner.'

Dewi drooped into a squat behind the tram.

'Fucked-up innew, boy?'

'I'm al'right,' he said.

'Bollocks! Admit!'

'What you on about?'

'Tough bugger, won't admit you're beat to the wide.'

'I'll tamp back. Keep your mouth to yourself.'

Irfon laughed into singing, '*Look down, look down that lonesome fucken road, before you travel on!*'
He said, 'Right, *Gymanfa*, let's get out on the main.'
'Hey, there's more wit than shit in Dewi Joshua after all!'
'Bloody Charlie Chaplin you are,' he said.
'Why not? Enough fucken creeping Jesuses in Moel Exchange.'
'Aye-aye aye-aye,' he sneered, weary to his marrow.

★   ★   ★   ★

Asleep on the couch after dinner, he dreamt Llew ran into Parc Villa while he lunged and stranded himself on the white, prodigal body of Elsie Kitchener. Llew whining, shivering like a trapped dog before he keeled over in a frothing dog-fit.
Zena shook him. 'Dewi, wake up.'
Consciousness brought relief, a benign spasm of glory.
'Crying out in your sleep. Bad dream?'
He said, 'I forget. Can't remember.'
'Come to think of it, haven't seen you in tears since you was in Infants' School. Tea's in the pot, won't be long.'
As usual they shared homely peace. Gas lamps softened the dark garden and from down below Dinmel Terrace came the windy gut-rumble of a train in Gaer Cutting.
'Reminds me,' she said, 'Llew Kitchener caught the quarter past nine from Dewinton Halt. I met Elsie outside Boots when I went to fetch Jeyes Fluid for the lav. Buckets and buckets I poured down there to clear it.'
'Llew's gone to stay with his sister in Birmingham. Will he get better, Mam?'
'Not by the seem of it.' She rotated her right arm. 'I noticed wastage.'
'Why Llew, for God's sake?'
'Bad luck, boy, no other reason at all.'
'Lots going away from Moel Exchange, blokes and girls. Mostly girls.'
'What else! Me and your father scrimped and scraped from the day we married in the registrar's in Matabele Crescent. I came

home from Chiswick three weeks previous for us to put the banns in.'

He said, 'Pity about Llew.'

'More than you can say for Elsie Kitchener.' Zena supped her tea as if it were salt water.

'What'll she live on?'

'Huh, there's money there, shares in Wills cig'rettes.'

'The Woodbines?'

'Believe you me,' she vowed. 'Left over from the time Elsie's father went 'round with housecoal. Delivered all over Moel Exchange. Ent they with the *crachach* in the Villas?'

'Park Villa, aye, nice, classy.' He pushed away from the table.

'Lav,' he said.

Becalmed within herself, she watched him pass outside the kitchen window. What will your mother live on when you put some girl in the family way same as your father did? Never saw the light of day, our first baby. Poor little mite.

★ ★ ★ ★

At five past eight he caught a tramcar to the Legion Club. After a quick pint inquiries led him to the Mason's Hall.

Said the doorman, 'Can't allow you in the Concert Room. Whist drive started at half-past seven.'

He signed the Visitor's receipt. 'I'll take a gander later on. Mate of mine, see, real shark with the cards.'

'No interference mind,' warned the doorman.

He dropped two pennies in the box. 'Course not.'

Followed a restless hour until ten o'clock. Club members ignored his name on the sheet. They hogged three tables, two billiards and one snooker. He wondered about Llew, scrupulously regarding him as *gone away* from Moel Exchange, a convenience not to be ignored if Elsie was playing whist in the Concert Room.

She was, partnered by Ossie Ross the Company checkweigher, his thick silver hair immaculately waved as a wig. Imperious Ossie's deep sunken eyes glinty above the meaty snout of his nose, his scooped jawbone jowly from well-being.

Her strange, incisive deceit came as a reward. Several groups were milling between card tables, the stage at the far end, and a nearside hatch where shutters clattered up to serve drinks. Elsie appeared to dither among chairs. Ossie marched, chest out like a celluloid guardsman, to the hatch. She triggered Dewi with her forefinger, upraised palm halting him when he was three yards away, and she made to wind by towards the stage with a sheaf of score cards.

'Quarter past ten on Sampson's Corner. Shh, off you go. Ossie's not safe.'

Funny that, he decided. If it came to the push I'd flatten Ossie in two minutes. Soft as pap sitting there all day in the weighbridge office. Understanding clicked as he walked to Sampson's Corner. Elsie feared a *stab in the back for him*. Whisper-whisper between Ross and Sid Ginty the manager. Fortnight's notice. Send Joshua up the road with his cards. Unless she meant something else. Anyhow, I'm stone sober compared to before.

And as before she disappeared in Parc Villa, changed into the long shining pink gown, returned to feed him with omelette, cold ham slices, baby beetroots and crusty bread rolls coated with butter. Now he *knew* Elsie in his mind, big tender Elsie leading him by hand to her bed (Llew forgotten, abandoned), surrendering and again finding himself in the warm, white woman.

Elsie, Elsie, Elsie—she flamed his life.

★   ★   ★   ★

For the first time since leaving Upper Exchange Council School, he lost a shift, simply grunted noises to his mother's shouts from the foot of the stairs. Too late when she bewailed to herself, 'Bound to sooner or later. I wish Theo was here.'

He slept until mid-day.

Zena demanded, 'Who kept you out last night? Brazen slut whoever she is.'

He said, 'I'm eighteen.'

'Look me in the eye! Guilty conscience is it? Who is she?'

'Mam, keep your nose out, if you don't mind.'

'Neither you nor your father ever spoke to me like that!'

'Al'right, sorry. See, this is my own business.'

'Mine too. I don't want some flag knocking at my door.'

Fearing estrangement but desperate against her, 'Leave me be, for Christ's sake.'

'Stop swearing! Pack your bag whenever you want!'

'Christ Almighty, Mam!'

'Stop swearing, you're not down the pit!'

'What bloody bag? I haven't got any bloody, Christing bag!'

Zena trembled as if afflicted. Too shocked to speak, she stumbled around the wind-tattered garden, Dewi behind her, ashamed, never having embraced, comforted his mother.

He brewed tea while she protested on the couch. 'Worry it is, worry about what's going to become of us.'

'Yeh, you've had your share of worry, Mam.'

'You carry on, boy, do what you think best, suit yourself. No more complaints from me. I won't complain. Sometimes I wish I believed in God. Can't though, can't, not since when I went into service. Slaves we were, silly *crots* of girls from Wales, all of us mad to get married instead of feeling homesick. Slaving all hours under the sun for the English, English and Jewish. *Duw*, I cried and cried, sick inside myself with *hiraeth*.'

His 'Aye,' of sympathy droned like amen. He said, 'Irfon Francis is moving to Heol Cerrig. More rooms for their five kids.'

'Genuine he is, one of the old families.'

'We are, Mam.'

'Yes, I can't see you catching a train for London.'

'I don't think about it.'

'Work in the morning?'

He promised. 'Right on the dot.'

★ ★ ★ ★

The Longwall cutter left a four inch deep swathe of powdery gumming in the faces. Half hundredweight blocks of coal rolled out from wrist leverage with mandrels. Three trams filled by 11 o'clock, they shared drilling the roof for shot firing.

'Mind you *awat* them brasses in the same place,' said Irfon.

He wrapped the threaded split cylinder brass core of the boring machine in oiled rag, hid them at the base of the fourth road-post back from the seam—Irfon's formula.

Working each side towards the top of the road, they hewed coal to the limit of the four-foot-six undercut. More trams, faster shovelling, more posts in the face, more coal dust spat with morning phlegm. Special weeks when the roof was shot-fired and cleared near the coal, they filled forty trams.

Casually sarcastic about rearing his family, Irfon gave him 7/6 trumps, sometimes 10/-, Dewi saying, 'Your Missis copes al'right, she's one of the best.'

Man among men his lifetime gospel, Irfon quizzed him like a friendly interrogator, 'Who you knocking off these days, Dewio?'

'Her father's a deacon in Carmel, if you want to know the truth.'

'Cunt-struck you are, butty.'

'I'd be like you if I was.'

'Weekends on the nest, me. Top hole every Monday morning to sort out the men from the boys.'

Big square shovels heaping coal into the tram, they worked like robots until, 'Race the bugger,' said Irfon.

Sloping lumps of coal inward, Dewi built a low wall of coal around the rim of the tram, Irfon topping up while he chalked their number on it.

Sunday morning he helped Irfon haul furniture from Tŷ-isaf cottage to Heol Cerrig, on a bogie of planks lashed to pram wheels. Hetty Francis and the children carried chairs, blankets, clothes, pots, pans and family treasures. The youngest kiddies hullaballoo-ed like nomads in and out the echoing rooms.

October's end in Moel Exchange, bracken reddening the hillsides, dry calms days, tough leaves crinkling on grimed alders clumped along the black winding of Nantglas. And after Guy Fawkes' night, conditions changed in the Four Deep. Fault in the seam to six feet, nine feet, twelve. Finally unworkable, unknown height. Sid Ginty brought in a Company surveyor. Decision: drive on through the fault. Seven foot rings. Arched girders braced with iron straps, butt-lagged and packed beneath a dangerous overhead mix of soft coal and shale.

The coal cutter remained chocked on its trolley out on the double-parting.

'Pair of headings,' explained Dai Greg. 'One on the straight, another off the supply road. Three shifts. Twelve men and twelve strong boys. As for choice, depends on Sid Ginty. My hands are tied, honest, on my life. Might be you'll get selected, some of you might, might not. As I mentioned, my hands are tied. Whoever's picked, they'll have to be extra steady. Bad ground up above there. We've seen it. Fact is, men, once we're through we'll start turning off new stalls, fetch the cutter down agen. Aye, God knows when though.'

Wyndham spoke to Irfon. 'Seems like we'll be signing on the dole with about hundred other blokes.'

Said Irfon, 'Sixty odd stalls finished, right back to the supply road. Fucken creeps, they'll be after Sid Ginty. Ass'ole scrapers, they'll drive these two new headings.'

Dai defended himself, 'I've no idea at all, swear to God.'

'Fucken snake-tongue.'

'True, Irfon, no idea so far. It's up to Sid Ginty.'

Zena Joshua's eyes deadened when she heard the news. 'Nothing left for you, son. Now there's no option. Better prospects anywhere than Moel Exchange. Prince of Wales is coming down, all a farce it is.'

Dewi felt victimised, deprived on dole money. He saw the Prince of Wales in the *Daily Herald*, read the piece of blue blood chicanery uttered in Dowlais.

Zena sniped from the kitchen sink, 'Spoilt beyond, that boy.'

On December 11th 1936, Edward VIII preferred wilful divorcee Mrs. Simpson to the throne.

It was an impoverished Christmas in 9, Dinmel Terrace. They exchanged presents; hers a sixpenny brooch, his a pair of Army socks from the same cheapjack under naptha flares in the pre-industrial cobblestoned precinct behind Dewinton Halt.

Fifty-four men maintained water pumps, stoked boilers, operated winding gear, serviced ventilation and worked on the pithead. One hundred and twenty-four colliers, collier-boys, hauliers and labourers worked two other Pencaer districts: West Vein and the Six Foot.

Humiliation blunted his energy, idleness his reasoning. He walked the pavements, played half-price billiards in Pencaer Institute, and drifted from his mother. Staring at the damp mottled ceiling of his bedroom, he wished himself gone 40 to even out the years between Elsie Kitchener's 43 and his 18. Her 'lovely boy' felt sickened.

Young men joined the Army. Families uprooted on one-way tickets to Coventry, Slough, the Home Counties. Empty houses in every street. Tramps passed through Upper Road to and from the workhouse in Union Yard. Depressed middle-aged husbands returned to chapels, prayers, hymn singing and raw-minded Old Testament deacons poured out *hwyl* in front room prayer meetings. Deprivation boosted religion and pilfering. The Communist Party thrived.

More than anything he missed the togetherness of men underground, the bonding, walking the main, old blokes on the double-parting discussing Moel Exchange events and all the wireless and newspaper world like gods talking. Sanguine commentaries between hewing coal far, far away from all sky. Butties and mates settling down for grub at 11 o'clock, blokes queueing to the lamproom, collier-boys chin-wagging outside the pay hatch on Fridays.

He felt disintegration. Winter nights he sneaked out to steal coal from trucks in Pencaer sidings—no loss to colliers, the trams had passed over the weighbridge.

Schoolchildren observed St. David's Day with singing and drama. Fewer then ever leeks or daffodils worn on the streets. Feudal Exchange Manor ruins marked a coincidence of history, steam coal a coincidence of Nature in Time out of mind. So generations of immigrants had mongrelised nationhood and withered the language. Habits changed. Traditions died. Memories carried stains left over from boom times and penury.

On May Day came a better celebration. One of the parallel headings broke through the Four Deep fault. For Dewi at first on Wednesday night, simply eye contact with Elsie at the close of a whist drive in Moel Progressive Workingmen's Club. She slow-nodded. He slow-signalled.

As they were barged aboard a tramcar she murmured inches from his face, 'You'll be back in work next week.'

He sat behind her, Elsie's black wavy hair shawling over her fur trimmed collar. Girlish in Park Villa pom-pom-pom pom-ing *The Blue Danube*, she waltzed him around the room.

'You sure, Elsie? That right?'

'Direct from Sidney Ginty himself. Nice little clique of us invited, mm, manager's Plasmarl on the Square. Gracie Ginty, she runs Dewinton Grammar board of governers. Sharp though, very straight forward. Gracie's from Bristol, thick twang still, the way she talks. Gracie never went to grammar school. Sidney married her because she speaks her own mind. All right, I'll cut it short. Fresh work soon in Pencaer. I put in a word for you, not for you personally, certainly not, *cariad*. God no! For Zena your mother, on her behalf, so keep quiet otherwise there'll be scandal. Worse than ever!' Forearms clasped around his waist, she heaved a massive squeeze, lifting him off his feet, panting, 'Lovely boy,' as their mouths clung.

Skulking lanes to Dinmel Terrace at 1 a.m., he thought, here's why Llew always landed a good place on the coal. She's well in with Sid Ginty, plus a few others besides. Yet I'm the one she's after when it comes to the real *gummel*. Me, Elsie prefers me. By the Jesus, she's great, she's ideal . . . He gloried in his throat.

Zena sat in darkness, waiting. 'Where you been?'

'Out.'

'I know out! Where? Whose house?'

'Nobody's.'

'Where then?'

'Progressive W.M. Club, Tonio's bracchi shop, up above St. Teilo Infirmary, Cefn Road to the old sheep dip, back around past Pencaer and down to Dinmel. I'll sleep like a log tonight.'

She frowned disdain. 'I don't believe you. There's some cheese left in the pantry. Cover it after.'

He wrapped a cheese sandwich in brown paper, squashed it in his trouser pocket against tomorrow's inevitable hunger.

Expectant limbo for three days. Sunday morning a Lodge committee-man came to the kitchen door.

'Dewi about, Mrs. Joshua?'

He said, 'What's on, Idris?'

The Fed. messenger strutted importance. 'Orders from Mr. Ginty. Start afternoons tomorrow.'

'On the coal?'

'Ask the overman by afternoon.'

'You don't know, you mean?'

Idris Stanton skewed his underslung jaw. 'Bloody cheek. Your name came up for the Four Deep.'

'So-long now, Iddie,' he said.

II

Isolate contentment crooned from Zena Joshua in the garden:
>*I was standing by a churchyard in the city,*
>*when I met a beggar old and grey,*
>*with his hands outstretched he asked the folk for pity,*
>*and this is what I heard him say,*
>*'O I wonder, yes I wonder'*

pausing to repeat,
>*'yes I wonder, will the angels play up yonder,*
>*will the angels play their harps for me,*
>*for a million miles I've travelled*
>*and a million sights I've seen,*
>*and I'm ready for the glory soon to be,*
>*O I wonder, yes I wonder,*
>*will the angels play up yonder,*
>*will the angels play their harps for me.'*

'Bootlaces, missis? Safety pins, cotton, hairpins, Old Moore's, hooks and eyes?' called a weathered faced packman at the gate.

'On your rounds agen then,' she said.

'Aye-aye.'

'Sorry, nothing today.'

He hoisted a scuffed, belt strapped suitcase. '*Bore da*, missis.'

'*Bore da*, mister,' and she cocked her head, listening, thinking, they're up early. She went into the kitchen. Quarter past six on the wall clock from Clarke's catalogue. Pray to God it isn't my Dewi—hobnail boots still stumping along Dinmel Terrace.

The gate latch clacked.

'That you, son?'

He said, 'Everybody out. Bloke killed up in West Vein. Ludo Gammon from the Cellars.'

'Damn damn! They came from Radstock, oh years ago.'

'One side fell in. They've laid Ludo out on a stretcher in the winding house.' Eyeing her sidelong, he clutched his lower spine. 'Smashed across here.'

'Tribe of kids left too,' she said, clinical, prescribing future with present grief.

'Bad ground up in West Vein, not solid top like it was in Number One before Llew went away.'

'Gone for good by the looks of it.'

He said, 'Best place on the coal always, for Llew Kitchener.'

Cynicism prowling her mouth, 'No surprise at all. Elsie goes gallivanting, flings herself at Pencaer officials.'

'People talk. Course Llew was a *trych*.'

'Stingy nettle pop,' she said, filling two cups from a screw-corked flagon. 'All the deacons in Moel Exchange won't stop Elsie.'

'Wonder how he's doing up there. Been away a long time. Last October when he went.'

'Elsie Kitchener'd know for sure.'

'I might as well go out of my way, ask her about Llew.'

'Watch yourself, she's looking for anything in trousers.' Zena sniffed regret. 'I should have kept myself tidy. Widows my age, they're roaming Moel Exchange like lost sheep.'

'I wouldn't stand in your way, Mam.'

They sipped home-brewed pop at the table. 'I'm not that daft,' she said.

'Well, up to you,' regarding himself as detached, immune to the notion of his mother finding a second husband.

'Son, take a squint at yourself, nineteen next week, not courting yet.'

'Wait 'til I'm driving my own stall down the Four Deep.'

'Theo and me, we picked up early on. Real nice it was in those days.'

He hung his head. 'Long walk from the Cellars to Brynrhedyn cemetery. I'll be going with Irfon. Find my black tie, will you, Mam?'

'I'll iron it ready.'

'My third funeral since I started with Llew in Number One.'

'We all end up in Brynrhedyn, some lily-livered who never dirtied his hands promising we're safe in heaven for ever and ever. Makes me choke. When you're gone you're gone.'

'I keep thinking about old Llew.'

'Yes, know why? Because you didn't have a father.'

'Aye, perhaps.'

'Tell me, boy, what d'you want for your birthday? Sports coat?'

They smiled away from each other.

'From the catalogue,' he said.

'The one you fancied,' Zena chuckling, her hands cowling her face. 'Harris tweed supposed to be.' She flipped out a measuring tape from a Coronation mug on the mantelpiece. 'Stand up, let's take your chest size.'

'My arms, don't forget my long arms.'

'Awkward. Only thing to do, order a bigger chest size.' Quickly impish, she tickled his armpit while adjusting the tape. He inhaled, held his breath. 'Thirty-eight inches, call it forty. *Duw*, boy, you're filling out, following after my side, all big lumps of men. I was the *dwt*.'

He said, 'Not bad, thirty-eight inch chest.'

'What counts is how you feel.'

Lightly jogging her elbow, 'Fact al'right.'

★ ★ ★ ★

Midsummer's day came and went, June flaming and expiring with drizzle sheeting the hills. Traffic men hooked out coaldust and muck clogging tramroad points on top pit. Scarlet fever travelled in Dinmel Terrace. Twenty-three diptheria cases in Moel Exchange. One smallpox death. He was old, one-time G.W.R. shunter and Band of Hope evangelist, carted away in a black van, spectators ranged out wide, his toothless widow screaming lament like a Breugel arrest.

Wearing new flannel trousers and the cut price Harris tweed jacket, he went to a Saturday night dance in the Legion Club. He had a date with Elsie for the following Saturday. Cheap day ticket to Aberselsig seaside. She wanted a dip in the sea, *lorch* on the beach with sandwiches, then find a spot deep in the dunes for some *bethingalw*. Fish and chips on the way back to the station. Separate compartments coming home to Dewinton Halt.

He recognised Ellis Mabon's shout in the Legion bar. 'You-there! How's it going?' Ellis in khaki, sun-tanned and heavy-shouldered, demanding, 'Pint for my mate!'

'*Iesu*, you're like a bull,' he said.

'Good packing, man. You ought to join up, get out of that bloody death trap. Seen Greta Picton? She's upstairs.'

Slow waves of shuffling feet overhead, Glyn Rupe's Five Stars playing foxtrots, waltzes and the Gypsy tango.

He said, 'We more or less jacked in before Greta went to West Ealing. Lost touch altogether since.'

'She's engaged to a copper, bloke from Carmarthen.'

A barmaid click-clicked the glass with her wedding ring. 'Yours, soldier.'

Ellis waved a ten shilling note. 'Have one on me, girl.'

'Ta,' as if buying a tramcar ticket. 'I'll take for a small Guinness. Home on leave? Nice too.'

Ellis coughed throaty guile instead of grinning, 'Hey, boy, been in any fights lately?'

'Cut it out. My old man used to stick his fists up, so they tell me. I'd sooner fuck than fight.' Instant chagrin gnawed his stomach. Bullshitter, he thought, then, 'Ellis, how long you down for?'

'Due back in Crickhowell tomorrow night.'

'They laid us off in the Four Deep. Big jump knocked out the district. Through it now, thank Christ. Opening up a new face. Slow suicide it was, on the dole.'

Ellis spread his hands on the counter. 'Ginty took advantage of me, the bastard. Nights regular behind that cutter. From then on I changed my mind about Pencaer. I went to the office. There's

Sid Ginty, skinny as a rake, cheeks of his arse on the table, firemen coming and going with their reports, and Ginty says, "The alternative is a fortnight's notice." I tried telling him I'd sooner work my own stall. Not a blink from Ginty. He gives it to me flat, "No man is automatically entitled to a stall when he reaches twenty-one." All I could think of was nightshift and bare money, so I put my notice in. Sink that pint. Let's go.'

Upstairs in the hall, Ellis elbowed his ribs. 'Look at her, comrade'—Greta Picton tangoing, old Lincoln the M.C. hooked over her, deadly serious, thickskinned, a technician of ballroom mummery.

He said, 'Rudolph Valentino.'

Ellis mimed snapping a stick across his thigh. 'Linc'll break her back.'

They stooged around close to the wall. Glyn Rupe's Five Stars flourished 'Gipsy Dream Girl' to a final double thump on the big drum.

Cautiously cocksure to Greta, 'Okay, stare me out.'

Primly tall, long-legged in court shoes, her head flinging rufous brown hair to stillness. Resistance straightened her flexible mouth, 'Well, how's Dewi Joshua this long time?'

'Why grumble? How's yourself, anyway?'

Ellis backed off. 'See you later, boy.'

Greta knuckled the top of her hip. 'Excuse me, I suppose you've let on to Dewi?'

'Yeh, that you was engaged. No offence, Greta.'

Smiling condescension, 'I am engaged, to Police Constable Mark Rowley. As for Mark's father, he's a farmer in Sylen, Carmarthen.'

Arrogant in lieu of loss, 'I'm tied up myself, on the quiet for the time being 'cause she's married.'

Ellis leered, gangsterish. 'Sly as a bloody fox.'

'Common-sense, man. We don't want trouble.'

Creases stitched the rim of Greta's lower lip. 'Married woman! Who'd have dreamt of such a thing?'

He saw Glyn Rupe timing 'Ha-one two three four,' for *Deep Purple*.

'Dance, Greta?

Their knees knocked.

'Drunk?' her nostrils flaring.

'Sorry.'

On tenterhooks he counted steps, turned, counting, slid into another forward glide, turned, foxtrotting, accurately skimming around other couples.

'Mark Rowley, ah?' he said.

'In the Metropolitan Police.' Thin gemstone ring on the third finger on her left hand. 'See!'

'Best of luck.'

'Thanks. Same to you, Dewi. Do I know her?'

Ellis was twirling, improvising with a girl from Station Lane.

'Doubt it,' he said.

Greta stiffened to ice queen. 'Try me.'

'Can't.'

'Don't be childish.'

They were boxed in beside the shuttered hatch as the dance ended. He said, 'Come down to the small lounge, let me buy you a drink.' He fisted his hands in the jacket pockets, 'Though I shan't tell you who she is, reason being I'm on oath.'

Greta poured distrust, 'God alive, boy!'

'Might take us a couple of years. I'm not old enough yet for a place of my own in Pencaer.'

'We're saving up, Markie and myself.'

'Lady's maid in West Ealing, that right?'

'Of course. Trained!'

Staid Club members with wives to match filled the narrow annexe lounge overlooking Nantglas.

'They're all eyes,' complained Greta, squaring her shoulders, breasts pouting above her folded arms. 'I only came home to see my father. He's bad again. Sherry for me, sweet, please. Terrible for Dad, he's gone like a skeleton.'

'Dust, aye, same as my old man. Great full back, Luke Picton used to be, trial for his cap before you and me were born. They talk about Luke playing rugger on the field where they built the Infants' School. Girl, look, you're not up the Smoke, so what if there's no sherry?'

Greta swam her hands above his shoulders. 'You're much bigger than I remember you, Dewi.'

'I've sprung up recent.'

'I don't like gin, can't a'bear the taste of whisky either. It's sweet sherry when Markie takes me out.'

'Know something, this makes me laugh.'

'Otherwise I'd sooner lemonade.'

He left her sitting next to a Pencaer gaffer haulier, a compo case, his broken wrist slung across his chest. The haulier's wife smiled no-nonsense, dabbing her brow with a black bordered handkerchief.

He brought a medium sherry.

Greta sipped like a hurried bird. 'Nice.'

'Good, that's all's behind the bar. Cheers, girl. Never thought I'd bump into you tonight.' He greeted the haulier's wife, 'Hullo there, Mrs. Lougher,' and '*Shwmae*, Leyshon, still in plaster then?'

Leyshon Lougher scowled down at his wrist. 'Complications.'

A soulful *Carolina Moon* duet began at a corner table, increasing to half a dozen in compulsive harmony.

Fervour robbing her breath, Greta moaned, 'Oh lovely, lovely. They don't sing like that in London.'

Gripe snapped from him, 'I don't know why in the name of Christ you went away.'

'Fool! Could I keep myself here?'

'I was on the dole for months.'

'Whyn't you shut up, boy!'

'Huh,' he said, thinking. We're same as before. There's no change.

They danced until Glyn Rupe played *Hen Wlad* on piano.

'See you home, Greta?'

'Look at you, like a tom-cat. Who's this slut you're going with?'

They were outside on the pavement. 'Ne'-mind, Greta, I'll see you on a tram. Long lay-in tomorrow, so I'll use my legs.'

'We'll *both* walk.'

'Righto, love.'

'Oh, you fool.'

He said, 'Not my idea, this.'

Her hand snaked inside his forearm, furiously clamped his

wrist, and then gripped palms, her stride to his, their thighs siamesed. They kissed in gloom between lamp-posts, the July night swarming rife as Africa.
'Dewi, I'm scared.'
'Nothing to be scared of—is there?'
'Y'know what I mean.'
'Ah?'
'I'll be late too.'
'Pardon?'
'Late in our house.'
Better late than never, he thought, pushing aside a ramshackle gate, on through sappy grass, around the roofless hulk of Plas Cistfaen to yew trees older than British Empire pink on maps of the world. Sympathy came sneaking at him, helpless regret for her tears, the cruel psalm of pleading, 'Please don't be rough, please, Dewi, please. Oh, *Duw* . . . oh, God,' fading to inert, muffled sighing.
Aftermath blanked his feelings.
'Excuse me,' she said, breaking his vacancy.
Ground level dark beneath the graveyard trees. He stared wide-eyed, anxious. Why me instead of him, the copper up in West Ealing?
She was scratching up his arm to his neck. Solemn from the dim round of her face, 'You are the very first.'
He said, 'Al'right, Greta?'
'Yes thanks. I felt nervous.' Searching for his mouth, her kiss skidded down from his left eye. 'I'm glad it's over.'
Headlong for truth, 'Obvious for Chrissake.'
She bridled, drifting in darkness. 'There's no reason to be foulmouthed.' He rolled away from a scuffling shoe. 'I must go now, Dewi.'
He found her outflung hand. 'Aye, okay, girl.'
They lingered at the parlour window in Victoria Street, Greta quietly impersonal. 'Goodbye then. I'm on my way back tomorrow.'
'So-long, Greta.'
'Dewi, what's her name?'
Rationalising his grudge, 'Look, you marry that copper.

45

Everything'll be guaranteed, see. Buy nice things for yourself and so on.'

'Tell me her name.'

Through the net curtain he saw Luke Picton propped up in bed. Faint lustre of light from a paraffin lamp on a brown chest of drawers. Ghost of a man, his hands like blanched roots on the patchwork counterpane.

'In a bad way, old Luke. There's no coming round for a man with the dust.'

Greta squeezed herself into the passageway. 'G'bye, Dewi, see you next year perhaps.'

Hand raised, he said to himself, next year? Next year? *Iesu*. 'So-long, girl.'

He wandered to Dinmel Terrace, thinking, Army? Like Ellis? Not on. My mind's my own in Moel Exchange. Good butties, decent mates wherever I turn. Never, I shan't be going away. I'm fixed for life, specially when I get a place down the Four Deep. Matter of fact, I'd work any stall in Pencaer.

Grinning seized tendons below his ears: Elsie diddled about for Llew Kitchener. She can do the same for this chick.

His mouth dried, creepiness shirring his bowels.

★   ★   ★   ★

Irfon Tŷ-isaf unlocked his toolbar. 'Heard the latest? They're fetching conveyors in. We'll be clearing stents, just chucking coal on the belt. No more stall work. No more fucken top holes. Cross parties by afternoons and nights, they'll drive on our supply road. Same goes for our gate road from the tip end. Teams, Dewi-boy. Shifters, packers, borers, waste men.'

'Ive,' he said, 'I can't follow what you mean.'

'*Raight*, al'raight, wait till the bloody thing comes. I had a stent in Cwmffrwd pit before the water broke in. Indeed to Christ, there's going to be fucken big changes down here in the Four Deep.'

'Changes, ah?'

Irfon cackled joy. 'More fairness all round. *Trychs* in Pencaer, they might as well blow their brains out. Only the boy on our tip end'll pick up a few trumps. True what I'm telling you, true.'

'When d'you reckon?'

Irfon went kneeling into the face, neatly sliding two square shovels and two patent mandrels ahead of him. He ticked off on his fingers: 'Dai Phil on the straight, Gomer North, Pete Lougher, Eddie Jones Batch, Evie Houghton, Barry Doughty, Will Williams, Archie Lougher, Wyndham Mabon Rhys, Teddo Moon, Dwgi Harding, myself, Cled Grant, Twm Lloyd, Pryssor Rawlins, Glyn Tarw Jones—who's next?'

'Eddie Jenkins,' he said.

'Eddie First Aid and Toby Watts. Eighteen stalls. They'll turn plenty more for sure. Once this face is all straightened out, then they'll start. Coal, there'll be coal pouring from Pencaer like the fucken sea.'

'Aberselsig,' he said.

'Hey, mentioning Aberselsig; when I was a boy, pushers from Sinkers' Huts used to go there whooring. They'd come back like a fancy dress party. Week later they was skint.'

He said, 'Sounds like you'd go for some sloppy whoor.'

'I'm not quibbling, sonny-boy. Where's that fucken haulier? Same it is every fucken Monday morning. No shape back there on the double-parting.'

'Shurrup moaning, man.'

Irfon yelled comical rage, 'Don't you give me any fucken lip,' tutting his pretence to, 'I heard you was out with some piece from up London. Luke Picton's daughter. What's she like on the job?'

'Bellow your lungs out on Moel Square, Ive.'

'It's just *clecs*, fair do's. There'll be no *clecs* when we're pushing up the daisies.'

They turned coal back to the top of the road until the haulier came. He shovelled automatically, conjuring ideas: himself and Elsie in public, the talk of Moel Exchange. Facing up to Zena. He cut off day-dreaming. Greta? Nowhere. Gone up the Smoke. Next Saturday, Elsie on the sands. Everything settled. Stick to secrecy.

Eleven o'clock behind the tram, fireman Dai Greg and Irfon were bickering.

'Daio, you've never seen a bloody conveyor face.'

'Irfon bighead, *you* won't be chargehand. I'll be recommending Gomer North.'

'Now there's a right *sioni-hoy*. Gomer'd raffle the cheese from under his foreskin.'

Dai spilled breathy splutters.

Dewi said, 'When's it due?'

The fireman spat on his cap lamp, rubbed it on his knee, wiped the glass dry with his shirt cuff. 'Take ages yet. Few months.'

'Near enough three,' said Irfon.

'As regards myself, Dai, when I'm twenty-one they'll put me on a stent instead of driving my own stall?'

'Corr-rect,' promised Dai, 'I'll see to that, don't worry.' He pivoted back to Irfon. 'News up in our cabin this morning, old Llew Kitchener kill't himself, took overdose.'

Dewi fought to loosen his throat. 'Who said?'

'Mrs. Kitchener to Mrs. Ginty last night in the Con. There was a meeting to raise funds for Moel Ward. Sid Ginty, he spoke on the phone to Gabe Coles the cashier, then from Gabe to his missis, then from Deborah to God knows along the line to our top pit cabin. Aye, Llew's a goner.'

He said, 'Llew was a good butty to me. I don't go with such as you, Irfon, and those who run him down.'

Dai Greg huffed rectitude. 'Bag of nerves since that stroke. Llew turned away from me in the 'Stute as if I was muck.'

Irfon swigged cold tea. Sagacity quietened him. 'Old story isn't it. They go do-lally. They slouch about town, they yarn all day in the 'Stute or the *bracchi* shops, tearing religion or politics to bits. All of a sudden they're missing, they snuff it quiet as mice. Llew Kitch, he commits suicide up there in Brum.'

Dai sloped away in a crouch. 'Well, men, do your best.'

Riding up in the cage and crossing to the lamproom, they talked about Llew Kitchener, old-timers who remembered his Bristolian father and Aberdare mother, who knew him as a boy in Empire Crossing Mixed School, even remembered the medal and certificate he won outright, never having lost a day's attendance. It was in him then, mule of a kid with boils like ally bompers on his neck, but every morning, '*Yma 'thrawes*, Miss,' no matter if he was drenched to the skin. Mystery how he married Elsie Evans from Rheola All Saints.

Zena sermonised at the dinner table. 'Your father would never do the dirty on Llew Kitchener's name, whether down the pit or anywhere else. Theo refused, he walked away from back-biting. He saw what went on, course he did. Spiritualists they were, the Kitcheners, yes, in Tabernacle before Tabernacle went Pentecostal. See, boy, the Spiritualists wouldn't pay the rates. Fell behind years. One from the other, you can't tell which is worst, Spiritualists or Pentecostals. "Their privilege, leave well alone," Theo used to say. Elsie soon put the block on Llew's Spiritualism.'

'What was she like in those days, Mam?'

'Elsie? Oh, top fashion, all the rage. She worked in Moel Emporium, from titivating the windows to manageress. Hoity-toity beyond, you'd never believe. But glands it is. Elsie's not the first, not by a long chalk. Big roly-poly woman by the time Llew fell for her. He'd be seven or eight years older than Elsie.'

'What if she told Llew about the Wills Woodbines shares?'

'We-ell, temptation, I mean for Elsie and for Llew Kitchener. Y'know, son, they wasn't a *real* married couple. They never walked the streets together.'

He said, 'Is she forty-threeish?'

'Not far off.'

'Think she'll marry agen?'

'I wouldn't venture guessing. No telling what she'll do.' Zena's square work-hand circled above his plate.

Relishing lamb's liver, fried onions and chips, 'Treat, Mam.'

'Caraway cake to follow,' the same hand tentatively rumpling his hair.

'Wish I could buy a new suit for Llew's funeral,' he said. 'Chalk stripe from the Fifty Bob Tailors.'

'This'll flabbergast you, Dewi. It's up in Birmingham next Wednesday.'

'Damn and bugger it.'

'Must you curse?'
'I can't go to Brum!'

III

Elsie stayed in Birmingham for a week. Saturday afternoon he went swimming in Cwmffrwd colliery feeder, the stone and mortar walled dam filling a pear-shaped pond two hundred yards above the abandoned pit head. Families gathered around a fire were singing *Swing low sweet chariot*. Mothers paddled with toddlers at the inflow. Schoolboys roved the banktop, warring with stripped bracken stalks. Young men and girls sunbathed in separate groups pending evening, pairing off to wander arm in arm, finding dingles beneath oak trees older than castles in Wales, ritual courtship older than Wales under mid-summer gloaming.

He practised jack-knife dives off the shredded branch of a lowly overhanging sycamore. Time after time he squelched through horsetails, climbed up to the branch, concentrated for Olympian perfection, launched, flexed and plunged, swam under water over murky peat-stained gravel, surfaced for a speedy trudgen back to the bogged horsetails.

Aware of a limited expertise from the age of twelve, he towelled himself. The camp fire families chorussed *Home, sweet home on the prairie*. Irfon Tŷ-isaf and his wife had children playing around them, leaping, barging, yelping 'Touch! You're on it!'

Hetty Francis turned potatoes baking in the embers. 'Dewi! Try one of these.'

He juggled the blackened potato from hand to hand.

'Pass the bloke some salt,' Irfon said.

'Reach it for himself, can't he!' She leered private triumph at Dewi. 'Shows what I got to put up with. This fella won't lift a finger.'

He took a pinch of salt from a screw of greaseproof.

'How's your mother?'

'Al'right, Hetty. She's potching hours on end in the garden.'

'Nice for her, better than moping indoors.'

'Yeh.' He fingernailed burnt peeling off the potato. 'Hey, Llew was buried up in Brum last Wednesday. They must have come to agreement.'

Irfon let seconds pass. 'Who's they?'

'Mrs. Kitchener and Llew's sister.'

Hetty sniffed, 'Funny arrangement. There's a family grave belonging to Elsie in Brynrhedyn.'

'It's what Llew wanted,' decided Irfon. 'That stroke broke him. The man didn't care at all.'

He said, 'Right enough.'

Irfon blew, 'Phoo-phoo-phooph,' around a steaming bolus of potato. 'Us two'll be stretched out next to each other in Brynrhedyn.'

His wife gritted, 'That morbid mind of yours.'

'Me morbid?'

'Out of order,' smirked Hetty.

Irfon thumbed his nose. 'Objection over-ruled. Address the bloody chair,' then, 'Scoot, you little bugger,' as his seven year old son flopped wetly on his lap. The child creamed angelic smiles at Hetty, writhing around to embrace his father's neck.

'Where to tonight, Ive?'

'Comrades' Club. You?'

'Do some pub crawling,' he said.

Irfon lifted the boy, held him balanced, sitting on his head. 'I'll tan your arse for you,' and set him into skelping free, into the reaching arms of their eldest son.

Hetty forked a chunk of potato to her mouth. 'Lovely kids they are.'

Irfon chested pride. 'Aye-girl, you can say that agen.'

Clear through a babble of children and water rose the desolate voice of the young tubercular wife of a Pencaer mains rider, *I'm alone because I love you*. The others left her soloist for a while, her twangy soprano out-pouring. Then soft humming finally released full-throated concord and running children held still, entranced, watching faces, grown-up brothers, sisters, mothers and fathers.

Dewi waited.

He said, 'Tarra, I'm off.'

Irfon and Hetty waved, dignified as aristocrats.

Walking across the dam wall, he wondered why Elsie hadn't come home to Parc Villa.

Locked door at 9, Dinmel Terrace, key under a Laughing Cavalier biscuit tin brimming nasturtiums on the windowsill. His mother's note on the wireless: GONE FIRST HOUSE TO RIALTO.

Good, why not? he thought, flashbacked to childhood, cosy receptive nights sitting beside Zena in the Rialto, Pavilion, Workmen's Hall or the Empire.

He layered corned beef between slices of bread and margarine. He felt lonely. In pain of loneliness. He starved for Elsie, keeper of his life. Closeness, he longed for closeness, everything else shut out. Throw the world away for Elsie. Elsie. Her, Elsie.

Bearable agony in his bedroom while changing into his best clothes (dark grey flannel trousers, white shirt and the sports jacket), shifting fractionally, foreboding staring back at him in the Woolworth's mirror, wet comb parting his hair, sloping short back and sides to left and right.

Loyal to his campaign, he explored Moel Exchange pubs. Eight pubs. Nine pints from three breweries, slur-footed by now, aiming for straightness, slack-lipped unlike his jack-knife rigour, vertigo treacherous, lurching by wall and railing yet still politely heeding, 'Goodnight, boy.'

'*Shwmae*, Dewi.'

'Howbe there?'

'How's it going then?'

'Al'right, butty?'

Or, 'Man, you're fucken loaded.'

'Right bloody state you're in.'

'Take it easy!'

Zena left him sleeping on the couch. During the night he gouted vomit, missing the backyard drain-hole. She watched him from her bedroom window, moonlight ghosting the unbunned mop of her greying hair.

'Leave it. I'll swill it down the sink in the morning.' And the chill stun of, 'Your father would be ashamed of you.'

Long gone Theo Joshua, moral maker of all his mother's days. Unreal Theo, a memory ghost.

Groggily sober at the table for Sunday dinner, he said, 'I'll be leaving, Mam, when I find a place.'

'Lodgings?'

'Yeh, somewhere not too far from the pit.'

'I'm not driving you out, remember.'

'Better if I go though. I can't stomach animosity.'

Her mouth tightened. 'You must come for a visit whenever you want.'

'Righto, Mam.'

'Yes, you're old enough to think for yourself. As Theo used to say, "A man's entitled to make up his own mind, that's how we live and learn."'

Dewi kept quiet, resenting preach-words from beyond the grave.

★ ★ ★ ★

Days sank away until he found Elsie Kitchener. Liptons Store was closed but she stepped out, wicker basket on the crook of her arm, the door clapping shut behind her.

Head-on, he said, 'Why'd you stay in Birmingham?'

'Various matters to do with family. She's bad too, Sallyanne's stiff as a poker with arthritis. Gracious alive, the way she's let herself go, just a smelly spaniel for company. As it turned out, my Llew preferred Sallyanne's two rooms and a scullery. I was tamping mad. Silly old woman, full of nonsense. There's those you can help, others you can't. Such rubbish.'

'Spiritualism?' he said.

'Mm, the way Sallyanne was brought up. Never bettered herself up there. I stayed in a guest house, all commercial travellers. You're looking peaky as well,' Elsie's dark eyes were searching. 'Anything wrong, *cariad*? Tell Elsie.'

'I'm looking for lodgings. My mother, well, we can't agree no more. Not that I'm blaming her. It's myself. I intend leaving home.'

'I see.'

'What about it, Elsie, what d'you say?'

She diverted mischieviously. 'We took in lodgers! Mrs. Gulliver and her little boy with calipers on his leg, then Roy Rawlins who joined the Navy, and my Dad's two half brothers, Hiley and Issac. They rode by lorry to Coventry. Mm, everybody took in lodgers when Cwmffrwd and High Seven and Pencaer were going full blast.' Elsie gave him a cream slice from the basket. 'Like a cup of tea? Tonio's cafe behind Liptons.'

He glanced around for witnesses. Puff pastry and custard melted in his mouth, the root of his tongue cloyed by icing. 'Okay, Elsie, Tonio's. Honest now, I'll pay you top lodgings.'

'Beside the point. Realise this, I'll be accused. My name'll be dirt.'

'Difference in our ages, you mean?'

'Good looking fella you are, Dewi, but I'm old enough to be your . . .'

'Wait a minute,' he said. 'Leave the stupid buggers talk.'

Delight enveloped her, teetering plumply summer-frocked on the pavement.

'Two teas, please.' She waggled her purse below Tonio's pencil moustache. 'Fresh mind, none of your *bracchi* tricks, tea boiled up.'

'Never-never, Missis. Nice to see you, Missis,' smiled Tonio. 'How's life, Dewi, on the up and up?'

'Not so bad.'

Tonio gushed, 'G'wan, sit down.'

Dewi pulled a chair out for her, Elsie pirouetting, winsome, 'There's polite.'

Hubris hardened his neck. 'I'm not worried about Tom Peps, they're everywhere in Moel Exchange. Know what though, if we'd gone to Aberselsig somebody would have seen us. Full charabanc load went from Lower Moel Outing Club last Saturday.'

'Mm, lucky them. Fools' paradise, Aberselsig,' which tumbled Elsie's memories: I'm still a Dewinton Sixth Form girl at heart, but he's never been the boy to match the kind of girl I was. I can *bring him out*, look after him for years. Years.

His head had no alphabet for the future. Warmth flushed him

when she paid for the teas. She'll take me in as lodger. Great heart inside Elsie. She knows the ropes, definitely.

'New craze at the moment is hiking,' she said. 'Crowd of hikers with knapsacks left the train once we were in the country outside Birmingham. Marvellous past-time really. I've been tempted. You interested?'

'On Sundays?'

'Weekends.'

'I'm days regular, six shifts.'

'Bank Holiday next week.'

Anxiety flustered him. 'Let's settle about lodgings. Straight yes or no.'

'I'd rather go hiking than take up crocheting!'

'Myself, I don't mind out-doors. What about the lodgings?'

Staring aside, 'For how long?'

'Aah, up to you, Elsie.'

Reflecting as if habitual, 'Two empty bedrooms in my house, gathering dust they are. Never has been much rowdy life in Parc Villa. Senseless creating over trifles, pandemonium every day. I like being *clean*. Work, eat and sleep, that was Llew. Never a thought besides. No picture shows, no mates to follow rugby or discuss things out in the garden. Night after night I felt pity for Llew.'

He said, 'Best heading collier in Pencaer, bar none. Surprised me when he went to Brum.'

'Mm, exactly.' She flashed a gamin grin. 'I've decided. You can move into the back bedroom.'

'Thanks, Elsie. Am I chuffed!'

'After August Bank Holiday.' Frown-eyed, she lowered her head. 'Sheets, blankets, pillows: where, where, where? The old chest. If the moths haven't been at them.' She flared remembrance, 'Solid oak chest off my mother when we got married.'

'I'll pay full lodge,' saluting victory like a boxer, his secret joy celebrating, Bloody great!

Elsie gripped his wrist, murmuring, 'Buy some french letters.'

Behind the counter, Welsh-born Tonio Carmello signalling the Cross as if blessing peace on earth.

That night he slept nose to the steady pulse in her white neck until dawn. Dinmel Terrace was deserted as he trailed home.

His mother called from the head of the stairs, 'Your tommy box is on the pantry stone. If you want breakfast fry some rashers.'

He said, 'Right.'

'She'll be the ruination of you, boy, whoever she is.'

'Mam, get back to bed,' he said.

Ten minutes before Pencaer hooter, she stood above him while he laced his pit boots. 'Go careful, Dewi.'

'Always am once I'm in the face.'

'In fairness to yourself because you've had no proper rest.'

'Don't worry. So-long, Mam.'

But shortly after 11 o'clock he slumped into forbidden sleep with a wad of blackcurrant jam sandwich in his mouth, Irfon Tŷ-isaf deliberately leaving him until the haulier's cap lamp came into the stall from the straight heading.

'On your feet, haulier's coming.'

He finished his sandwiches kneeling, hewing coal.

'Feeling bad?' inquired Irfon.

'Nuh.'

'What's up then?'

'Went to bed late.'

'Chasing skirt was you?'

'Yeh.'

'Ne' mind, kiddo.'

They filled six trams and timbered the face, Irfon offering advice, 'Get your head down early tonight, else you'll fuck yourself up in a heap.'

'Whyn't you take a megaphone 'round the streets?'

'Never yet met a big ram good for anything besides.'

'Quiet, for Chrissake.'

'Whatsamatter, backache?'

Quid pro quo, his joky insults. They ridiculed, cross-talked, striding sleepers up from the Four Deep and out along Pencaer main to pit bottom.

Zena Joshua feigned haste, saying, 'Pie in the oven, gravy on the hob. I'm off into town.'

'Okay,' he said.
Again, 'I must go. Sale in Parade bazaar, six-pence off towels.'
'Catch a tram.'
'Single back home,' she said. '*Cawl* day tomorrow, so it's butcher-shop then Ffynnon Stalls for veg.'
Breaking Zena's discipline of almost six years, he ate his dinner before washing in the wooden tub. Timeless to himself in time, in place, Dewi chanted while scrubbing his head: '*Dah dee dee-dee, dah dee dee, dah dee dee, dah dee-dee-dee, dah dee, dee, dah dee . . .*' and relinquished *Goldmine in the sky*. Contorting his arms to soap his back, he finally, carelessly growled frustration. Next week Elsie'll wash my back. She might. Might refuse. *Iesu*, I've never been in a full size bath since I was pupped. Recovering the song, he baritoned stentorian, '*We will sit up there and watch the clouds roll by, when we find that long lost goldmine in the sky.*'
Outside the high chickenwire garden fence, his neighbour whistled the tune in fine style, fluting tremolo glissades, extemporising, ranging beyond scope of the lyric.
Benny Lowry Whistler, skinamalink of a bloke. Bone idle. Too lazy to button his trousers.
After emptying the tub, Dewi sprawled into welcome sleep on the couch.
And thereafter the week wore out to Saturday.
He saw Irfon scuttling fast back to the tram.
'Ive?'
'Give us a hand!'
Overhanging top coal tumbled in slab-glossy lumps. Timbers creaked, whined to thin seeps faint as bat-squealing.
'Bit of a squeeze,' he said.
'Not much if we keep our lugholes open. There's a break down my side. First look, we'll chuck this lot into the dram. I'll turn it back. Don't you wander from the top of the road. Just fill.'
'It's squeezing al'right, Ive.'
'I'm not fucken deaf.'
'Only ignorant.'
'Watch your mouth, spunkface.'
'Listen, bomby-head,' he said, 'if we dab a few posts up close

to the coal, by the time we work the stent off there'll be space for a flat and for the cutter to pass through tonight.'

'Can't odds it,' agreed Irfon.

'Want me to fix some posts up?'

'Both of us. Bastard this is. I thought we'd have a cushy weekend shift.'

Safe behind the tram, they hatcheted five Norway posts and lids. Meanwhile the roof pounded.

'Where you bound for Bank Holiday, Ive?'

'We're taking the tribe to Aberselsig seaside. Excursion going nine o'clock.'

'Hiking's all the go these days.'

'Bloody mad.'

He sledgehammered a post upright, estimated a yard distance, and indented a firm base for the next post.

'See, width of my finger in this break,' said Irfon.

'Flat should hold it.'

'Hark!'

'Roof's sounding off down to Cled Grant's stall,' he said.

'Pouncing, aye. Mind what I told you. Stay close to the dram.'

He chalked their last tram at 2 o'clock.

'Take five, Dewi, then we'll put the flat up.' They sat on their heels, resting, listening, the squeeze lifting, moving away, Irfon chatty now, 'Lovely weather, be nice for the kids. I'm not much for the sea myself. Too bloody big. Where'll you be Monday?'

'Not far.'

'How far?'

'Old Roman road.'

'We crossed over there during the twenty-six strike. Three of us went begging in Pontyllan. The women came out with Swansea loaves, fresh eggs, pats of butter, jam and treacle. Us singing *Pen Calfaria* in the gutter, but not a bloody penny. We spent two nights under sacks in a timber yard. Almost froze. Mostyn Jones caught a sheep by the Roman road, kill't it with his knife from when he was in the War. Don't let on, right? Dead now, Mostyn, killed in this pit. Billy Fish was with us. Went to Canada, Billy did. What a runner, blue streak over a hundred yards. Good bloke all round.'

'D'you cook the sheep?'

'Course! Fetched it back home all chopped up clean and tidy inside our raglans. Raggedy fucken raglans, take it from me.'

They hammered the corrugated steel flat in position across the broken roof, parallel with the seam.

'She'll serve,' said Irfon. 'Collect up the tools and we'll be away.'

On top pit Dai Greg came out of the officials' cabin. 'Well, men, old Luke Picton's gone.'

Irfon Tŷ-isaf cursed the universe. 'Luke suffered, Luke had to fucken suffer it.'

IV

They picnicked in a copse between the moss and sedge-pocked Roman road and ground level ruins, pounds left over from the Middle Ages. He cooked sausages four at a time in the clip-on lid of a Bijou Camp Kit, on a fire of dead oak twigs. Elsie tended two small side-by- side saucepans: potatoes and runner beans. A throwback Elsie Kitchener, her strange off-key mezzo soprano leaping sensation inside his chest. She squatted like a Red Indian woman, belly pouched on her thighs, self absorbed, slewing up her head, *Myfanwy* drawling from her red-lipped mouth.

'Everybody's favourite, *Myfanwy*,' he said.

She rummaged pepper and salt from her knapsack. 'Last time we came up here I was in Dewinton Grammar.'

'Oh?'

'Mm, with Gorwel Pomeroy.'

'Corn Stores?'

'Their son.'

'I remember Pomeroy's Stores near the Mortar Works.'

'He died young. Nineteen.' Elsie strained the vegetables. 'They worshipped him.'

'I don't understand shoppies,' he said.

'Move, Dewi! Plates!'

He opened his knapsack—her present from Moel Sports Goods.

Elsie served. She manoeuvred a knob of butter on his beans. 'Pepper to taste,' and after a while, as they were eating, 'Speaking truthfully, it was too much for Gorwel, fending for himself amongst strangers.'

'How come?'

'In Aberystwyth University. As for myself, terrible! I didn't want to go away. They gave in to me. Oh, I was a cheeky bitch. Girls from Dewinton Grammar had to leave, go into service. I *wouldn't*. I refused.'

He braved his spirit. 'I reckon you're the smartest of all, the loveliest in Wales.'

Wriggling glee, she pulled to him, their teeth slicing the sausage popping from her mouth.

He felt removed without trace from his mother, from every man and boy in Pencaer pit. Four switchback miles below the high, disappearing Roman road was the August Monday town without tramcars, shops, three Council libraries, three institutes, and the men (mostly) who caroused or quietly enjoyed Bank Holiday in clubs and pubs. Others waited for dancehalls or cinemas to open.

Afterwards he scoured the Made in Sheffield Camp Kit with handfuls of grass. Elsie packed them in a wicker basket. While she relieved herself behind a nameless cairn, he pissed on and scuffed earth over the crinkling embers.

'Quick!' she cried.

'I'm douting the fire!'

'Fox!'

He raced, saw the ruddy blur inside summer bracken, then leaping low across cropped turf, escaping again into tall ferns.

'There's a beauty.'

She flounced excitement. 'He watched me peeing!'

'I can't tell a dog fox from a vixen, but don't panic, he won't tell nobody. Let's cool off in Pwllmelyn.'

Tiered below the sunken ruins, moraine rockeries of heather and whinberry overlooked the round pond in a hollow of scree and patchy moss. Only fleet whirligig beetles printed the still water.

He undressed to his underpants.

'We might catch cramp,' she said.

'Aye, it was a good-size feed.'

'Strip off, shall I?'

'Yeh, c'mon, strip off.'

'Huh, horny.'

Hurling screestones doublehanded like a mole, he cleared a strip of yellowy moss and lichened earth.

She flapped out a towel, offering, 'Bless my soul,' to his dense passion, sanguine helpmeet, earth mother and layer-out, committed since consciousness conquered seasons millennia before right and wrong. She thrilled to the craving in his eyes, yet gripped his nape, 'Wait now,' and later, 'Be still, *cariad*.'

Foundered in gawp, he watched her standing shin-deep, splashing, scooping, scrupulously splashing, skimming water down her thighs as she stepped out, delicately foot-stamped him off the towel, drying herself, pausing half-turned, inhaling-exhaling to bland pronouncement, 'Dewi Joshua, we're better shaggers than hikers.'

Which galled his feelings. 'Lay off that kind of talk. We're a pair, we're two lovers. Comes natural whatever you think, but I don't want to argue. Lovers, for God's sake. I love you Elsie, always will, if I drop dead this minute.'

'Watch what you say, mister.' She kneeled, lowered herself slow motion, prone on the towel. 'Massage my back for me.'

'Massage, righto.'

'Where I can't reach.'

He rubbed between her shoulder blades then rapidly pummelled the edges of his hands up and down, up and down until the soft flesh pinkened.

'How's that, girl?'

'Mm, nice. Now do us both a favour, jump in the water.'

'Aye, makes me feel horny agen.'

He dived shallow, thrashed a few strokes, filled his lungs, porpoised up and over, down through lifeless chill, peering narrow-eyed, groping algae-covered sandstone rubble—*Iesu*, she can read my mind.

Floating, sighting her along his torso between the held-stiff vee of his feet, he said, 'Coming in?'

Elsie slept.

He lay beside her, shivering. He paced off, swung his arms, jogged on the spot, thinking, we didn't bring our bathers. Just one towel. She planned this from the beginning. Same as she did with the bloke Pomeroy. Can't remember Gorwel Pomeroy. Before I was born. As for Llew, he'd never stroll up here. No chance. Old Llew . . . and I'm with his Missis. Bloody hell. By the Jesus Christ Almighty.

Warm-bodied, staring down at his penis, 'You're doing al'right.'

★   ★   ★   ★

Bank Holiday night-time when he left 9, Dinmel Terrace, his belongings wrapped in brown paper parcels, his pit clothes, boots, tommy box and tin jack in a hessian sack.

Zena sniffled misery. 'Well, your life it is, but you're making a big mistake with Elsie Kitchener.' Zena dry-washed her hands. 'Take care.'

'Mam, you keep on worrying.'

'Goodbye, son.'

'So-long, Mam.'

He slept in the back bedroom, jolted himself awake at 6 a.m., chocked the alarm clock and padded down to the kitchen. Frumpily morose in a plaid dressing gown, Elsie said, 'On the hob.'

'Hullo there, girl!'

'I shan't be getting up this time of day.'

He snatched the plate from the hob to the table. 'Poached egg on toast. Good-oh. Look, it's no bother, I'll manage every morning so stay in bed.'

She stammered yawning with the back of her hand. 'I intend to, mister.'

At five to seven he leapt sprinting from a tramcar. The top pit banksman grumbled, 'Get in the bloody cage. Last bon down.'

Walking on, he came alongside Wyndham Mabon.

'*Shwmae'n mynd*, Dewi?'
'Great, man. What about Ellis?'
'Right on his toes at the moment. It's that fucken Hitler. Two loonies, Hitler and that dirty waster slaughtering his own people in Spain. Bastards should have their breath stopped.'
'Think there'll be a war?'
'Bound to if you read the papers. Don't forget, four men from Moel Exchange gone to fight in Spain.'
'Aye, Communists, plenty in Wales. I'm not interested in politics.'
Wyndham grunted disapproval.
'Whenever you write to Ellis, tell him all the best from me. He did me a good turn once. Where'd you go yesterday?'
'Me and the wife started on a chicken cot out the back. I got some nice Rhode Island pullets coming from Twm Ray's ranch up by Cefn Road.'
He said, 'Twm's bloody hacienda, *braddish* nailed on off-cuts from Pencaer sawmill, more bark than timber.'
'It's the fresh eggs, Dewi. What's in your face this morning?'
'Full cut should be.'
'Your butty's on in front.'
'I'll step on it, catch up with him.'
Wyndham nodded, 'Fair enough, boy.'
Irfon was building the roadside gob wall, his greeting impartial, 'Aye-aye.'
'How's it looking, Ive?'
'Like a palace.'
'What d'you say we pitch in together on this top hole 'til the haulier comes? I can throw left hand better than you.'
They worked side by side, kneeing round-nosed shovels into roof debris, Irfon saying, 'You should have seen me doing overarm in Aberselsig. No puff left at all. Knackered I was.'
'Can't do the overarm myself, Ive.'
'Sun caught Hetty, she's like beetroot 'cross her shoulders. Tossed and turned all night. She saw you coming down our *gwli*.'
'What time?'
'Late. I was out like a dead man.'

Temptation stirred but he waited until they were sitting behind their third tram at grub-time.

Irfon reached into his pocket. 'Here's a stick of Aberselsig rock for you. Hetty thought of it.'

'Ta, thanks. Listen a minute, I'm in the Villas, lodging with Elsie Kitchener.'

'Jonnack?'

'Honest.'

'Gawd fuck me drunk. Now I've heard everything. Bust-up with your mother Zena, or what?'

'No-no, no-no.'

'Been to bed with her?'

'Well-aye, sometimes, now and then.'

'Digging your grave with your prick. Christ, we've seen it times galore.' Irfon raised his water jack, 'Cheers, Cetewayo, and the best of fucken British.'

'She's my woman, Elsie is.'

'The old *trych*'s not long in his box either.'

He said, 'We've been sparking for ages, matter of fact since the time we met in the Legion Club, long before Ellis Mabon joined the Army.'

'Clicked straight off then?'

'Aye,' and coldly truculent, 'I'll have a go at any bugger who tries taking the piss out of me.'

'Dewi-boy, never let it be said your father reared a jibber.'

He gnawed the hard sweetmeat. 'Theo didn't rear me. I can hardly remember my father.'

'No matter,' said Irfon Tŷ-isaf.

★   ★   ★   ★

At the end of the week he gave Elsie thirty shillings.

'Twenty-five will be enough.'

'Thirty bob, full lodge,' he said, 'Two quid when I'm working my own stall.'

She lightly jabbed, held her forefinger on the nub of his chin. 'When you're twenty-one you must sit the fireman's exam. I'll teach you the maths.'

'Firemen,' he said, 'they get ballockings off the men and off management. Fact is, decent officials in Pencaer, they're sent afternoons or nights. They can't take the ranting and raving on dayshift. Understand, Elsie, sometimes it's pure nerve showing who's boss.'

'You'll be a boss too.'

'I don't know.'

She folded his palm on two halfcrowns. 'I'll teach you.'

'I want to pay my way, though.'

He fell into her smothering hug. 'Shh, hush hush. Remember now, my word goes in Parc Villa.' Elsie disengaged herself to pour tea.

Time ahead stretched baffling. He thought, if she's *always* in the right, I'll be a loser. I'll lose mates. Just like our coppers booking men for swearing or singing *The Red Flag*, or putting the half-nelson on blokes after stop tap, men they grew up with in school.

★   ★   ★   ★

War wreaked far away from Moel Exchange. *Their* planes flew over at night. The siren wailed from the A.R.P. centre, a spare engine shed commandeered from the G.W.R. And Dewi felt older than twenty, guest of Sid Ginty in Plasmarl, with a small tumbler of beer in his hand, paper doily crumpled in his other hand. He was finding the manager's eyes above Mrs. Ginty's tightly permed hair. Swift awareness in Mrs. Ginty's turning face, offering him a tipped de Reske.

'No thanks. I don't smoke.'

'Time draweth nigh,' announced the pit manager, checking his pocket watch. 'Ladies and gents, hooter in five seconds.'

Whistles piped discordant from engines in the shunting yard, Pencaer hooter louder, prolonged, booming on and on.

Elsie kissed him on the forehead. 'Happy New Year.'

'Happy New Year.'

'Lovely boy.'

'Lovely girl.'

'I'm tight.'

'I'm not, not so far anyhow.'

Her eyes swoony, 'Mm, what a handsome swine.'

He said, 'I'm breaking new ground.'

He watched her pecking kisses, clinking glasses. Carefree. At home in Plasmarl. We're opposites, he thought. She's full of pep. She's full of faces. She's on stage. What kind of bloke am I? Learn. Find out. Be yourself, for Christ's sake.

Frizzy haired Mrs. Ginty emphasised, '*Happy* New Year!'

'Happy New Year, Mrs. Ginty.'

'Gracie to my friends.'

Her handshake kindled free-speaking. 'How are things, Gracie?'

'Come, I think we should have a chat.' Her fingers wriggled over the funny bone in his elbow. He saw Sid Ginty's Mining Engineer's diploma framed on the wall. Gracie smiled her mouth. 'My husband's study. You don't want that.' She dropped the doily into a waste paper basket. 'Another drink?'

'Please.'

'Whisky?'

He resented rictal fixity in his grin. 'To loosen my tongue?'

She poured Johnny Walker into a fresh glass. 'Soda?'

'More the better.' Clicking his tongue, 'I'm not used to shorts.'

'What are you afraid of?'

Slowing his words, 'Nothing that I know of, either in Moel Exchange or down under.'

Her eyebrows arched, supporting thin mazy creases to her hairline. She blinked, disarming, 'Hurrah, the famous Welsh arrogance. Arrogance and cunning mixed together. I'm not sure if it's a blessing or a burden. Some men talk big because they feel small. Now to business. My husband would like to promote you to time-keeper in Pencaer office—wait a moment! On the understanding you attend night school classes.'

'I get it, Elsie's influence, only she's mistaken. By next New Year's Day I'll qualify as fireman. That'll suit me, fireman's ticket. I know the work and I know every collier in Pencaer.' Whisky firing defiance, 'Daresay my name'll be dragged through the mud a bit more, but I've been through it already. There'll be rows, arguments in the pit, but eventually I'll sort things out.'

Sid Ginty's slanted head appeared and withdrew from the doorway.

In the plush velvet, balconied lounge they were singing *Should auld acquaintance be forgot,* likewise on blacked-out Moel Square, celebrants circling hand in hand, children darting, yelping 'Happy New Year!' for pennies.

Gracie caught his elbow again, 'Young man, you are a tribute to Elsie,' hustling him from Ginty's study, and he cross-armed between Gracie and the cashier's wife, longshanks Deborah Coles wearing a puce frock down to her shoes, rucks from neckline to waist camouflaging her bony frame: *For auld lang syne, my dear, For auld lang syne, We'll take a cup of kindness yet, For auld lang syne.*

Gracie wiped her eyes. She stared upwards as if alone.

Her stance reminded him of Zena. 'You al'right, Gracie?'

She moved away, ''Bye for now, Dewi.'

Elsie came queenly between dark jacketed shoulders. 'Enjoying the party?'

He said, 'Hey, there's no other collier ever been invited to Plasmarl.'

'So there!'

'Another thing, love, forget about time-keeper. A sixteen year old girl could book in shift work. Do as you promised, help me tackle the School of Mines exam in Twrgwyn, then I'll be dishing out orders from the cabin.'

Sid Ginty smacked decorous handclaps, 'Ladies and gents, take your partners.'

'Let's show off,' he said.

Company checkweigher Ossie Ross towered his silvery maned head. 'May I, Elsie?'

He said, 'Wait in the *gwt.*'

Ossie's thumbs hung in his waistcoat pockets. 'Rather crude, Joshua.'

'Yellow,' he replied, stoic as a hangman. 'More bottom in a pom.'

She insisted, 'You two, that's enough.' Then Elsie cut loose, stylish, slow foxtrotting around the lounge.

Proud, he thought, saying, 'When I'm carrying a lamp we'll make a date for the registrar's office in Matabele Crescent.'

'Lamp?'

'Safety lamp, goes with a fireman's ticket. Oil lamp for testing gas.'

Delayed response, rapt Elsie singing, '*Those autumn leaves, all red and gold, and when you're far away...*'

'I won't be,' he said.

They flowed past Sid Ginty, cigar butt cupped in his hand, shouldering through heavy window drapes from the balcony as the wiren wailed.

Ginty voiced, 'Dah-amn.'

Gracie pleaded. 'For goodness sake, spare a thought for those poor people in London.'

And Dai Greg, 'Three nights back, fire bombs all over London. It's a crime.'

Guests moved into groups, Dinah Shore winding down the lost-cause sentiment of *Falling leaves*. Sid Ginty switched off the gramophone.

Seated cramped on benches in the cellar of Plasmarl, Elsie elected herself M.C., urging entertainment until the All Clear.

Gabe and Deborah Coles sang *I'm forever blowing bubbles*.

Elsie, 'We now call upon our famous elocutionist, Mr. Ossie Ross!'

Ossie recited *The green eye of the little yellow god*.

Near the end of Gracie's demure *Flow gently, sweet Afton*, the All Clear sounded.

Dai Greg complained, 'Work tomorrow,' as they returned to the lounge.

He said, 'Where's the cutter?'

'Gate road on the trolley. Full cut right down the face.'

They were queueing towards Sid and Gracie: 'Lovely party'— 'Goodnight, goodnight'— 'Happy New Year'— 'Really lovely; goodnight.'

'Irfon and me,' he said to Dai, 'between us we'll throw ten tons on the belt tomorrow.'

Ginty tightened a complicit smile at Gracie's, 'You must come again,' turning her face to cat-rub cheeks with Elsie.

'Surely,' remarked Sid Ginty, lifeless as echo, as if excluded from human affairs.

Gracie smiled her mouth again.

As they walked to Parc Villa, high flying bombers hummed like turbines in the black sky. Elsie clung to his arm, her high heels stuttering to his long-striding Pencaer main gait.

'Awfully nice party. You made a good impression, mister.'

'Think so?'

'I *know* so.'

They went straight to bed, his hands and mouth exploring her body, but Elsie slept, disappeared. Lusting in darkness, he too went lost until the 6 a.m. alarm rang into his head.

★ ★ ★ ★

Irfon taunted, 'You're using that shovel like fucken Frankenstein.'

'We were in Plasmarl last night,' he said.

'*Duw*, boy!'

'Big do. All the *crachach*.'

'By Chrise, well-in then, butty. Don't spread it 'round.'

'You should have been there, Ive.'

'Get fucked.'

They shovelled coal onto the sliding belt.

He said, 'It was good.'

'Lotsa grub?'

'Salmon sandwiches, ham sandwiches, beef, cheese and tomato and onion sandwiches. Enough biscuits and crackers to fill a couple of curling boxes. Booze, you name it. Christ knows where they finagled the food coupons. Mrs. Ginty took a shine to me, reckoned Sid wanted to make me time-keeper.'

The belt jerked, rollers squealed, colliers bawled, 'Who's chuckling them big lumps on?'

'Fucken senseless!'

'Too tired to pick up a fucken mandrel!'

Irfon spat Ringer's juice. 'Elsie Kitch pull wires, ah?'

'I turned it down,' he said.

'You'd be called up, butty. Youngster from the pay office in khaki already.'

'Yeh, I was in Empire Crossing school with Tim Owens. Tim

never joined in anything, not even marbles. He'd watch us playing Catty and Dog.'

Gomer North came down the face. 'Too big lumps, they're roughing the top out on our tip end.'

Irfon tenor-shrieked, 'We'd be fucken stupid, wouldn't we!'

Said the chargehand, 'Every bugger's complaining. Just telling you same as the rest.'

Instantly mollified, 'So long as you're not picking on us,' said Irfon.

'Orders see, every man-jack of us. I gotto put my foot down.'

'Bollocks to Dai Greg. I didn't come down the river onna fucken plank.'

Gomer the North Walian repeated orders throughout the face, then he returned to his stent.

At 11 o'clock thirty men and boys went to the gate road. Another dozen sat in the supply road. Dewi lolled, stolidly munched, drank most of his water and rested mindless until twenty past eleven.

They cleared their stent by 2 o'clock.

He dozed on his knees, left leg buckled under, left shoulder against a post. Irfon ape-lolloped up the face to help Dwgie Harding clear his stent—Dwgie, born in Moel Exchange, whose grandfather Cadwgan tramped from Cardiganshire with Irfon's grandfather, Bible-haunted Irfon Francis.

'Okay,' he said, without moving.

Irfon gently smacked his ribs, 'C'mon, Elmo the Mighty.'

'Aye, be right there.'

Rain bleared the town as they walked to the lamproom.

'Out tonight, Dewi?'

'Con Club. Concert for evacuees.'

Irfon mimed another soft punch. 'Fucken 'vacuee yourself.'

Grinning Colgate teeth in his black face, 'Elsie's on the committee. Secretary.'

'Faaquen roll on. Hardly any 'vacuees in the bloody Villas.'

'S'long, Ive.'

'Raw eggs, boy. Build your strength up with raw eggs.'

V

Contract saloon buses ferried shift workers (girls, wives, grandmothers) to the Arsenal 29 miles away on Rhos Estate. Zena Joshua served in one of the canteens. Elsie avoided yellowing her face and hands. She supervised, signed for meats, vegetables and tinned supplies in the British Restaurant outside the G.W.R. Central.

Winter hardened as the Essential Works Order squeezed. Labour Exchange queues now meant only crocks, cripples and introvert outlaws. Conscientious objectors became colliery labourers. A few rock bottom desperates maimed themselves. Exempted civil servants sustained patriotism by edict, drafting men and women under the Order. Great War veterans trained the Home Guard, up down and roundabout two football fields. Lacking bullets, they manned pillboxes on the outskirts of town. Lieutenant Ginty and Sergeant Coles organised and delegated duties from a room in Pencaer Institute. Innate bureaucrats operated from Moel Exchange Council Offices, granting allocations, awarding favours by unwritten statute.

Methodist and Baptist congregations prayed for loved ones in uniform. Two churches, Catholic and Church of England, prayed to the same deity with ritual fervour.

Death and destruction belonged elsewhere.

Germany invaded Denmark, Norway, the Netherlands, Luxembourg, France. Until Dunkirk, St. Valery and the fall of France, Pencaer colliery prospered. Dewi bought a good as new second-hand 500 ccs Triumph motorbike. He swotted plain black leather bound text books borrowed from Dai Greg, Elsie at his elbow, critical, uprooting his largely *Daily Herald* ethos. And she demeaned the worth of his coal-face six years with Llew and Irfon, the root and branch spread of his experience. Week after week into months. Each to each they reconciled in bed. But aggravations lingered, seeding acrimony. Meanwhile she unravelled jargoned mysteries of the Mines and Quarries Acts. Step by step she manipulated layers of his feelings. Slow as a chameleon he moved, connected theory to reality. She as if by divine right, thinking: The more he hurts, the more I hurt too. He's man enough. And I'm the woman who found him. Because I'm Mair Evans's daughter.

One evening in early July, Ellis Mabon knocked on the door. He was hangdog, recoiled, his face raddled raw pink from forehead to his khaki collar.

'They tell me Dewi Joshua lives here.'

Dewi bundled past her in the hallway. 'Ellis! You're home!'

'I've been keeping my head down. Too much fuss in Chapel Street, as if I'm in a bloody zoo.'

She wagged a small clenched fist. 'Wyndham Rhys's son?'

'Right. These blotches on my face, they came from food poisoning. Fancy a stroll 'round, Dewi?'

Aversion flattened her tone. 'He's studying at the moment.'

'For fireman,' he said. 'Be with you in two ticks.'

Doleful Private Rhys as they walked under avenue trees towards High Street.

'*Iesu*, you've lost some weight, Ellis. What d'you say to a few pints in the Legion Club?'

'I've just come out of dock. M.O. said lay off the beer. Straight now, how does it look?'

'Good Christ, man, you're not blind.'

Ellis pawed his face. 'Fuck it. Rotten stinking fucken meat, spew and fucken spew and no more shit left to come out of my ring. Fucken shambles it was.'

'When? Where's that, Ellis?'

'Inland, before they took us aboard off Dunkirk.' Ellis dragged, slow-paced as a decrepit. He squared his shoulders, protesting like a child reaching for belief, 'Cut off see, no grub! We ate leaves, mouldy chaff from stables and troughs. Worst, them fucken ducks, been dead ages, stinking fucken rotten, stinking, stinking . . .'

He said, 'Take it easy. You're al'right now, you're home safe.'

Ellis blared, 'Dopy bugger, you don't know what bastard day it is. Same goes for my old man and the old lady.'

'Al'right, take it easy,' was all he could say.

Ellis swivelled about-turn on the pavement. 'I'll be off back to the house.'

'See you tomorrow,' he said.

'Leave me be for a spell.'

'Righto, that's okay, Ellis.'
Ellis marched away.
He said, 'Let me know then.'
Elsie opened the door. 'Keep at the homework. If I'm late, go to bed.'
'What's on, girl?'
'Whist drive. Unless you concentrate you won't pass the exam.'
'Slow but sure,' he said. 'You might jib before me.'
Shrilling irritation, 'Remains to be seen!'

That night he awoke as pallid dawn expanded, brightening the bedroom. Worry lurked. I'm lucky. Lucky so far. Three meals a day. Warm bed with Elsie. Regular job down the Four Deep. Stent of my own three months from now.

Her nasal moan changed to *achchch* in her throat, to peaceful breathing.

Ellis. Bloody hell, Ellis Mabon, he's tormented deep inside himself.

Sleep failed him. He sidled away from her and went downstairs. Bare feet up on the table, he reasoned out his flesh and blood. I'm not brainy, never was in school, mug neither, otherwise I'd be shoved from pillar to post. Whatever crops up, I'll take it on. I'm good in the coal face. Plenty good for her upstairs. I'll hold my own. I'll do my whack. Definitely.

Remembrances invaded. Old Llew explaining why and how to put up a pair of timbers. Sound the top, sound the coal instead of slashing at it like a man with four arms. How to sink sleepers. Lay a pair of rails. Hole under the stank. Keep the gob wall straight. Pull a quick dram-full if needs be. Measure posts. Flats. Build and pack a cog. Rig up a boring machine. Drill six-footers, six pills and one det, go careful at first with the ramming clay, ram it home firm to finish. Above all, put the block on clever bastards. Or some fireman too chesty for his job: 'Don't let any bugger walk over you.'

Only I can't be a *trych* like old Llew. Old Llew forgot how to spend money. Forgot Elsie too, except very likely she forgot him first.

Tugging into his pit clothes from a locker in the bathroom, consciousness crowding his mind: I'm fucking a *trych*'s wife . . .

widow, *widow* for Jesus' sake. As for love, I don't know much about that. Never a hint about love down below. Otherwise in Moel Exchange, just cheap bloody lies, stuff from what goes on in the pictures.

Ellis Mabon, he's been to his limit. Good bloke. He's near the edge. Ellis though, he *knows*. We're happy as pigs in shit, nowhere near what he's been through. Even my old lady, she's better off now than before Theo my father was laid out.

First kick and the Triumph cough-coughed. Second kick she roared. Watch it, he thought, no petrol coupons left.

Dozens of colliers were ganged around the officials' cabin on top pit.

'Three shifts on, three off,' said the stooped overman as if evangelising, 'which means you'll be able to claim dole money for three days. As Mr. Ginty put it, don't make sense raising coal if they can't sell it. See, boys, we're up agenst the wall. There's no trade out from the docks. Tonight you'll see notices all over town. Better three on-three off than shutting down till we lambaste those fucken Nazis.'

Without hope or option they grizzled pros and cons in the cage, tramping the main, on the double-parting, at grub-time and while wives or mothers scrubbed their backs on the hearth. Dewi invented washing his back criss-crosswise with a length of soaped towelling, the way he dried himself.

When Elsie came home she groped a small pork pie and four sausages from poacher's pockets inside her coat. She said, 'Gracie believes Pencaer will close before the end of the summer. These things are meant to try us. Now, I suggest you've got to move fast.'

'Where to? Army? I'd sooner dig ditches down Cox's Farm.'

'Rubbish, mister. They'll need *some* men in Pencaer. Safety officials, winding house, pumpsmen. Any others?'

'Electrician, fitter, boilermen.'

'How many?'

'Days, afternoons, nights.' A sudden glimpse of Llew pitched alive inside his head. Llew's raw obsession: Fill out coal. And since gone forever. 'There's the lamproom,' he said. 'Compo cases only. One bloke on crutches, another two canting sideways on sticks.'

Elsie acted, she sat down, chin on her palm like Rodin's massive *Thinker*.

He heated milk for making custard. They shared cooking and cleaning as inevitable. Both worked. Unseasonable *cawl* simmered on the kitchen range. Treacle pudding (British Restaurant) and dried milk custard for afters.

Serene at the table, Elsie spooned aside shiny surface rings of mutton fat. 'Elton Nixon,' she said, 'he's the eldest.'

'Paddy Nixon, corns on his hands like black leather. Cranky old Paddy, he keeps a bull terrier in a cask outside of his back door.'

'I must speak to the manager.'

'Ginty?'

'He won't be in Plasmarl when they close Pencaer. D'you know, long ago Selina Nixon worked in Pencaer stables. Selina Price in those days, very friendly with my Auntie Megan. Megan Coslett—*her* mother was Madame Powell-Coslett, bel canto soprano, Weston Super Mare. Megan herself, she married Rupert Harris, Tŷcoed farm.'

'Mervyn's father?'

'Mm. First of all I'll try Selina. She owes me favours from when I took on Moel Emporium. You see, lovely boy, I think Elton is ready for old age pension. You could be boilerman, stay nice and comfy with me in Parc Villa.'

Amazement clowned his face.

Curt from Elsie, 'Not the least bit funny.'

Folded arms pressed against spluttering, he said, 'And we'll still have cheap loads of coal.'

'Zena can have them.'

'Aye, my mother, unless all this falls apart. Don't get me wrong, I'd stoke the Titanic. Easy after the Four Deep.'

Sadness stilled his unWelsh eyes: we're strangers, Zena and myself.

Elsie counted off on her fingers: 'Pencaer, High Seven, Garw, Pontfedw. Four pits for closing down.'

'According to who?'

Curls jiggling on Elsie's head, 'Deborah Coles actually.'

Boilerman, he thought. It'll make a change from packing the gob and shovelling coal off my knees.

*   *   *   *

The four pits closed a fortnight before his 21st birthday on September 7th. Clinching proofless nepotism, a Labour Exchange clerk handed him the green card, H.M. Government's clearance, exemption under the Essential Works Order. Three shift workers fired one Pencaer boiler. Four boilers left to rust. He learned the job from Elton Nixon, the old man's last slow-motion eight hours freeing him after forty-two years in colliery stokeholes, another fitly contented, albeit sometimes choleric, pinchpenny pensioner for the rest of his days. Elton's bog Irish father died from phthisis in Union Yard workhouse. Elton and four sisters grew up in a Barnado's Home. Their mother, Sylvia Nixon, had drowned herself in Cwmffrwd colliery dam.

In the way of mankind everywhere, civvy street fiddled, despite carnage past reckoning. World statesmen puffed themselves following stars, leaving lesser souls the perdu rationale of galaxies.

And Elsie miscarried a two month pregnancy in the British Restaurant staff lavatory.

Dewi overheard her puling grief in Dr. Hector Tibbs's surgery. The next day Hector Tibbs entered Parc Villa after a single sharp thump on the lion's head door knocker.

Elsie confessing as before, 'I thought I was starting on the change, Doctor.'

He felt humbler than proud, Doctor Tibbs's rapid backhand wigwag bidding him leave the room.

He leaned over the ironwork garden gate, swung it open for the crofter's grandson, professionally isolated to oracle: 'Have a care, laddie. Use french letters.'

'Sorry, Doctor. Forgot, just forgot.'

She flapped the prescription. 'Tonic, iron tonic! Oh, I feel so ashamed.'

Hugging her close, 'I'll sleep in the back room tonight.'

'Love me, *cariad*?'

'Word of honour,' he said.

While preparing dinner they sang *Hutsut rowlson on the rithela* with Gracie Fields on the wireless.

'She's wonderful,' enthused Elsie. 'The way she puts it across. Oh, I think she's out on her own.'

He remarked off-hand, 'Good voice, old fashioned style.'

Akimbo for confrontation, 'Are you saying I'm old fashioned?'

'Don't put words into my mouth.'

Up on the balls of her feet, rhythmic to regal dismissal, 'Thenk you, mister.'

'Steady, Elsie.'

'What does that mean?'

'No need, is there? Rowing over nothing at all.'

One behind the other they served fish rissoles, potatoes and parsley sauce.

'How do you find Doctor Tibbs?' he said.

'Mm, thick from the neck down.'

He twin-pointed his knife and fork, seriousness ageing his high cheekboned face. 'Sorry about this trouble, love. My fault. It's up to me, right?'

Soliloquy while slicing a rissole, 'Men, they think they're in charge of life itself.' She stared at him. 'Women, we run everything. Always have, always will.'

Leave it, he thought. You're in the middle of nowhere.

'Water's gaining fast in the sump at pit bottom,' he said. 'Our pumps are working 'round the clock but they can't keep the water down.'

'Sid Ginty's gone away.'

'He'd tell us where it's coming from.'

'On Civil Defence.'

He cupped his ear. 'Where'd Sid disappear to? No fifth column in Moel Exchange.'

'Well, Gracie kept the secret. All she came out with was "South coast."'

'Must be tunnelling. The man's a mining engineer.'

Elsie forked a piece of rissole onto his plate. 'I miss Gracie Ginty.'

He thought, Aye, more real than Gracie the comedienne, then

he changed course, 'Ellis Mabon's back in dock somewhere near to Swansea. Army, Navy and Air Force hospital. He's bad with stomach ulcers. Like a lath gone. Mrs. Rhys catches the west Wales bus on weekends. Wyndham himself, he's working in the Arsenal, him and my old butty Irfon. Unbelievable, colliers clocking in with thousands of women.'

'Hundreds at least,' revulsion crooking Elsie's mouth. 'We don't see men with yellow hair and faces and hands.' Footsteps in the front porch smoothed her distaste, soothed her murmured, 'Who can that be?'

Deborah Coles sang, 'Anybody ho-ome?' She opened a leather bag stencilled with weeping willows.

'Chocolate Rolls!' cried Elsie.

'Dozen!' he said. 'Where from?'

Lanky Deborah stalked, innocent hands clasped to her pudendum. 'Ask no questions. Walls have ears.'

Elsie kissed her cheek. 'You're a gem, Deborah.'

He filled the kettle. *Iesu*, dozen Chocolate Rolls.

At eight o'clock Deborah and Elsie went to the Council Canteen. Two bachelor scrooges were selling clothing coupons.

En route to Pencaer stokehole at ten o'clock, he propped the Triumph outside his mother's house.

'Hullo, stranger.'

'I know I should have called in, Mam. No excuses.'

'Nights I see.'

'Days next week.'

'Elsie feeling better?'

'Gone to the Canteen with Mrs. Coles.'

'Awful about the baby.'

He corrected a headshake to solemn nodding.

'My grandchild.'

'Would have been, aye. Doctor Tibbs said act of God, nobody's to blame.'

Zena strained warm smiling, 'How are you, boy?'

'Great,' he laughed spontaneously. 'I'm stoking 'cause Elsie pulled strings.'

Thrill wriggled her slender shoulders. 'I pinch tea and sugar from the cookhouse.' She reached a caddy from the mantelpiece, spooned tea into a brown paper bag, twisted it tight. 'For you and Elsie.'

'Mam, you're the goods. Now I must skate. G'night. Look after yourself.'

At the door with a timorous gesture stroking his arm, 'I'm so pleased for you, Dewi. Goodnight, son, and thanks for the housecoal.'

Minutes later he straddle-walked the Triumph into Pencaer's empty blacksmith shop. Torchlight blinded him as he switched off the headlamp.

'*Shwmae,*' he said to the man shadow. 'Switch off, you'll fetch the bloody A.R.P. up here.'

Irfon Tŷ-isaf whispered, 'Dewi Josh! Seen Willie Bob Ochr the watchman?'

'He'd be in the cabin this time of night. Does his rounds later on.'

'I'm after a hatchet shaft. Used to be a few tool shafts up agenst this wall.'

'Hatchet shaft, Ive?'

'For fence posts. I joined Gaer Allotments Association. Dig for victory, right?'

'I'll look around in the stores.'

'Locked solid, boy.'

'Key's in the cabin,' he said. 'I'll drop a shaft in your house tomorrow night.'

Solitary in the stokehole, unaware of loneliness, he reflected piecemeal smidgens of lost yesterdays and mysterious tomorrows. He felt the quietening between himself and Elsie. Gossip over and done with. No more shit-spreading. We've taken the muck in Moel Exchange, now we're same as man and wife anywhere. Just one thing. I know damn all about those Wills Woodbines shares. Yet money's for spending. Elsie's is on paper. She'll talk when she's ready. If my old lady knew, it's not news.

Hard trodden clinker underfoot, he barrowed cooling ashes by starlight, backfilling polluted marshland out to the parish track rutted from horse and cart days. Before seeing him, Dewi smelled the watchman's pipe smoke.

'Al'right, Willie?'

Bow-legged, tub-bellied and short-armed, the bootlicker watchman said, 'They'll be sending for the mechanic unless I'm much mistaken.'

'Can't say, Willie.'

'There agen, they might be gone bankrupt.'

'Never,' he said. 'Elsie reckons Ystrad and Talbot Mining Company went into armaments from the start.'

'She don't miss a trick, that's a fact'—Willie Bob Ochr following him into the stokehole, deviously impartial, watching him rake the firebars and shut the oven door with a quick shove and upward heave from the palm of his hand.

'Cwmffrwd was flooded out,' said Willie. 'With us it's the sump filling up.'

'You work in Cwmffrwd?'

'Not me, boy. I was put on a steady job with Mr. Pomperoy the seed merchant.'

He stared at the pressure gauge. 'Pomeroy's son, what he die of?'

'*Duw*, very very intelligent, Gorwel Pomeroy.'

'How old when he kicked it?'

'Young, terrible young. Consumption. They fumigated all the Corn Stores.'

'Was he courting?'

'Courting indeed! Ah now, *Mrs*. Pomeroy, she ruled the roost behind closed doors.'

'She *cwtched* the young bugger then?'

'I don't poke into other's business, if you must know.'

He wheeled the barrow sharply: skedaddle, you bloody creep.

Said Willie, 'Sorry to be in the way.' He fingered his soiled red and white cravat. 'Gorwel passed away in their front room upstairs, yes he did. Big funeral, length of High Street.' He lofted his nightstick as the siren moaned. 'Them oilworks agen!' And Willie went rubber-soled in and out the deserted workshops on the silent pithead.

German bombers thrummed, unknowable as star drift, while Dewi unlatched a cupboard in the officials' cabin. Brass key plate stamped STORES. Then back to the stokehole for his Mari Lwyd night lantern: candle stump wax-stuck inside a tin, nailhole perforated bottom, with a wire loop handle. But no hatchet shaft in Pencaer stores. Stacked pipes, flanges, fishplates, blast bags, patent mandrel heads, shackles, barhooks, oil drums, signal wire, insulators, boring machines, coils of cable, pit-rope collars, valves, drills, spanners, two electric motors in crates, cramp nails, road gauges hanging from wall pegs, rolls of brattice, oil buckets, hand pumps, tramwheel grease, bundle of safety sticks, nuts and bolts for repairing tram-planks.

He relocked the stores and sprinted to the cabin. 'You there, Willie?'

Silence.

Dewi hung the key on its hook in the cupboard.

Back in the stokehole, he realised Llew's tools were in Parc Villa. Full set on a toolbar hidden in the *cwtch dan stâr*. Llew's hatchet to Irfon. Good turn for a good bloke.

He increased the draught, raked the sparking coals level, banked up the fire, re-adjusted the damper and slammed shut the door. Buttoning into his jacket, he strolled outside. Redness profiled the northern horizon, a blaze from Llangroes oil works forty-seven miles away. Another mouthful for Lord Haw-Haw, the sneering shit.

VI

'Dead man's hatchet,' said Irfon. 'Don't wish bad luck on me.'

He said, 'What's the matter, afraid? I searched right through the stores for a bloody shaft.'

Irfon cuffed his shoulder. 'Cool down, butty. *Diolch* a lot. Let you have some fresh veg next season.'

'How's life in the Arsenal?'

'Loading department, me and Wyndham. Doctor on Rhos Estate told him he's got 'stagmus.'

'By the Jesus.'

'Chances are it'll wear off so long as he doesn't work in the pits. Who'd have thought they'd have shut down Pencaer, ah? Say ta-ta to your fireman's ticket.'

He said, 'Come in handy some day.'

'Hetty! Hetty, make us a cuppa tea, please!'

Mrs. Francis came from the middle room. 'Dewi Joshua, there's nice to see you.'

'Brought a hatchet for Irfon,' he said.

'Good God, Doctor Crippen to the tee.'

Irfon ran his wet thumb along the cutting edge. 'I'll build a fence that'll stop a bloody elephant.'

'What's the latest on Ellis Mabon?'

Irfon fisted the palm of his left hand. 'In a bad way, Ellis is. Once they discharge him he might go in for a government training course, only the boy's weak as a kitten.'

'Pity, pity,' said Hetty, lightly kicking Irfon's ankle. 'Mind out, man.' She swirled the teapot and left it on the fender, saying, 'Three minutes.'

Muted *thwoks* of ping-pong in the middle room, and he though, never a game of any sort in Dinmel Terrace. I don't play games except billiards now and again. Lost interest. Can't even win playing whist with Elsie the fanatic. Stoke Pencaer boiler by day, afternoons and nights, few pints whenever I feel like it, Elsie on gin shorts. Ride her bareback whenever she feels like it. *Iesu*, I'm narrow before my time . . .

Dewi waived this review to zero.

★   ★   ★   ★

As if competing for dread with the air raid siren, Pencaer hooter boomed a ragged S.O.S. on Boxing Day night. A jettisoned land mine erupted sphagnum moss, cotton-grass, peat, stones and clay, cratering the watershed two miles from Moel waterworks.

Elsie slept, the soft palping of her lips barely visible. He went downstairs. Men were running the white frosted avenue. A half waned moon pendant below twitching stars.

'Dewi!'

'What's up?'

Dai Greg, full-time A.R.P. warden (his C4 medical result

creased in his wallet), rattled the front gate. 'They've bombed Devil's Bog and there's water broke through from the old airway return in Glas Tump!'

Elsie appeared on the stairs, archetypal Venus, plaid dressing gown roped around her middle.

Staggered hooting continued from the roof of Pencaer winding house.

'Flood-out!' shouted Dai. 'C'mon, Dewi, all hands!'

'Be careful!' cried Elsie.

Four hundred yards west from the pitshaft, above the parish track, men and youths with shovels and picks floundered knee-deep through torrent.

'One man, one voice,' they were saying, demanding, expecting a leader with nous or bravado.

The shallow hillside glimmered darkly, clouds shredding across the half moon. He knelt in scree, picturing the terrain down the Nantglas from the neglected airway tunnel driven into Glas Tump, stone arched by Cornish masons in 1881, after sinkers had spent two years winning Pencaer steam coal seam. Dai Greg squatted, forearms on his knees.

He said, 'We'll turn it from the mouth. Let's move, fetch pills and dets and fuse from Pencaer powder-house. Now, Dai, give orders. Tell the men to start digging a gutter far side of the airway. But leave the mouth alone. Explain to the men. You and me, we'll lay some charges, turn the water.'

'Where to, for Chrissake?'

'Down to Nantglas. Got your bloody tin whistle? Blow it!'

They rolled stones, flung turves and clumps of bracken, the ditch raking slantwise away from Pencaer pit-head.

He broke into the padlocked powder magazine with a sledge-hammer. Half past one when Dai again blew his whistle. Two charges, ten pills each, wadded with clay in holes scooped under the far side wall of the airway return tunnel, three yards of fuse from each detonator. As the shouting ceased, Dewi and Dai lit the fuses.

'Hold hands,' he said, running, and they flopped together behind a sunken boulder. Two simultaneous cracks. Earth and pulverised stones whined and hissed the frosted night. Nobody moved. Then low gabble on Glas Tump. Yells broke loud, ringing to triumph. Men leapt like demoniac clowns, digging into hummocks, tumbling stones, and the wide-spreading subterranean water began scouring its own gully down to Nantglas.

Daylight brought women, children and pensioners.

'Broke through from up Cwmffrwd,' they were saying.

'Must be Cwmffrwd.'

'Same as before,' they said, old-timers rheumy and grey.

'Bound to be the Cwmffrwd body of water'—ex-colliery officials watching Nantglas doubling its flow, iron rust riming the banks forever-after, humming and hawing consternation while a dozen low-lying back kitchens were swamped to their firegrates; upper Nantglas well nigh sterile forever too, as far as Time comes and goes everywhere.

To no purpose a fire engine jangled in from Rhos Estate. By now Elsie had won esteem. She organised a van supplying tea and slices of bread pudding on Pencaer pit-head.

'Aye,' they were saying, wet-legged, shivering, 'Dewi Joshua was on to the right idea from the start. Used to work down the Four Deep with Irfon Tŷ-isaf.'

'I'm fucken perished.'

'We saved Bute Row and Bryncae Street and Parish Bridge and Dinmel. Main pipeline from the waterworks comes across Bute Row top end.'

'Gaer Cutting, don't forget,' they said. 'There'd be no bloody trains.'

'Theo's boy, he read the signs.'

'Too fucken true.'

'Living tally with Mrs. Kitchener.'

'Give her a medal and all.'

The town crier stumped with his handbell. His proclamation threatened, 'By orders of the Council, you must boil water from the taps 'til further notice! Remember now! In case you catch typhoid!'

Dewi worked his afternoon shift. He didn't want any more palavering. Councillors, they stayed in bed or Andersen shelters. Elsie gloried, vaunting him in the British Restaurant. *Her* lodger.

Platonic actually. Of course platonic. Moel Exchange hero for the time being. And on the bus to Rhos Estate Arsenal, Zena Joshua smiled ineffable pride. 'Famous,' they said. Her son, only child of her lost husband. Different men, different ways, but goodness in both deep down. Her wilful son, testimony to/of herself—herself saved from poverty by this War. She was independent. No doubt whatsoever in Zena's mind.

Another white frost night, Willie Bob Ochr calling 'Hoi!' as he stood pissing in the dark. '*Duw*, you it is, Dewi. I bet you feel ever so pleased, going by all the talk. They tell me it was pelting out of the old return.'

He said, 'Pit bottom's back to normal, few inches of slurry in the sump.'

'But it would have filled up all the pit and drownded us out!' Fear and cant brought Willie's hand clutching Dewi's forearm. 'Lucky for us you was there! I could see it like in chapter seven.'

'Leave off, man,' he said.

'Genesis! The flood! We'd all be gone, all gone!'

'Willie, bugger off.'

'Me and the wife, we prayed for you, boy *bach*.'

'G'night now, Willie,' then, '*Shwmae*, Ike. I barrowed a couple of loads ready for you.'

The watchman hopped aside from stoker Ike Houghton's cruiserweight heft.

'Righto. Now you ride home on that bike.'

Principle, he thought, custom and practice from Elton Nixon. Two barrowloads from the bunker for the on-coming shift.

Shared pause, waiting for Willie to drift elsewhere.

'Notice up in the 'Stute,' said Ike. 'Some bright cunt down from London, more war effort blah-blah. Fucken shower. Work? They got no idea. G'wan, Dewi, put your head down.'

'Roads slippery tonight, Ike. See you, butty.'

Minutes later, rounding out from behind the deserted colliery stables, he clicked up a gear as she stepped off the pavement, white scarf flagging him down. The Triumph racketted. He closed the throttle.

The mohair scarf wafted under his chin. 'It's me, Greta. I don't want us to be seen. Where can we meet?'

'Where's your copper then?'

'I've heard about you and Mrs. Kitchener. For shame on you, Dewi.'

'You're way behind the times, girl. Where's the copper?'

'Markie went to pieces after old Mr. Rowley died. Drove himself sick. Fuss fuss, I couldn't bear it. When they gave permission for Markie to leave the Force to run the farm in Sylen, we decided on separation.'

He cut the engine. 'Oh aye.'

'Honest to God, Mrs. Rowley's a proper witch. I'd be afraid to eat food in that farmhouse.'

'You'll soon get a job in the Arsenal.'

'I'm starting Monday.'

'Good. Your old lady still about the place?'

'She's busy all right, I mean for her age. As a matter of interest by the way, don't you want us to meet one night?'

'This is the pot calling the kettle black,' he said. 'Didn't you mention shame?'

Greta flounced, stamped, 'Ych, it's bitter cold.' She drew the scarf across her mouth. 'I'm broad-minded these days.'

'How come?'

'There's a war on!'

He lunged down on kickstart. 'So long as you don't blame me. All the best, Greta.'

Muffled behind the scarf, 'You cheeky bloody pig.'

* * * *

Rosebay willowherb flew south-west from Gaer Cutting to colonise the vacant half acre of Pencaer timber yard, bark-mulched for forty-six years. Couch grass gave way to rushes in waterlogged patches on top pit, where the wheels of discarded trams seized in caked grease.

Dry weather cripples, lungers, and ailing moochers absolved from everything scavenged slag heaps for ribblings, splintered posts, scrap iron, worthless scraps of conveyor belt. Ancient, familiar crises of work and money triggered the dispersion of Moel Exchange men, of women if they refused employment on

Rhos Estate. Ellis Rhys wandered, closed face, furtive in libraries and Pencaer Institute. Mice chittered unheard in Plasmarl; Corrugated zinc sheets were nailed to door jambs and window frames front and back, herbaceous plants and bushes pilfered from the beech hedged garden, the hedge itself butchered for kindling.

Music While You Work in the Arsenal, everybody willy-nilly sponging up *Chattanooga Choo Choo*, the Andrew Sisters followed by *Still of the night* from Victor Sylvester.

Tranced at the bathroom mirror, Elsie hummed *These foolish things* while plucking out single greys from the towelled mop of her wavy black hair, information from Ossie Ross concentrating her mind. Councillor Ossie (Labour, Ward 4) after three nominations for office. Lonely Ossie, life-cursed by a Plymouth Brethren mother and a backslider father who embezzled Pearl Insurance Company, and disappeared the night before Ossie matriculated in Dewinton Grammar School.

Ossie: 'Surveyors are inspecting Cwmffrwd.'

'Really?'

'Let you know the outcome.'

'Ever so obliged, my dear,' she said.

'My pleasure.'

'There's a good man, Ossie-love,' craning towards him, dapping her lips on his cheek.

'I have always looked up to you, Elsie.'

Her childlike hand pat-patted his strange androgynous coiffure. 'After all, we're two of a kind, sort of, mm? I'm not saying physically.'

And she heard Dewi grunt himself awake. He came into the bathroom.

'I'll be working another doubler,' he said. 'Albert Mort's still down with 'flu.' He bent over the wash basin. 'What's the time? *Iesu*, I caught up with some sleep today.'

She yanked the elasticated waist of his pyjamas. 'Gone nine o'clock. You'll be dead between the legs.'

'Joke,' he said, lowering his head, whoofing explosions until warm water filled his ears. He spouted a needle-streamed inch at her face while grabbing her around the buttocks.

'Don't make me blush, lovely boy!'

He growled between her breasts.
Elsie shrieked, 'Carry me!'
'Hi-yup!'
He wobbled, tried hooking her bodyweight higher in his arms, finally collapsed backwards beneath her on the bed.
She hymned, 'Beautiful,' planting his entry. 'Your cock is beautiful.'
His fleeting shock stammered. 'By the Jesus . . .' Then engulfed, ready as she plunged, plunged down on him, plunging to shuddering sprawl, careless as Eve before funk crucified Adam.
He was twenty minutes late in the stokehole.
Left pensive, waiting for news, she planned strategy pending the re-opening of Cwmffrwd. Of Dewi Joshua, colliery official. Traditionally, schoolteachers, firemen and shopkeepers occupied the Villas.
Ike Houghton hitched up his belt. 'They gotto sign on another man. I'm not working doublers with this fucken rupture of mine.'
'Twelve hour shifts, Ike. What d'you say? You could use the money.'
Ike stroked his groin. 'I'll be in Moel Ward agen.'
He said, 'Give it a try till the weekend. By Sunday Albert'll be on his feet.'
'Bugger might take advantage once he's on the Sick, make sure he puts in his three waiting days. Can't blame Albert nor anybody else either.'
'Ike, you with me?'
'Might as well, aye. You like having your own way, Dewi, on the quiet.'
They worked 12 hour shifts for three weeks. Influenza left pleurisy, left scars on Albert Mort's lungs already damaged by sulphur fumes. Thereafter Albert cultivated his garden, dug for victory on Sickness Benefit.

★   ★   ★   ★

The turning world brought Spring to Wales.
When the Company agent moved into Plasmarl, General

Meeting notices went up in institutes, post offices, clubs and pubs. The agent guaranteed jobs for colliers, repairers, labourers, hauliers, winders, one electrician, one fitter, one farrier/blacksmith, two wagon repairers, maintenance pit-men and lamproom men. A new engineer/mechanic was modernising the screens. G.W.R. platelayers were extending the siding. And Lester Mackie acknowledged Cwmffrwd's underground water now flowed into Nantglas, the *why* of it left to mystery.

'To start off first of all then, Mr. Mackie,' said the former chairman of Cwmffrwd's obsolete Lodge, 'you're after experienced heading men and borers to drive these new headings, one up towards North, the other back West towards the old Five Foot district. Am I right in my contention?'

'Absolutely, that's why I'm here this evening, Mr. . . .? I didn't get your name.'

Ernie Bolshie Spiller deflected the agent. 'Makes no odds at the moment. I'm just explaining to these men. Most of us are members in arrears, goes without saying, but that won't be your personal problem, Mr. Mackie. Later on, well, management will have to, y'know, sort things out, do your own picking and choosing.'

'Obviously,' the agent impassive as if responding to himself.

Addressing the meeting from below the stage, Ernie Bolshie removed his beige slouch, peacock's eye feather in the hat band. 'Don't let's fool ourselves'—he thumbed at the agent, 'this gentleman wants hard heading men. Take it from me, some of us earned our keep in Cwmffrwd North district before the big water broke in. Therefore, what it means, it means taking precautions. It means wearing a mask no matter about the extra sweat. I'm saying if you don't let the dust settle after shot-firing, silicosis will get you. Few months on bloody cough mixture and you're finished. Understood?'

'Well done, Ernie,' they said—ex-miners labouring long hours on building sites.

'We know the story, Ernie,' from skilled colliers doing fetch and carry jobs, sleeping two hours a day in crowded trains and buses, or living away from home in hostels.

'Sit down, Ernie.'

'Take the weight off,' they said.

From the floor of the Institute's upstairs hall, they queued on-stage, the happy-go-luckiest crocodile of men since pre-War, signing on for shorter hours, better wages and exemption from call-up.

Dewi's name went to the colliery office via Deborah Coles, prodded by Elsie to invite the agent's wife to a night out in the Conservative Club. Chamber of Commerce charity buffet and Olde English dance in aid of renovations to Dewinton Grammar School.

He waltzed with Mrs. Prudence Mackie, a robust woman with the glottal blur of her upbringing in Caernarfon. Shy too, by contrast. Her son was in the R.A.F., training for navigator. One daughter, driving instructor with the A.T.S., another daughter teacher-training in Middlesex. Matter of factly she said, 'When they want advice they ask Mr. Mackie; they turn to me for family matters.'

He assumed interest, 'Such as?'

'Birthdays, weddings, funerals. Our children have eleven uncles and aunties. Where do you live?'

'Um, Parc Villa.'

'Ah, the Villas.'

'Mind if I call you Prudence?'

She shook her head, abrupt, her small blue eyes secretive, mistrusting the vigour of his left hand between her shoulder-blades.

He went on, 'Not that we'll bump into each other in town. Don't suppose you'll be staying long either, once they find a manager for Cwmffrwd.'

'You mustn't be rude, young man.'

Gusting soft laughter close to her country-woman's face, 'Like gypsies, ah! Only you and Mr. Mackie won't be selling pegs and tissue paper flowers 'round the doors.' Then quickly, 'Sorry Prudence, sorry. That was cheap.'

Bafflement whimsied her smile.

Yet he persisted, 'As you can see, there's not much side on us born and bred in Moel Exchange. We're pretty blunt. Comes with being nosy.'

She stepped away from him at the buffet table, murmur garbling from her like a troubled teenager. For no reason Llew Kitchener silenced into Dewi's mind. Gawky old sick-man Llew before he went to Birmingham to commit suicide. Llew unbuckling his york straps outside the lamproom, another shift done with, five more trams of handcut over the weighbridge, another top hole cleared. Coming or going, nobody walked alongside Llew. *Shwmae* sufficed in passing. *Trych* they called him.

Tinned salmon sandwich to his mouth, he looked around for Deborah Coles.

'I'd like to butt in for a sec., Deborah. Something I wanted to ask you. What's *trych* in English?'

Deborah ogled post-menopausal mischief. 'Greedy, *trachwantus* means greedy.'

'Had to be,' he said. 'Couldn't mean anything else. I've been around the floor with Prudence. What d'you think of her and Lester Mackie?'

'The man's efficient. He's too fast for Moel Exchange.'

'Here today, gone tomorrow, ah?'

Deborah cantilevered from the waist, leaning down to him. 'We'll have to wait and see.'

'Kerr-riste, Deb, you're stone-walling like Lloyd George.'

'Watch that mouth. Remember the company you're in.'

'Aye, Elsie's put her foot down.'

'Be grateful, Elsie saved you from the Army.'

'Who's disputing? I'm booked for Twrgwyn School of Mines. My own fault if I don't pass the exam.'

Deborah trembled upright, dismay scraping from her throat as the siren groaned to wailing. She hurried across to Gabe Coles, hooked onto his arm, miseried with fear, and Pencaer's ex-cashier comforting, stroking her knuckles. Gabe from Llwyn Villa who had nom de plumed himself into a profitable, illegal tote business, with runners distributing TOP DIVI football coupons throughout Moel Exchange and factories on Rhos Estate.

Came the far off summer-thundery whumps of bombs dropping on Llangroes oilworks.

'Kill or be killed,' said Lester Mackie, hands in pockets, his slashbacked hair gleaming ebony as if montaged to the healthy white smoothness of his face. 'How are you? We haven't been introduced. You're Dewi Joshua.'

'Pleased to meet you, Mr. Mackie.'

The agent folded his arms. 'My father was killed on the Somme in 1916. My mother had the letter on November the fifth: *I regret to inform, War Office reports Sergeant George Mackie presumed killed in action, Lord Kitchener expresses his sympathy.*' Lester Mackie unfolded his arms. 'We are a lethal species, stuck on Darwin's ladder with blood on our hands.'

He said, 'No relation to Llew Kitchener, that Lord Kitchener with a big tash. I started work with Llew. As for my own father, the dust took him when I was a kid. I don't reckon we're dangerous though, Mr. Mackie.'

Head-shake convincing himself, 'Consider the evidence. Politicians and patriots sanction murder disguised as moral necessity. Murder comes easy, it's older than heaven and hell. Murder blossoms from *Homo sapiens*, his intelligence anarchic to kingdom come.'

'Yeh, politicians mostly, the ones in charge,' he said. 'I'm not much for politics. Elsie neither, come to that, but she'll hold her own against anybody in this kind of discussion.'

The Company agent intoned courteously, 'Of course, I'm sure.' Touching Dewi's shoulder at arm's length, 'By the way, our conversation has been confidential.'

'Definitely, Mr. Mackie.'

'My son would accuse me of treason.'

'I've forgotten what you said, Mr. Mackie.'

'Unlikely.'

Dignity between them, gravely punctilious.

Prompted by the All Clear, Glyn Rupe's Five Stars played *Moonlight and roses*.

He sidled through heavy blackout curtains to the balcony.

'Dreadful,' they were saying—two wives of civil servants and two retired schoolmistresses, ex-Dewinton Grammar School scholars flapdoodling at the red glow low down in the northern sky.

'Oh, it's you, Dewi. Isn't it cruel!'

'Dewi, isn't it beyond!'
He agreed as if they were drowning behind glass.

*   *   *   *

War came quixotically nearer to Moel Exchange; the American ack-ack unit bell-tented on Cape Cefn. Easy-talking, sauntering fellows with money to spend. Four whites and a negro attended Bethany Baptist Church. *En bloc* they went by Christian names in town. There were no quarrels, fist fights, the traditional option of young colliers confronted by confident strangers.

VII

It was abnormal. Foul slurry and rotten sleepers underfoot. Sopping wet everywhere, his mandrel sounding baggy roadsides for another pair of twelve foot rings, and he thought: shan't ever again set eyes on the likes of this. Seven headings, eighty stalls, airways, five hundred yards of main, all under water for thirteen years. Since I was in Standard 1. Spent six weeks in Bethlehem Isolation Hospital that summer. Scarlet fever. Long time ago. There's no going backwards in life. Yet here we are, opening up Cwmffrwd. As for the underground lake, close on a mile across to Pencaer airway return tunnel in Glas Tump. Lester Mackie wasn't bothered. Not his handwriting. No flies on Lester. Kept his nose clean. Away too, gone off like a packman. Be another six months before we start filling out coal.

'Ready when you are, butty,' said Chris Prior.

They pushed a tramful of debris forward, spragged the rear wheels. Chris gripped the half ring to his chest, lifted it clear while Dewi placed a hardwood sill beneath the foot of the ring. In turn he lifted the second half.

'Ease her down,' said Chris.

Both halves sloped against the tram.

He climbed up on the debris. Chris levered back the half rings until the heads were aligned. Dewi slotted in the fishplates.

'Reach me the nuts and bolts,' he said.

Chris Prior was forty-eight, with a cauliflower ear from front row rugby, triumphs of his heyday referred to as honourable in Moel Exchange. He had two soldier sons. Two married daughters worked in Rhos Estate Arsenal. A spinster daughter was in the Land Army. Mrs. Prior kept chickens and a registered pig.

Tightening the fishplate bolts, witfully repeating himself, 'Take six months before we start filling out coal.'

Chris fingered the teeth of his pit-saw. 'Ne'-mind, it's a steady job. I'll cut some lagging timbers.'

'Where you been working, Chris?'

'Four of us unloading duff in Aberselsig power station.'

'On bonus?'

'Not a red meg.'

'Donkey work, ah?'

'Long way there and back home was the trouble.'

He tested the ring for movement.

'Wedge, Dewi?'

'Few,' he said, 'then she'll stay firm while we lag up the sides.'

'Sledge?'

'Course I want the bloody sledge.'

Chris threw the sledgehammer. 'Watch your feet and less fucken lip.'

'*Manno manno* fucken *shenko*!'

Chris appealed, 'Keep your moss on for Chrissake.'

He vaulted down from the tram. 'You gerrup there. I'll cut the wedges.'

'Listen, ask anybody, they'll tell you I don't go in for aggravation.'

Patience, he thought, the patience of bloody Job. You'd swear we were putting up Crystal bloody Palace.

He said, 'Chris, this pong put you off your grub?'

Earnestly intent, Chris hammered wedges above the head of the ring. 'S'all on my clothes, Missis tells me.'

He paced backwards, pausing to sight along the last three pairs of rings. Chris Prior leaned forward, his cap lamp shining on the new ring.

'Do?'

'Dead on,' he said. 'Let's start lagging.'

Chris swung down to the hitching plate. '*Duw*, these sides are like caccy poop.'

'Needle's stuck on that record, Chris.'

Shift after shift, the same slimy reek. Then pipe fitters hung sectional steel pipes on suspension chains from the rings, flexible canvas bag at the end, and fan-driven air purred overhead at the work place. Bitter cul de sac cold. They wore woollies, long-johns, overcoats and oilskin leggins until they branched off, turned North into new ground—the silica rock of Cwmffrwd. And another small airway looped, tunnelled through a twenty inch rider seam, circulating ventilation back to the main.

Chris, randomly annoyed, '*Twp* as ass'oles, expecting us to wear these masks all day long.'

Said Dewi, 'Take some getting used to. Like the fella who invented Christ's cross, the bugger who invented these masks never worked in a hard heading.'

'No comparison. Too far fetched.'

'What if there'd been bullets when that Pilate bloke turned his thumb down?'

'You're all to cock, man,' said Chris. Mask lowered to clear his chest. 'I can't fucken breathe proper.'

'Stick it out, Chris. One thing, we're under solid rock, pair of rings here and there will do the job.'

Chris uneasy inside his mask, 'I always refused hard headings. How do we use these boring machines?'

'Let's fetch the blast bag on. I'll show you.'

Working off a platform of posts and sleepers, they drilled a chalk-marked pattern of 26 holes, compressed air (blast) powering the drills. Rock dust spilled down, powdery, innocuous as white pepper.

'Fucken deadly stuff,' muttered Chris.

He said, 'Can't odds it.'

'I know blokes flaked out in their twenties from silicosis.'

'Ernie Bolshie gave us warning. Take precautions.'

The elderly fireman brought tin canisters of pills, and detonators in a leather pouch. Behind him, a teenage boy hooped over the weight of two buckets filled with firm moist clay for ramming into the holes, hand-rolled like blunt lengths of sausage, rammed home behind the pills and dets with a length of broomstick.

They huddled in a manhole. Elias Roberts pressed the plunger. Earthquake noise boomed the heading. 'All fired,' said Elias. 'Same time tomorrow. Pick them buckets up, son.'

They waited for the dust to settle. Chris trailed him to the dismantled platform. He grabbed his tommy box and water jack. 'Bugger this. We'll hang about in the manhole.'

''Lias might check back.'

'You'll be saying the same about me after we knock through to the Five Foot.'

'I don't get you, Dewi?'

'I'll be carrying a safety lamp.'

Chris rollicked, 'Hoo hoo hoo, you fireman, who'd a' thought!'

'Aye, right.'

Hunkered in the manhole, he said, 'Sprays, butty; in modern pits they spray water. Same goes for anthracite coal down west Wales. When my certificate is up on the wall in Parc Villa, I'll be arguing in the office for water infusion.'

'He's a mean, tight bugger, Hubie Taylor the manager.'

'I can be a bit of a dictator myself, Chris.'

'You're talking like a quim. They all renege once they're carrying a lamp.'

He grinned, 'I'm fucken civilised, don't forget.'

Waning dust and cordite fumes drifted past the manhole.

Accurately timed, they reached pit bottom at half-past two. On Cwmffrwd top pit, 'Give me those drills,' offered Chris. 'I'll take 'em across to the blacksmith's shop.'

He saw his pale speckled clothes in the dark green windows of the lamproom. Like a baker, except this is rock dust. The killer.

After late evening tea he went to the back bedroom, Elsie's stand-offish omen seething his wits. Pass the fireman's exam or do a flit to Dinmel Terrace. Sleeping, he nightmared her hooked fingers clawing out his heart, purple like a plum dripping blood, tossed up and down in her palm, and higher, her head flung back, mouth gaping wide. She swallowed his heart behind dribbling skeins of blood, her throat rippling as she gulped.

He silently screamed himself awake.

Alarm bell at 6 a.m., Elsie hullooing, 'Deh-wee! Beans on toast on the hob!'

'Okay! Ta!'

Elsie slept until 8.30. She entered the British Restaurant at 9 o'clock, sailing the aisle between breakfasting night shift workers, early morning cleaners and old folks, garrulous, dour or negative as shadows, elderly survivors from the war to end all wars.

★   ★   ★   ★

They cleared five yards a week in the hard heading, with a labourer helping to fill out the debris.

One mid-Autumn morning Elias Roberts confronted them on top pit. 'Careful does it today, boys. We're almost through. I'm under instructions, one of you supposed to carry this.'

Dewi took the Davy safety lamp. 'How d'you know there's gas?'

'Just in case, boy. Might be a pocket of firedamp. What I want you blokes to do, bore three-footers. I'll be firing near enough grub-time.'

Said Chris Prior, 'Book me a stent once we're into the Five Foot.'

'You've earned it,' agreed Elias.

And I've earned my fireman's certificate, Dewi decided.

It was eerie, unreal, locked to hope as they walked on after the shot-firing, old Elias rasping small coughs, youthful for all the lost flesh of his ageing frame when they saw stone-powdered mashed coal and the flashing, lispy rustling of the impacted Five Foot seam.

Chris shouting from inside his mask. 'We've done it!'

'Through,' he said.

Elias as if praying inside the grotesque muzzle of his mask, 'Well done, men, well done.'

Dewi punched up his fist. 'While the smoke clears I suggest we finish our grub back in the manhole.'

The following day, comedy verged on catastrophe. They were working off the last pillar of coal, Chris central in the heading, grunting, humming to himself. Consciously aware, unconsciously fearless, Dewi glanced at the safety lamp hooked on a post. Peaceable humming gouted to husky roar: Chris vanished, toppled down, forward rolling to avoid injuring his face, his eyes and head. Bent over himself, Chris bawled, 'Watch yourselves!'

The safety lamp dimmed, hung low like liquid gold on the wick.

'Gas!' he shouted. 'Come on out! Gas!' yelling, 'Run! Run! Run!' Chris and the labourer stumbling past him over muck and coal, fleeing the heading and around to the main, and still running thirty yards to a ventilation door, where, inside the door, Elias and a haulier were righteously discussing a nationalised coal industry.

'Gas,' croaked from his parched throat.

'On the phone, Percy,' ordered Elias. 'I want the under-manager down here.'

Hitching his pony to an empty tram, Percy the haulier crouched on the gun. 'Gerron, Prince!'

Prince steadily trotted the main back to pit bottom.

Half-past twelve when Morris Crewe the under-manager and two firemen strode the hard heading on to the Five Foot seam. Dewi's safety lamp was out. But by now the trapped methane had dispersed. Leading the way, bright safety lamp held high, the under-manager scrambled over collapsed coal. All together behind him, they heeled down into old workings.

'We were lucky,' said Morris. 'God damn, mining shouldn't depend on luck.'

'Hold on,' said Dewi. 'Not Elias's fault. He told us yesterday. Obvious there was a touch of luck. Couple of minutes and we might have had a whiff to knock us out.'

'This gas could have been tapped.'

'Should perhaps, aye, no doubt.' And going on, he revealed his tack: 'I swotted it up for my exam.'

Which evoked sardonic snorts, growly chuckles of official togetherness.

VIII

Day-shift firemen were waiting for him in the new brick and concrete bunker style office on Cwmffrwd top pit.
'Look at this, another Company lackey.'
'Hubert Taylor's blue eyed boy.'
'Elsie Kitchener's more like. No offence, Dewi.'
'Day shift, the jammy bugger. They sent me afternoons for three years before I came on day-shift.'
'You-are, Dewi, sit over by there.'
'Another fucken dot and carry on the books.'
He said, 'Most of you remember when I was Irfon Tŷ-isaf's butty down the Four Deep in Pencaer.'
Elias Roberts suggested, 'Give the fella chance to settle in.'
This was supported by overman Rhidian Coslett, 'Same as all of us learnt. Any mistakes, Dewi, make sure you come to me first. Us officials, we stand between the men and Mr. Taylor's office. You follow?'
'Bank on it,' he said.
'And don't antagonise the men. *Safety* first and last. In between I want coal up the pit. Team work, see. Very important we work as a team.'
'I won't let you down.'
'Go with Elias for a week. You're on your own after as regards responsibility.' The overman signalled his officials out of the bunker. 'Once you make a decision, stick to it unless there's a dead cert option.'
'Right, I get the gist,' he said.
'Set example, Dewi. Any bloody scruff bullyrag you, chuck the book at him. Gain respect the way you know best. It's got fuck all to do with opinions from the Fed. Ours is a mouthy job but you've got to know what you're on about. Final word, try not to drop any of my officials in the shit. Might tamp back on you in years to come.'
Resentment welled. Who does Coslett think he's talking to?
As if Elsie prompted behind his eyes, he said, 'You've laid it on fair and square, Rhidian.'

★ ★ ★ ★

Squatting beside Elias, he journeyed from pit bottom in a tram hauled by a swaggy fetlocked main line drafthorse. First ride in, he thought, since I left school to work with Llew.

Elias seemed to be dozing.

'Any problems in your district, Elias?'

'Only thing on Hubert Taylor's mind, full trucks in the siding. I used to be back on the double-parting a lot. Say there was a haulier missing, what I'd do, pitch in, ride on the gun for a shift. Haulier myself years ago. Gone past it now. When I was a youngster over in Mawr Drift, you'd see officials turn to if there was a man short. Dog eat dog these days.'

'You reckon?'

'Sutainly, boy.'

He said, 'Always been sort of dog eat dog.'

'Speak as you find.'

'Meaning what?'

The main line haulier shouted, 'I'm fetching from Yorkie's heading!'

They climbed out of the tram. The old fireman flagged his arm but he kept on trudging, 'Go in Oliver's airway, prime the little pump, start her up. Save my legs, see boy. And test for gas. See the braddish is all right. I'll be on the double-parting.' Elias paused, 'You had a shitten start with Llew Kitchener.'

He filled a rickety bucket with sump water, unscrewed the filler cap, primed the pump, replaced the cap and triggered the switch down. Normally this was a labourer's job. Water hissing from a leaking manifold died to glassy wreathing. Rhythmic glugging sang inside the 2 inch pipeline. He studied the brattice nailed to a heavy wooden frame. The stiff sheets wafted ghostly, controlling airflow back to the main. He ran his fingertips over nailheads around the frame. Slowly walking away, he held high the Davy oil lamp. No gas. Safe.

Shitten shart with Llew? Cranky old bugger, Elias Roberts. Chapel man once, bible in his fist every Sunday according to Zena. She *turned*, by God she changed to vinegar after Theo died. People live in the past though. Not me. But Elias, he's straight enough. Paddy round him.

From the double-parting they went up through nine stalls to Chris Prior's heading.

'Leave him to you,' said Elias.

'Yardage, Chris?'

'Hey, Dewi, how's negotiations on the new job?'

'Two yards?'

'Aye, book two.'

'Timbers?'

'Four six'n half road posts and a cog up my left side there. Elias suggested it. Broken stuff coming like *mum-glo*.'

'Pills? Dets?'

'Fired twice. Ten pills in all. Two dets.'

'This your second dram, Chris?'

'Second aye.' Sitting on his heels, Chris rocked contentment. 'You and me, Dewi, we made a great job of it knocking through to the coal. See that slip coming down the face? Peel the clod off and she drops out lovely.'

'Better than unloading duff in Aberselsig power station.'

'Daft fucken game.'

Elias wheezed into crouching out of the face. 'Mind you keep to the point in this heading, Chris.'

Chris Prior came wriggling past the tram. 'Say, Dewi, you married yet? You said once you had that lamp you'd be marching Elsie down to the registrar's.'

'Later on perhaps. Keep it quiet.'

'Aah, I get what you mean.'

'So-long, Chris.'

Back on the double-parting a haulier was beating his pony with a sprag.

'No more of that,' Dewi said (Elias grunting encouragement), 'or you'll be reported.'

'More pull in my granny,' argued Shink the haulier.

'Fucken dram's down to the axle,' he said. 'Where's your yard pieces?'

Three lights were coming one behind the other on the straight heading.

'Now's your chance to show how good you are,' he said. 'Jam

those tee-head pieces under the front wheels. Me and Elias, we'll shove from the side.'

Splay-legged, rumps against the side of the tram, they heaved while the pony lowered, hooves gouging for purchase in hard-packed hollows between sleepers, the haulier screeching, 'Giddup, Caesar! Giddup! Giddup!'

The tram lurched, slewed inwards, hung poised as if sentient, and slid forward onto the track.

'Whoa-boy! Whoa Caesar! Stan' back!'

'Nice bit of scheming,' said Elias.

The other three hauliers jibed the pony beater.

Shink bawled, 'Fucken rail sprung out back there!'

Elias stroked Caesar's shivering neck. 'Shackle this dram to the journey, you're blocking up the double-parting.' He warned Shink again, 'Use more sense next time.'

Dewi laughed, 'Silly cunt you, Shink.'

'Lost my rag for a minute.'

'Aye, lose your fucken job next.'

He stood with Elias while the hauliers shackled full trams to he journey. In strict sequence they hitched to empty trams before returning to the stalls.

Silence came quickly. Rats squealed in the gob wall behind the horse trough.

Elias hunkered from tiredness. 'Take a look at the rails. Bag of cramp nails under the feed trough.'

He propped the short pieces of tee-head rail inside a ring.

'Elias, this sleeper's all split.'

'Will it last out the shift?'

'Never.'

Carping under his tongue, the old fireman waggled a loose cramp nail from the end-riven wooden sleeper. 'They'll be back any minute.'

'Want me to lay a new sleeper?'

'No time.'

'While the hauliers are on grub. What we'll do temporary, fix a stayer from the ring out to the rail.'

'Careful then. Instead of drams off the road somebody's leg'll get broken.'

The stayer held.

'Clever,' approved Elias.

He loped to the nearest stall for a heavy mandrel and a sledgehammer. Fifteen minutes later he cramp-nailed the rails to a new sleeper, the hauliers eating and jeering at Shink's, 'That Dewi's like a fucken American devil.'

'Good on you, boy,' said Elias.

His mint conviction: I shan't ask a man to do anything I can't do myself.

★ ★ ★ ★

The persistent north-easterly subdued Moel Exchange. Fine snow scudding from blanket grey skies, thickening to muffled white-out. And fire raged through Sinkers' Huts from end to end. Everybody escaped. Eleven families slept in the strippng room extension behind Pencaer Institute boilerhouse. Salvation Army and W.V.S. supplied food and blankets. Hubert Taylor donated £7, the unTory Conservative Club £10, payday collections outside Cwmffrwd office made £21.11.6. The Council Medical Officer appealed for volunteers to accomodate the homeless. Four children were adopted, eight thereafter reared by grandparents, aunts and uncles. Three marriages broke up. Nine dogs and seven cats were put down. Mal Rogers the Institute caretaker was sacked for interfering with 13 year old Cissie Watts. From a short list of five, the job went to Idwal Murphy, top pit haulier and treasurer of Moel Communist Party.

Snow and more snow, outlying farms cut off, sheep perishing squashed together, stained by droppings under snowdrifts behind drystone walls. Two Infants' Schools closed. Women raided coal trucks in twilight. Bakeries rationed bread. Tramcar drivers went on strike for 12 hours. Snow sooted on pavements. Shopkeepers blamed Council officials. For three days at noon, a mongrel bitch howled in Brynrhedyn cemetery. Ellis Mabon took the bitch home and Wyndham began despising his son. The bitch escaped from Chapel Street, found refuge with a befuddled old spinster in Gaer Row.

The upper reaches of Nantglas vanished. Powdery snow

crisped on glaucous ice windows sheeted above midstream runnels. Braziers burned in the sidings, overlooked by bonfires near tramroad junctions on Cwmffrwd top pit. Gangs of day-wage labourers shovelled snow, trenching footpaths to workshops, winding house, weighbridge office, timber yard, manager's office and the First Aid shed.

Pioneer Corps soldiers arrived in lorries. They cleared Sinkers' Huts site. Charcoaled baulks, flagstone floors, kitchen sinks and lavatory bowls sank from sight in rust-water bog below the G.W.R. permanent way. The swaddies sang *Roll me over in the clover* while erecting Nissen huts for six families. The Sinkers' Huts weren't insured. From common utility to swift extinction. A G.W.R. ganger had collected weekly rent. The remaining families eked out, found cellar apartments, ceased carrying the stigma of Sinkers' Huts.

Snowploughs charged, staggered, charged in Gaer Cutting, and the mineral line continued freighting steam coal.

Despite rumours, shortages and blackout, war remained distant. Work, food, sex, clothes, small privileges, cinemas, club and pub life were more real than Winston Churchill. His romantic death-wish oratory fell transient as gossamer. Moel Exchange had been by-passed by Roman legionaries one thousand, eight hundred and fifty years ago, and eight centuries later Exchange Manor's crenellated walls powered feudal Cethin Dewinton families, blood lines short-lived from humdrum diseases. Caretaker landlords came and went, succumbed to mortmain or pillage. While Nelson battled against Emperor Napoleon 1 of France, cartloads of Exchange Manor masonry went into building Plasmarl and town houses for tradesmen, for dealers in wool and meat, for churches and chapels and merchants of Christianity.

★   ★   ★   ★

Dewi and Elsie celebrated winter's end in marriage, frowned upon by the lady registrar in Matabele Crescent, who was in turn rebuffed by Elsie's suggestive gaiety. Ossie Ross and Dai Greg stood by, witnesses in dark serge suits.

Zena learned about the wedding from Edwin Fowkes, neighbour to Dai Greg in Druid Uplands. Sunday-free, she deliberately stared at her tattered, sogged garden. Zena devoting her reedy, tone pure soprano to *Stormy weather*, distraction against moithering about Edwin Fowkes, storeman in the Arsenal. Lonely widower. Lonely widow. Her lodger. Perhaps. First tell Dewi—or let him know later? Take the chance. Proud Edwin. Tough as old boots, the pair of us . . . '*Since my man and I came together*,' Welshy strident, '*Keeps rainin' all the tuh-hime, keeps rainin' all the tah-ime*,' as he back-heeled the garden gate, came striding to the kitchen door.

'Hullo, Mam.'

'I was thinking about you.'

'Me too, that's why I've come, let you know I'm married to Elsie.'

'Well, there's lovely for you both. Edwin Fowkes told me though, in work. Might as well spill the rest while I'm at it. Edwin's going to be my lodger. Steady man he is, no frills and fancies.'

'Great. Real good sort, Edwin, pumpsman in Pencaer after he broke his leg up in the Number One. When's he moving in?'

Zena mocked herself, 'Take ages potching through the furniture.'

'Edwin's?'

'Preferable to these bits and pieces of mine.'

'Make a bonfire.'

She smiled, unlike his mother. Zena's pale features shed travail. She blushed.

He said, 'I'll put the kettle on.'

At the table they gossiped in the old familiar way, her farewell kiss on his cheek memorable as he strolled to the Villas. He could not recall another in all his days.

Boys and girls came scooting out from Horeb Sunday school. He counted them. Sixteen kids in best clothes. The lay preacher's sing-song, 'Careful-careful, careful-careful, careful-careful. *Shwd i chi*, Dewi? How's Mrs. Joshua your mother?'

'She's okay. You still doing your bit by night in the watchman's cabin on Clyne Road?'

'Job for life, Dewi.'
'So-long, Geraint.'
'God bless, Dewi.'

Elsie had her feet up on a maroon leather pouffe. Her breathing whiffled a corner of *The News of the World* sloped across her bosom. Tiptoeing between doors, he went through Parc Villa to the bumpy back-garden lawn. He unlocked her never-used 12 feet x 8 feet greenhouse. Flog it, he thought, wheeling the Triumph out to a red ash lane above Nantglas. Buy a second-hand motor car. Bar Hubert Taylor and Buff Hooper the Company mechanic, I'll be the only man in Cwmffrwd with a car.

He cleaned the plug, sandpapered lead connections, wiped condensation from the dynamo, listened to the dry whoofing of the kickstart before tickling the carburettor. Fifth kick she growled into roaring. Pleased with himself, adjusting the choke, he low-geared up and down the lane. Rickety old-timers with slow-moving dogs were on parade. Sometimes he stopped to chat. When Elsie came out, he shouted, 'Back in a few minutes.'

He rode up to the waterworks tower, full-throttled the straight half mile to the filter bed, and went home.

Windmilling his arms, 'Should have put my clobber on.'

Elsie wanly puffed, 'Phoo-oh . . . look at the cutlets, please.' From wordless moaning she complained, 'I'm coming unwell.'

'Stay where you are,' he said. 'Leave the dinner to me.'

After a while, from behind closed eyes, 'I love you too, *cariad*.'

He forked the lamb cutlets, turned them, poured some fat into a frying pan, switched off the gas and replaced the meat tin in the oven. Gravy next. Smooth paste of fat, flour and gravy browning. Splash at a time, he stirred in boiling water from the potatoes. While the gravy simmered he drained the potatoes and cabbage. Glancing at Elsie: *Iesu*, she's bad all right. 'Elsie, don't go to sleep. I'm serving up. C'mon, love, everthing's ready. Hark at this! Edwin Fowkes is moving in with my old lady. It's taken her all these years to get over Theo my father.'

Elsie approved as if human nature needed a rinse and a flap in the wind, then her mood came doleful, 'Oh Lord, these flushes. Change, change, I'm definitely on the change.'

He remembered Llew's sepia photograph hanging above the sideboard. Old Llew, deadpan mug on him, centre parting in his straight black hair. Gone from sight, laid face down under blankets in the chest upstairs. Solid oak. Off her mother. Day by day, night after night with Elsie, yet she's twice my age. Forty-eight. Exactly twice.

'You'll get over it,' he said. 'Dinner's ready.'

He sat below the large studio portrait, Spanish Elsie smiling white teeth. Flowery Elsie, temptation sparkling her eyes. Yet I seldom even realise . . . aye, true, she's middle aged.

'Nice cutlets from the Coop.'

He said, 'Yeh, taste rich, hardly any fat.'

'So Zena decided at long last. What's he like, Edwin Fowkes?'

'Decent bloke. Gammy leg from a bump in Pencaer.'

'Think they make love?'

'None of our business.'

'I'm nosey,' she said.

'No dispute, only don't rake up the dirt.'

'All right, all right! I wouldn't dream of such a thing. Just spec., that's all, hoping they'll be happy. I mean, what else besides? Men and women are awfully different. We're separate. The beauty is when we join, make love together. Everything outside of coming together isn't worth much. It's either bickering, pretending to be polite or chit-chatting about whatever.'

'You've sorted it out, girl.'

'Guh-url indeed.'

Arms hooped wide, he scratched his armpits. '*Shwmae*, Jane. Me Tarzan.'

Elsie gloated, 'That's what I love best in you. Down inside you don't damn well care what anybody says.'

'Depends what I'm up agenst.'

She cracked bird-like alarm, 'Me!'

Searching for candour, 'I'd put you queen of Wales.'

Elsie's happiness lowered to derision.

'More intelligent by a mile,' he said, 'than this fella.' He looked over his shoulder. 'Same Elsie up there as you are today.'

Chewing delicately, pouting her lips, 'Mm, we're all over each other in bed, give or take when I'm fussy, selfish to be honest. *Then*, when that photograph was taken, the '26 strike brought misery. My Dad had the biggest coal-round in town. Who could afford coal? Not many. After the strike, two years afterwards, he had five horses and carts delivering housecoal. My father Caleb, Caleb Evans from All Saints Place, he made huge success. Her up there on the wall, guess her age?'

'Twenty?'

'Twenty-one, and never been done!'

'What about Gorwel Pomeroy?'

'Poor Gorwel, the pity of it.'

'Did he?'

'Only tried a few times. Always in torment he was, shaken to his roots.'

She brought a plate of apple tart from the pantry.

Dewi resolved his opinion. 'The kid didn't stand a chance with T.B.'

'Cold blooded you are, mister. But still, fire killed off T.B. in the old Huts. Say when,' she said, spooning cream on his slice of tart.

'Luxury. Where from?'

'Ossie left it in the Bee Arr office for us. He's matey with the manager of Pegler's. As I was saying, when Gorwel died I cried like the rain. Oh, I may sound flippant sometimes, but Gorwel was sensitive, very refined for a boy.'

'Wrong place, Moel Exchange.' He grinned behind a mouthful of tart and cream. 'Your Dad made a packet by all accounts. Who went first, Caleb Evans or your Mam?'

'Women live longest. My Mother was eighty-two.'

'Where'd the *dwsh* go after she died?'

Elsie held her lower lip puckered between forefinger and thumb. She blinked wide-eyed, tears magnifying her pupils. 'We agreed from the start, didn't we? No children. Well, I was the only child. You too. My Mother used to beg me: "Have a family." Oh God, my Mam, she *pushed* in our house. Her motto was: Shilling's worth of business is better than a guinea's worth of slogging underground for somebody else. Her word was law in All Saints Place. She warned me when I married Llew.'

He said, 'I'm not with you, Elsie.'

'Regarding children! Once, she screamed in my face, "If you can't have children by Llew Kitchener, find another man!" Mair Evans, she followed life. She believed in *life*.'

'You've lost me agen.'

'I never wanted children from Llew! Never never!'

'Right, we agreed between us two. We settled all that,' he said. 'Referring back though, what I meant was, the money your old man supposed to have made when he worked the biggest coal-round in Moel Exchange.'

Her right hand hung poised with a spoonful of apple tart and cream. 'Lloyds Bank of course.'

'Oh aye. Mind telling me how much?'

Tilting the spoon to her mouth, 'Quite a lot actually.'

'Anyhow,' he began, 'stands to reason it's nothing to do with me. I've no intention of meddling in your affairs. Shan't argue about some of your ideas either. So long as we're straight with each other, suits me. I listened to enough moans about money from my old lady in Dinmel Terrace.'

Elsie watching him across the table, 'Over seventeen thousand pounds.'

'Jesus, that's a shaker.'

'Gilt, *cariad*.'

'What?'

'W.D. and H.O. Wills shares. My mother started buying them when I was sixteen, five years before that photograph was taken.'

'Hey-hey, now there's a woman. She's the long-headed one who . . .'

Elsie interrupted, 'Mair Evans could barely write her name. She ran away from my grandfather's house in Margam. He used to ride horseback over the mountains once a month to collect her wages.'

He rubbed his forehead. 'Those days are *gone*. No going back either.'

Obstinately, 'She worked in Jessop's brewery.'

'By Exchange Manor?'

'Jessops became Moel Orphanage until it was knocked down

by the Council when they brought in tramcars before the last war.'

He said, 'Elsie-love, let's *forget* about the past. I'm thinking of buying a motor car. What d'you say?'

'Mm, would be marvellous.' And, 'Mister, sometimes you think like a machine.'

'Cash down?'

'First I'll have a chat with Ambrose the Garage.'

'I'd rather inquire from our mechanic, Buff Hooper.'

'Phebe Hooper's *Annibynwr*, quite sociable, but he's a Tory candidate, any excuse for bad manners.'

'The man's top notch. Buff built the new screens when we opened Cwmffrwd.'

Elsie discarded modesty. 'Leave the matter in my hands.'

'Fifty-fifty cash?'

She returned to the couch. 'We shan't get upset about the money. I shan't drive either. Ambrose Adams will teach you to drive.'

'Hah, oh for the open road!' he said.

★ ★ ★ ★

Without warning in high summer, a curt statement in every pay docket: 14 days notice. Hubert Taylor disappeared from Plasmarl. Under-manager Morris Crewe took charge. The Company began dismantling, loading out equipment. Men went sick instead of registering as unemployed. Lumbar and stomach complaints recurred, old injuries or ailments guaranteeing minimum weekly income until they were laid off Benefit and had to register. Then they were compelled to take one of three job offers, invariably away from home, labouring for low money. Eight young colliers joined the Army.

A heavy wooden lid was clamped on the pit shaft.

Fortnight's wages in hand on the final weekend, Dewi packed suitcases, ration books, petrol coupons, torch, black market tinned fruit and corned beef, butter, tea, 1 lb sugar, dried eggs, soap, toothbrushes, the Bijou Camp Kit, towels and bathing costumes in the light green 1938 Rover. Elsie wore a yellow bandana.

Neighbours cheered, 'Lovely motor car!'

'Be good!'

'Bye-bye then!'

'Tarra!'—Elsie waving as they caroomed past the Villas with schoolkids briefly sprinting alongside, Moel Exchange shrinking rearward as the Rover gulped mileage and the ancient Roman road lost itself in landslips, scree, stands of alders, birch, ash, oak and rough pasture molinia.

From Swansea (the bombed town alien as phantasmagoria) to cockle-smelly Penclawdd. Elsie swanked style in cafes and guest houses. Together they felt like explorers verifying the half-known. Lukewarm sea tanged their bodies. They slept on wilful, stolen liberty, each morning a day-door to the same principle. Disregarding newspapers and wireless news, they sunbathed side by side on beaches. He read detective stories and improved himself with a Pelican paperback: *Science and Everyday Life*, but he didn't want to understand Communism. Elsie kept a diary, she sent letters and picture postcards. She protected her whiteness with coconut oil. Her breaststroke swimming had the leisurely hauteur of second nature.

One night on the headland above Pwlldu, footpicking behind a hooded torch, they were halted by shouts.

'Stand still! Don't move at all! Keep them covered, Dorien.'

Elsie laughted in her throat.

He heard himself muttering, 'For Christ's sake . . .'

The Home Guard sergeant bulked shadowy. 'Identity cards?'

He said, 'What d'you think we are, spies?'

'Must be their big car,' said invisible Dorien.

Elsie prised the torch from his hand. She approached the sergeant. 'Mrs. Joshua, Parc Villa, Moel Exchange. You'll find these cards in order. Actually my husband is an official with the Ystrad and Talbot Mining Company.'

The sergeant's peaky face hung spectral as he checked their identity cards. '*Diolch*, thank you, Mrs. Joshua.'

Said Dorien, 'Bad enough in daylight climbing up from down there.'

'Satisfied?' he said.

Elsie's roving torch found Dorien's legs. 'As a matter of fact, last week we spent a day on the beach. We followed the brook down the valley. Ever so charming really.'

'Careful with that torch,' warned the sergeant.

'We didn't meet a soul—did we, darling?' She insisted, 'My husband is an official with the Ystrad and Talbot Mining Company.'

'Only doing our duty, Mrs. Joshua. Goodnight both.' The sergeant clicked finger and thumb, 'On your bike, Dorien.'

Boot soles snicked gravelstones, then two rear lights glowed dimly, flowing away in summer darkness.

He cooped his arm around her waist. 'Before this war we used to say "It's a free country". Seven times we've been stopped by the Home Guard since we set out.'

'They're looking after us. Terrible thing is, there's no end in sight.' More possessive than erotic, she cupped his testicles. 'Let's go home.'

Four hours later he reversed on a concrete patio outside the front bay window of Parc Villa. Elsie giggled, stepping through a scatter of newspaper and letters in the hallway.

'My first real holiday,' he said. 'Enough money in my pocket to go and do whatever I wanted. We'll be on the Gower again next summer.' Arms at crucifix, he snapped his shoulders back several times. '*Iesu*, I feel strong as a lion.'

She said, 'Like a Greek god.'

'They never lived on the dole.' Teeth bared at his framed deputy's certificate, 'I scratched my brains out for that piece of paper.'

'Mister, you've learned to give orders. What's more, you don't fall asleep after dinner every day of the week.'

'Nothing to sing about,' he said. 'Haven't crossed words with any man in my district so far, touch wood. God damn, why'd thy have to close Cwmffrwd?'

Their unpacked suitcases were left at the foot of the stairs, dawn lightening the transom window above the door, stillness everywhere, Moel Exchange asleep.

He skidded two letters across the table: statement from Lloyds Bank instantly slotted in her handbag, and a directive from the

Ministry of Food. Blandly aloof she accused the Ministry of supplying pigs' swill to the British Restaurant.

His buff enveloped letter requested information re. Dewi Saul Joshua. His occupation. His current address. His employment record since 1934.

He said, 'They're quick off the mark. All these questions because I haven't signed on the dole yet.'

Elsie pondered sightless, fingers of her left hand breaking a Marie biscuit, the point of her elbow pivoting a crescent of crumbs. Rousing, she dunked the half biscuit in her tea, saying, 'We'll have to see Mervyn Harris, Tŷ-coed. His father married my Auntie Megan.'

'What's this about Tŷ-coed farm?'

'Sheep. We'll buy some sheep. Once you're registered they'll leave you alone until the war's finished.'

'All I know about sheep, they'll jump a six foot wall to get into some poor sod's garden. Oh aye, and mutton goes in *cawl*.'

'Learn, boy! Sooner the better!'

'Hey there, Elsie . . .'

'Or would you rather march off in khaki and come back home useless for the rest of your life, like Wyndham Rhys's son?'

'Ah, Christ, poor Ellis.'

'*Think* then,' she said. 'Decide what's best. The Germans are sure to lose. They're mad, mad as a pack of dogs. When it's all over people will start forgetting. Easier to forget, go parading to the cenotaph on Poppy Day, some clever kid who never saw blood blowing the Last Post on his bugle, and Salvation Army girls hoping for a date, and our M.P. making promises—his father was a blackleg and his mother was a flag—and the police inspector looking as if butter wouldn't melt in his mouth, and old hypocrites from the British Legion Women's Section trying to remember their husbands because it's all gone down the shoot. All gone from the Great War by the time this war started. Now, *we* must put our heads together. Sunday tomorrow. We'll drive out to Tŷ-coed farm. I'll have a chat wth Mervyn. Make arrangements.'

He resisted puppet-nodding: it's coming straight off her tongue like Lester Mackie the agent in Plasmarl. As if she's convinced

113

inside her head. No sons or daughters, not even old Llew to disagree, argue against her, due to the queer lump stuck in the gut. Even my gut. All I've got to do is give way whenever she opens her mouth. *Iesu*, Elsie, you're putting years on me.

'Okay,' he said, 'I'll run like a *milgi* rounding up sheep.'

'Sneer if you want to, mister.'

'By the Christ, woman, we've been through everything since I moved into Parc Villa with my tail between my legs.'

'And stuck it out, boy, made them shut up.'

'There you are then. Proof,' he said.

Mouth to mouth in bed, Elsie's threnody sighs for their Gower holiday night-times—her lush siren body Dewi Joshua's and his own hers in Moel Exchange Sabbath day-time.

Meanwhile knowing, jealous or smug neighbours passed by the green Rover outside the front room window.

★   ★   ★   ★

Autumn filtered space by timed space. Nettles withered inside the mossed ruins of Exchange Manor. Vandals hacked one of the rugger goalposts. Thieves ransacked the A.R.P. headquarters.

While autumn lost colours the town's chief executive bought two more terraced houses in his common-law wife's name; Arabella Cules, divorced daughter of a former Councillor banned *sine die* from office subsequent to receiving stolen goods: 2,000 bricks, cement, sand and chippings from the Council yard. The chief executive had seventeen rented terrace houses, and presidential entry to Uplands Park bowling green. He also had a *good name* in town. 'No side on Jacob Tanner,' they said. 'Rag, tag and bobtail, he'll buy them a pint. One of the best, aye.'

Boyhood myelitis left Jacob with a slightly flippering right leg, spur of his own jokes on the bowling rinks. His hegemony richly baritone, 'Come in, Elsie! Well now, good to see you after such a long time. What's the problem exactly?'

'Permission,' she said, 'for Dewi to put a gate and a stile across the old path through the wall coming down from the Quarry. I'm referring to Bluebell Woods. Your surveyor downstairs, he tells me it's a right of way. As you know full well, Jacob, once upon a time only courting couples went through the field to the Woods, but now there're more rodneys about than ever before.' Elsie glared for equity. 'Sheep stealers, Jacob, as God's my judge.'

The chief executive boomed, 'Haa,' from below sphinxate grey eyes. They are Dewinton scholars, shared the same mould.

'My husband pays rent for the field, *all* of it!'

'Um, Elsie, the Estate Office is in London.'

'Yes, as we were informed by my Auntie Megan's son.'

Louder, 'Haa, Mervyn Harris!'

'Yes-of-course, Mervyn rents his mountain grazing from Britannia Quarries Estate. That field is ours by law!'

Jacob playing his persona, 'Stile each side of the field. *Two* stiles, Elsie. Comply with the order. Afterwards then, d'you see, depends upon usage by the general public.'

Elsie had to change direction, inquiring, 'I don't see much of your Bella these days. All right is she, Jacob?'

'In the pink, manner of speaking. Dewi likewise, I believe.'

Change again. 'Dear Lord, I wish they'd settle this war.'

Jacob Tanner interlocked his fingertips across his waistcoat bulge. 'By the way, you must come to the Pavilion next Sunday night. Charity concert in aid of the Mayor's Fund. Arabella has booked wonderful artistes. Olwen Jones the soprano, Pryssor West clarinet soloist, Clayton Merchant playing his jazz medley on piano, baritone Chester Ringer who toured America before the war, Verdun Hewitt on the zylophone. Ten artistes altogether.'

'Mayor's Fund, Jacob?'

'For memorial statues.'

'Indeed?'

'To all our local boys.'

'Jacob, the war's not over yet.'

'Three bronze figures in the forecourt down there. Life size.' The chief executive timed three jaunty salutes: 'Soldiah. Sailah. Airman. Arabella wants to bring culture to Moel Exchange. Outside my remit of course, the business of culture. She would like to improve our status.'

'How much will they cost?'

'Estimates vary at the moment. All monies will be open to

public scrutiny. Arabella loves works of art. She's corresponding with candidates at her own expense.'

Smiling friendlily, 'Candidates?'

'Meaning sculptors, quite right.'

'They'll cost the mint, Jacob.'

'Come along Sunday night. Starts at seven o'clock. Perhaps you and Dewi might like to join us for supper afterwards?'

'Awfully kind of you, Jacob. Let you know as soon as possible.'

They shook hands across his desk.

'Two stiles, please, Elsie, for the sake of peace and quiet.'

Standing in the Council Offices hallway, she examined blistered varnish on the heavy double doors, varnish fading like watery gravy stain on the cracked lower panels. She paced to the gate pillars. Three yards. Twenty yards along the Offices from corner to corner. Sixty square yards of daffodils every Spring, planted by the Girl Guides. Elsie preoccupied herself walking short cut lanes to the British Restaurant: Gracie Ginty's one and only public speech before presenting certificates to the Girl Guides. Deborah Coles like a plank in that silly uniform. The first crop of daffodils stolen by scruffs from Sinkers' Huts. £5 fines to set example. One kid sent to Borstal. The Hollings boy, Marcus, paratrooper Marcus Hollings, killed somewhere . . . Arnhem. Who broke into the station ticket office. Joined the Army from Borstal. Never came home again. When? Not when Ossie Ross sang *Bold gendarmes* in the Recreation Centre Go-as-you-please. Long before. Mm, when Llew bought the greenhouse. One of my fads. Ten years ago. Three huge statues for the Council staff to goggle at. Ten years gone by, October or November 1935. Daft. Too daft for words. That Bella Tanner, she's diabolical. Divorced by Archie Cules for adultery with the G.W.R. station master who transferred himself to Severn Tunnel. Yes, divorce turned to fester in Arabella's mind.

Dewi brought the same news down from his ex-railway guards' van quarters in the lane above Tŷ-coed farm: Mervyn Harries's wife had tickets for the concert. 'Strokes,' he said, 'Bella pulls more strokes than Doctor Goebbels. Tell you something, Elsie, I'd sooner spit coal dust than tend bloody sheep. If I can find a bloke to take over, I'll go hobbling on the buildings, concrete gang or barrowing, humping or scaffolding, I'm not fussy. Some steady bloke preferably on the Sick so's nobody'll be any the wiser. Honest, all day long I'm like a hermit.'

She said, 'Stop, I don't wish to hear complaints. There's a public right of way across our field. You'll have to make a stile by the gate and another stile at the edge of Bluebell Woods. All red tape but its compulsory.'

'They know what they're up to, the wasters. Out on the job before first light of day. I found where they skin 'em, ditch below the Quarry. Must take a couple of strong fellas lugging a ewe up there. Makes me feel like murder. Mervyn says forget the police. First, up to me to catch the bastards.'

'Sleep in the van.'

'I've kipped in worse places underground. They pick bad nights, rain and fog. What I'll do, ask Ellis Mabon to take turns. Good mate Ellis used to be.'

Elsie raised her forefinger. 'Pay the man. I'll put it down in writing. Do not risk friendship.'

'Guts might be knocked out of Ellis though, state he's in since he cracked up. I'll take a mandrel shaft, no sense tackling two or three men in the dark.'

Sunday evening and Elsie warned, 'Mind your language in the Tanner's house.'

He said, 'Ta, love.'

'No sarcastic remarks to the Mayor either, regardless Mat Richards is pure rag-and-bone as a Councillor.'

'Thorough shit the time he was on Pencaer Lodge.'

Narrowing her eyes and mouth, 'Behave civilised and don't interfere when I'm talking to Bella Tanner.'

'Something on the agenda?'

'I checked in our reference library, every copy of *Exchange and District Leader* for 1935. Bella ran a sweepstake followed by charity concerts in the Gaiety and the Rex. Her cousin, Iolo Rice the undertaker, he built the Recreation Centre for Boy Scouts, Girl Guides and for Clyne Harriers. But Moel *Welfare* paid seventy-five per cent for the Rec. to be built.'

He said, 'Bunch of dummies in the Scouts when I was a kid.'

'Dinmel Terrace left its mark on you, mister.'

'I'm not a blaggard and I'm not a *clec.*'

'1935,' continued Elsie, 'when the Girl Guides planted hundreds of daffodil bulbs in front of the Council Offices. In charge of parks and bowling greens at that time was Bella's husband, Archie Cules, who divorced Bella to live with Gladys Rudge, whose father kept the Masons' Hall. Later on, when Gladys died from TB in Talgarth Sanitorium, Archie Cules went away. Nobody ever saw Archie after Gladys's funeral.' Elsie lapsed into reverie, 'From what goes on, I believe TB people are more itchy. Men turn into stallions, girls seem like their fannies are on fire.'

'Elsie, you *know* every damn thing.'

'Perhaps Bella's still trying to spite Archie, get rid of him from her system. There he was in his best suit, showing the Girl Guides how to plant the bulbs. Those daffs every Spring remind her of Archie, 'specially with Jacob Tanner stuck in his office above the flowers . . . *because*, lovely boy, Bella's father, Councillor Mog Mayhew, kept the sweepstake money and coaxed Archie to steal bulbs from the Parks Department. Of course it was all brushed under the carpet.'

'Kerr-riste-almighty.'

'There's a tiny bit more. Steve Rudge is Gladys's son by Archie Cules.'

Said Dewi, 'My age, Stevie. Sharp as a razor before he stepped into long trousers. He went to college from Dewinton.'

'Cambridge University with the backing of Gladys's father.'

'What's Stevie, officer in the Welsh Guards? They took a pasting at Dunkirk same time as Ellis copped his lot. Where's Stevie now?'

'Away somewhere, invalided out of the Guards. All the Moel Exchange Rudges are dead and gone. Are we ready? Let's go to the concert.'

During the interval in the Pavilion cinema, hands waved, low calls floated, extravagant greetings were shared. Bella crossed, mincing on ankle strap wedge heels below the stage, wayward in her fiftieth year, rotund eyes insectile, her crimson mouth the wound of rapacity.

'Ridiculous bitch,' murmured Elsie while twiddling her fingers to Deborah and Gabe Coles.

'Clayton Merchant next,' he said. 'All out honkytonk, everybody shiggling in their seats.'

'Mm,' equalled Elsie's disinterest.

Two slingshots east from the Pavilion, Iago Swift and Dai Greg were on the Cooperative Store roof, shop manager Iago fearful of Dai's authority—soft light escaping to the wintry night sky from a grilled vent in the dormer roof of the book-keeper's cubby little office.

Iago nailed a piece of tea chest three-ply over the vent.

'See my point,' says Dai. 'I'm not criticising your blackout in Miss Abraham's office, but you forgot to cover *this*. I spotted the light from my bedroom in Uplands. Taken me ever since to trace it to you.'

'Gold Flake, Dai?' says Iago. 'We'll pop into Miss Abraham's office. Nice cup of tea and a cigarette.'

'Aye, parky tonight, bites into the bones up here.'

'Dear God,' says Iago, 'ding-dong scrap going on somewhere above those American ack-ack guns on Cape Cefn.'

Says Dai Greg, 'They tell me those American boys are messing about with our girls night after night.'

Iago returned hard-earned Calvaria chapel innocence, 'I don't know anything as regards such as that. Cup of tea now, Dai?'

The sky cracked invisible shivers. 'They won't give in,' approved Dai. 'Bloody Christ, there's one on fire!'

At first on high, trailing stabs of flame chased by searchlights on Cape Cefn. Three lancing beams criss-crossed, cohered, the lone German plane, lost through frailty or chance (bomb racks emptied above the Severn estuary), careering slantwise, its tail changing from brilliant comet streak to clouded red.

Dai cried, 'Gerrinside!'

Iago Swift stumbled backwards from chesting the dormer door before thumbing the latch.

The searchlights cut out one-two-three.

Bedlam violin shrieking violated the star-prinked sky. Iago crept, stood head and shoulders above Dai. They watched the Hienkel 111 raking down on Moel Exchange. White-heat married the explosion. Dai and Iago were confounded by deafness. Street screams penetrated. Flames sprang, climbing through raging smoke.

'Where's that, Iago?'

The Coop. manager named the rooftop jigsaw: 'Hodges, wireless shop, Post Office, Sports Goods, Midland Bank next to Olivers . . . it's further away, aah, yes, I know, it's the Pavilion.'

Dai clutched his arms about his head. 'Elsie's in there!' He huddled over himself, quaking.

A fire engine clanged down below.

'God have mercy,' says Iago. 'Mrs. Swift and myself, we never buy tickets for Sunday concerts, goes against our principle. Shall I make a cup of tea for us, Dai?'

IX

Unlike his father dying slowly in his mother's arms, Elsie's endmost consciousness sighed, 'Dewi?' as if in dream before she passed beyond reach. He too collapsed then, a falling ceiling board ricochetting off his head, toppling him sidelong, facing the shard of galvanised roof truss spiked into her neck below her right eye.

They were at the edge of carnage, twelve seats inside the central aisle, plaster hailing down as joists crackled overhead, fourteen dying or dead, another thirty-four injured, trapped survivors howling loud anguish at the handful of fire-fighters and A.R.P. wardens, without experience of air raids. The Hienkel 111 stood upright on its tail stump against the caved-in left hand wall of the Pavilion, the nose section buried in flames above the wallplate. Two fire engine crews hosed the burning roof. November darkness intensified in swathes.

Nearby clubs emptied; habitual weekend drinkers were digging out victims. Council lorries ferried wounded to St. Teilo Infirmary behind Exchange Manor ruins.

Jacob and Bella Tanner escaped quickly through an exit in the undamaged side of the cinema. Ossie Ross too, from the Gents adjacent to the exit.

Jacob hurried away, Bella left weeping, her wet hankie smearing the cupidity of her mouth, runs in her stockings from scagging seats, laceholes, buckles and heels when she sprawled, kept her momentum, charging past three Councillors and their wives to the side door exit.

Inside the intact foyer, the police inspector ordered one of his Specials to look after the hysterical box office cashier, wandering the pavement with a Gladstone money bag in her hand. The Special locked Daisy Pomeroy (long dead Gorwel's first cousin) in the police car with a blanket over her head and shoulders.

When Dai Greg arrived, he saw Dewi being stretchered into Moel Ward ambulance van.

'Dewi, where's Elsie?'

Brusque from panic, 'Go about your business!' said the police inspector, turning back into the cinema.

Dai climbed into the ambulance.

The driver lightly bomp-bomped his fist on Dai's rump.

'Relative?'

Dai indicated the badge on the sleeve of his tunic. 'What's that gotto do with it for Jesus Chrissake?'

'Out then.'

'Where's his wife?'

'You her relative?'

'No!'

'Better see Doctor Tibbs.'

'How's Dewi Joshua?'

'Concussion so far as we know.'

'Man, where's Elsie?'

The driver scowling bitterness, 'Nothing anybody can do for her. Great she was, in the British Restaurant. We lost a good un. You Dai Greg from Uplands? C'mon out, Dai. No room see. Only relatives allowed.'

Iago Swift joined a hand-to-hand gang passing lumps of masonry, lathes, plaster, ceiling boards and broken seats across the aisle. Dai saw Dr. Tibbs swinging right leg, left leg, fitly hurdling himself over seats.

'Excuse me, Doctor: Elsie Joshua?'

'In the mortuary. Very sad, Mr. Greg.'

Dr. Tibbs went along the row. Dai followed him to Idwal Murphy, Pencaer Institute caretaker crouched like a foetus under a thwart jumble of boards holding up blocks of masonry.

Tibbs said, 'Are you hurt?'

'Gemme out, I'm choking.'

The Doctor pokes his arm through to Idwal's face. 'We shan't be long. Stay calm.'

Dai blew his whistle. 'You with the pushbike lamp! Up here! It's Idwal Murphy!'

They heaved dressed stones into the row below. Then Idwal's head rose in spastic jerks through the slot in two boards. 'Bloody Germans, the bloody bastards.'

Soft whimpering whuffed from his nose as they levered him upright.

Dr. Tibbs' hands were on Idwal's chest. 'Breathe deep, fill your lungs. Can you walk?'

'Walk, aye, gimme a minute.'

'Mr. Greg, take him outside.'

They shoulder-armed Idwal to the front pavement, where the W.I. had a van at the curb.

'Fetch this man some tea,' ordered Dai. 'Who's got the fags? Give Idwal a Woodbine.'

Back inside the cinema, he heard Dr. Tibbs announcing from the stage, 'Clear the aisle! Keep the doors open! Any nurses? St. John Ambulance?' He pointed, 'I want you there!'

'Ladies' toilets are smashed to smithereens,' they said.

'Definitely.'

'Send the bloody Yanks in.'

'Leave the Yanks be! Those boys from up Cape Cefn went there straight off!'

They said, 'All the bodies are over in St. Teilo's.'

But, 'Live in hope,' they agreed, bunching along below the stage behind the only First Aid man in the audience, who earned a shilling a week for carrying his small tin box of bandages, tourniquet and a morphia capsule before Cwmffrwd pit closure.

Dai Greg tailed away, ducked below Iago Swift's armswing—

Ah, God damn, never be the same without Elsie. Never the same. There's no justice. No rhyme nor reason. She trusted me. We both did. Trust, like Elsie took me for granted. No hope. Why am I wearing this tunic, these trousers? Doesn't mean anything. 'Come on down to earth,' prayed Dai, who hadn't been to chapel since leaving school at fourteen to work as a bucket and brass pump oilboy on Garw pithead. Bring back Elsie. Cruel this is, too much, awful, awful. 'Come down to earth.'

Bachelor Dai snivelling head-down, desolation rucking his anthropoid brow as he walked to the mortuary wing behind the Infirmary, over-darkened by windbreak pines.

'Very first brought in from the Pavilion,' said the boilerman/gardener/mortuary attendant.

'I must see her, Ricky.'

'Word came on the phone from Moel Ward. That fella Dewi Joshua, he'll be al'right.'

Dai said, 'I want to see Elsie.'

Ricky Thomas turned the sheet back off her face. 'She went quick. Know who's been here already? Ossie Ross the check-weigher and Mr. Jacob Tanner.'

Dai was grinding his teeth. He saw sepia-purple stains around her eyes, nose and mouth. 'What killed her?'

Ricky covered her face. 'Piece of metal in her neck drove in like a knife.'

Dai sobbed walking home to Druid Uplands. His 87 year old Pembrokeshire didicoi mother soothing without touching him, 'There, there, boy-*bach*, there, there now, there there. Broke your heart she did, yes indeed, broke to pieces. Pity too, pity for Elsie Kitchener from the Villas. Too much she was. Law unto herself, wouldn't take no for an answer.'

Dai's fingers dragged the greying gingery hair straggled across his baldness. 'Mam, she married the boy Joshua!'

'What's in the blood must come out. No matter though, *mae wedi cwpla*, all finished it is for Elsie Kitchener. You'll come 'round, David, by-and-by you'll feel much better.'

But Dai fell asleep in his tears, Mrs. Greg placid as doldrum, waiting until she drew the counterpane up to his chin—the old

123

didacoi woman sold for three guineas to a Cresselly farmer's wife in 1869, who ran away with the farmer's son when she was 16, then left him too for a wanderlust Scotsman, railway navvy turned ticket clerk on the G.W.R. station, and they flourished step by step from one room in Lower Road Cellars to the semi-detached in Druid Uplands. Four Greg infants were in Bryn-rhedyn cemetery, last born Dai the sole survivor, Elsie his only worship.

★ ★ ★ ★

Ten hours into Monday morning, Ellis Mabon crouched from window to window outside Moel Ward, looking for Dewi.

'Come at the proper visiting time,' warned Sister Blod *merch*-Gethin.

'Few words with Dewi Joshua, please, nurse?'

'Can't 'til six o'clock. Come then. You one of the Mabons from Chapel Street?'

'Ellis Rhys, aye.'

'Six o'clock to eight o'clock. Remember what I'm telling you, he's in shock.'

Ellis hoarsed a stricken laugh. 'I've had some myself.'

Sister Blod waved him away.

Ducking below the sill, spying from the corner of the next window, he continued searching.

Screens! Dewi's behind bloody screens!

Riled by dread, Ellis marched into Moel Ward, rapped three times on the Matron's door, doubled in, saluted, saying, 'Sorry about this, Matron. How bad is my mate Dewi Joshua? That him behind those screens?'

Amazonian wife of the wealthiest butcher in town, she led him out to the entrance.

'Go home and stop worrying about Dewi. We're keeping him in because he's lost his wife. Understand?' She grasped his hand. 'How are *you*, Ellis? Pleasure to meet one of our brave lads from Dunkirk. Well of course we're proud of you, Ellis.'

Panting breaths twitched his lips. 'Puh-puh-puh . . . I'm looking after Dewi's sheep up behind Tŷ-coed farm.'

'Wonderful, I am so pleased,' her hand squeezing his arm.

'I'll come back at six o'clock.'

She held to her collier father's vernacular, 'Dewi will need a good butty like you. He'll fall into grief on his own there in Parc Villa.'

'When, Matron?'

'By ambulance tomorrow. Be there, Ellis, you take care of him.'

He promised, 'Do my best. My opinion, everything depends on luck.'

Lax hands on her bosom like Churchill, 'Mind out for yourself and Dewi.'

'I'm al'right personally. Thanks, Matron.'

★ ★ ★ ★

They were unwanted during visiting hours, his mother and Edwin Fowkes, Ellis sitting bent forward on the other side of the bed.

Swollen eyelids betrayed him, Zena saying, 'I know it's hard, especially now.'

Edwin, 'Too early yet, too soon to make adjustment.'

And Ellis, 'Anything you need, give me the nod.'

'Another friend of yours?' Zena scarcely smiling at Ossie Ross approaching with Sister Blod *merch*-Gethin.

'How are you, Dewi?'

He said, '*Shwmae*, Ossie.'

The tall checkweigher balled his hands, wrists crossed high on his chest while he wept forlorn as a child, Sister Blod leading him away, glancing sternly at the visitors, Dewi sealing the enigma, 'Poor old bugger.'

Zena and Edwin supplied transient sympathy.

'He'll learn to take it,' said Ellis. 'Listen, boy, following instructions, Mervyn showed me how to tackle the job. There's a stile by the gate in the wall. The other one'll be done too, take my word on it. Honest, banging in those posts took me right back to the Four Deep.'

Zena and Edwin harboured worry.

'Mervyn Harris, he's a real all-rounder. About tomorrow, let me have the key then I'll fix things ready for you in Park Villa, get some grub going. What d'you say, butty?' Ellis grimaced appeasement at Zena. 'I'm Dewi's shepherd, in case you didn't know.'

'Yours for good if you want, Ellis, the whole flock,' he said. 'Just sign your name. Ask Mervyn. He'll explain. See, aah, see the solicitor, name of Simmons on Moel Square opposite Plasmarl.'

Ellis Mabon mumbled refusal.

Forthright Edwin, 'We'll leave you to discuss private business. Let's go, Zeen.'

'You rest, boy,' she said.

'Rest up,' repeated Edwin. 'Whatever you're short of from the Coop. or Pegler's, give us a shout. Ask us.'

'Yes, don't act too proud like your father.'

His rage flickered and died.

'No need for that remark, Zeen,' Edwin's locked knee swinging out his leg as he hurried her away.

Vacancy annulled turmoil. Strangeness of 'Zeen', his mind acknowledging, So-long, Mam.

Said Ellis, 'We'll gas about this idea some other time. Key, if that's okay with you?'

'Top drawer by there.'

Ellis took Parc Villa front door key from the locker.

'I'm down,' he said.

'Aye, for good reason.'

'Right down.'

'Aye.'

'Ellis, would you join up agen?'

Eyes glassy as marbles, Ellis wriggled ugly despair, 'Nuh, I wouldn't, but sometimes I wish I was back in the mob.'

'I don't know what to do,' he said.

'Well, Matron asked me to look after you.'

'She's brainless, talking through her arse'ole.'

Backing away, keys jingling, Ellis huffed his panting, then, 'Like the rest, she don't know any different. See you, butty.'

Vacuity returned.

Irfon Tŷ-isaf came loud-voiced, Sister Blod shaking her fist, 'Be quiet, you're disturbing my patients.'

Irfon replied, 'Sorry, Blod. Hey, *merch*-Gethin, remind me to Ishmael your father.'

Sister Blod's stubby jaws jutted, her thick lower lip reddened, pressed below her round nostrils.

'Bastard Ishmael Gethin,' muttered Irfon, 'he marked his own number on Hector Rimmer's dram. We chucked him out of the Fed. Worst a collier can do, mark another man's dram. Blod's mother saved him from the sack; she went crying about Ishmael's bad nerves to the manager. Before Sid Ginty's time in Pencaer. Hood was manager, Donnie Hood from down West, big fella built like the side of a shithouse.' Irfon leaned closer, 'What the fuck am I chopsing about? What I came to say, Dewi-boy, me and Hetty, we're sorry you lost Elsie.'

They exchanged gently repetitive, fatalistic shoulder punches.

Irfon rubbed snot off his nose. 'I'm no use at this.'

'Me neither,' he said.

'The way you and Elsie came out best agenst all the stirrers, by Christ . . . Look, why'n't you spend a few days with us 'til you sort yourself out?'

'Ne'mind, Ive.'

'Sure now?'

'Sure.'

'Righto.'

'From now on I'm on my jack,' he said.

'There's no knowing, son. Depends.'

'Visitors all out, please. Time, please,' called Sister Blod *merch*-Gethin.

Irfon turned at the door, palm raised like a tribal chieftain. 'All the best.'

★   ★   ★   ★

Two minutes silence in the British Restaurant.

Stilly grey November Friday noon in Brynrhedyn cemetery, Dewi across the grave-hole opposite Lyn Pratt, the Ebenezer minister rolling his basso, Zena sending her thin, waily soprano into *O frynia Caersalem*, the slow hymn sonorous from a hundred throats, Ossie Ross copying the barvura of Lawrence Tibbet, and tone deaf Dai Greg scrupulously miming his lips.

'Ashes to ashes,' promised Lyn Pratt.

Dewi's senses fled inwards.

'Dust to dust'—dust to dust, dust to dust, dust, the Cwmffrwd killer.

'Amen.'

'Amen,' confirmed believers.

Amen, let be, they said, ex-Dewinton matrons frankly eyeing him as one of themselves, coequal, Elsie's catch, truth be told her match, the man she took from Dinmel Terrace.

Fancy man on Zena Joshua's arm too. So there!

In Parc Villa he clenched on emptiness, leaving ritual grief to Deborah Coles, to forty-three mourners, a Moel Exchange cross section upwards from the Ebenezer chapel of her childhood baptisim.

Until, 'Dewi, please stand here,' ordered Deborah.

She ushered them out by name, murmurous with handshakes into the hallway, Gabe Coles at the front door, and they thronged the pavement before dispersing without a backward glance, hurrying against the cold November afternoon.

Constrained, proud of her role, Deborah said, 'Satisfactory I think. It went off all right.'

'Thanks, Deb.'

'Be a good chap, don't try anything silly.' Deborah sniffled distress through tears while buttoning her black astrakan collared overcoat. 'Elsie wouldn't want you to go to extremes.'

Gabe tugged the corners of his pinstripe waistcoat. 'Shh-shh, my dear. Dewi's sensible, proved it ever since we've known him. Goodbye now, Dewi.'

He closed the ironwork front gate behind them. Clean up, he thought. No. Leave it. Aye, clear the table. Wash the crocks. No. You're on your jack. This is it. Elsie smiling on the wall. The Spanish girl. Girl then. Long before I was thought of. Elsie Evans. Elsie. My Elsie.

Lost for always.

Thin rind of moon crawling above motionless grey clouds as

he walked from the Rover to their Bank Holiday picnic site. He felt contained, blessed in pilgrimage. Black caked earth shrinking inside the small stone circle of their camp fire. He spun around to her silent shriek: 'Fox!'

'*Iesu*, I could have sworn . . .'

Sense, for Christ's sake stick to reason. Think first. They were Spiritualists, the Kitcheners, old Llew's family. I can't take the idea of spirits.

Then she stifled his blood with *Myfanwy*, his eyes shut tight against the world, stock-still, his hands clasped to his belly.

Silence filled in.

He felt grief-trapped. Madly relentless he rounded Pwllmelyn pond, fiercely crushing remembrances, screestones rattling underfoot, kicking at tufts, bits of stick, clumps of moss, but he failed, surrendered himself to endless loss.

Pilgrimage as benediction curdled to woe. He wandered back to the car. Cloud smothered the moon. Darkness tempted peace. Invisible land. The premise stayed: I don't know what to do.

Don't know what to do.

And later, don't know, don't know, when Ellis Mabon came to Parc Villa.

'Say, Dewi, Mr. Simmons wants to see you. He's all right, Julius Simmons. Straight talking fella.'

He said, 'I'm not fussy.'

Ellis screwed anger into the defensive, inured shield of his face. 'Isn't that beside the bloody point? The man's gotto see you!'

'Elsie's will, the fortune left her by Caleb and Mair Evans.'

'Why tell me, boy?'

'I'll call in his office.'

'Ten o'clock Monday morning without fail.'

'*He* said so.'

Ellis pulled his twisted grin. 'Now don't play silly buggers.'

'Lay off.'

'Three times I came knocking after they all left this afternoon. Where you been?'

'Took the car out.'

'Beautiful machine, that Rover.'

'Want it? She's yours.'

'Shurrup, or I'll be gone through that fucken door.'
'Let's go for a run tomorrow.'
'I got work to do.'
'Mabon, you're too fucken good to be true.'
'Shut it, Dewi.'
'My mistake,' he said.
'Mind if I put a record on the gramophone? I played a few after seeing you in Moel Ward.'
'This one, Ellis.'

Can't help loving that man of mine, the velvety power of Elisabeth Welch—his first supper in Parc Villa, omelette and slices of ham on a wad of fried bread. Elsie nibbling crackers spread with honey. O Jesus Christ. One-to-one down on the rug. Elsie found me. We found ourselves both.

He went outside, butted his forehead against the door jamb, blinding torment stylised short of suicidal, harder and harder until blood ran down his face, Ellis saying, 'Won't get shot of it that way, butty. Comes back on yourself wherever you turn. Take a squint. I've been a loser for years. There's no fucken cure.'

'Let's clear off. Go somewhere else.'
'I know when I've had enough.'
'Gower coast. Get pissed every night.'
'No thanks. Wipe your chops.'

Tick tick tick tick ending Elisabeth Welch in Parc Villa.

'Sentimental,' accused Ellis. 'That bloody record started you off.'

Jocose versus despair, 'Hey, old Llew's upstairs, poor sod's hidden under blankets in the oak chest.'

'Ah?'
'Photo of Llew.'

Snarly from Ellis, 'What you expect, for fuck's sake? Everybody goes. Nobody escapes. Get a hold on yourself, you sloppy bugger.'

Surly, 'Mouthy bastard you.'

'Stay down on your knees then, there's no fucken answer.'

'I don't know what to do though.'

'Fuck all, mate, say fuck all, just carry on. Come indoors, wash the mess off your face. You'll have a pair of shiners by morning.'

Ellis played record after record while they yarned about men, coal, headings, stalls, high spirits and extremity.

He said, 'Anyway, you're well on the road.'

'Can't trust myself yet.' Ellis sat bowed, pressing the sides of his head. 'Load of shit stuck inside.'

'There's no answer, no fucken cure. Right?'

'Right.' Swishing his long thin shepherding stick, Ellis went to the hallway. 'So-long. Mind you call in Julius Simmon's office Monday morning.'

'See you.'

'Do yourself a kindness, lay low, don't force things.'

'Find a job, me. No way I'll stay idle.'

'Forget about joining the mob, Dewi-boy.'

★ ★ ★ ★

Empty Plasmarl, two cats squalling behind the hedge, Willie Bob Ochr locking the front door, wheedling, 'Lovely funeral, Dewi.'

He crossed to the solicitor's office.

'How do you do,' smiled Julius Simmons. He sang up and down to his secretary. 'San-dra!' and, 'Cup of tea, Mr. Joshua? Two teas, please, Sandra.'

Simmons was thirty-six, smooth-faced as a woman. Dewi resisted awe. This pure and clean expert, brown hair as if polished, wearing a black pinstripe you'd never see in the Fifty Shilling Tailors. Bloke with melted butter instead of blood in his veins. Laid-on style like Ronald Colman. Elsie dealt with him. Myself likewise. As Irfon Tŷ-isaf used to say when the roof was pouncing like gunfire, cogs squashing like sponge cake, 'Cool head and a sharp hatchet.'

Sandra left the office.

'May I offer you my condolences.' Gravitas impenetrable glazing hazel-stippled eyes as Julius Simmons reached a formal, slow handshake. 'Your wife was a sterling character in our community.'

I know it, mate.

'For the foreseeable future, I would advise a continuation of the policy as effected by your tragically deceased wife. Yes, quite.

Indeed, the same policy adopted by Mrs. Mair Evans, with whom my predecessor conducted business.'

He said, 'That would be your uncle, old Aaron Simmons. Aaron went to court with miners who couldn't pay rent during the '21 strike. We grew up with that story.' A sudden sense of wastage cold as sand oppressed his spirit. 'Excuse me, I can't stay much longer. What did Elsie write down, what did she say?'

Julius Simmons exuded aplomb. 'You are the sole benefactor. The entire estate belongs to you.' Again, 'San-dra! Aspirin for Mr. Joshua. He's been injured. No problem, Mr. Joshua. We can easily arrange another appointment. Thank you, Sandra.' He slipped two tablets into Dewi's mouth, held and tilted up the teacup. 'There, finish your tea. Not to worry. Leave everything in my hands.'

He recrossed Moel Square. By Jesus, I'm groggy. What to do? Where to go? Elsie-love, I'm senseless. Elsie. Elsie-love.

'Boy!' Hetty Francis pulling his arm. 'What's the matter for goodness' sake?' She urged him from the road to a cane chair in Luigi's Restaurant. 'Bad, you bad? Shouldn't be out on your own, you shouldn't. Where'd you get those black eyes and that lump on your forehead?'

'I'm all right, took a tumble.'

'Had breakfast? Ah well then, that's it. Empty stomach will make you feel dizzy. Look like a ghost you do. Best come back with me. Tarra, Luigi.'

Feeling low in the Heol Cerrig house, staring children coming and going while Hetty served porridge from a cast iron saucepan.

'This'll line your insides. Roasted cheese and chutney to follow.'

'Wait, Hetty. I can't eat your rations.'

'Do unto others,' she said.

'What?'

'Irfon thinks a lot of you, reckons your principle is in the right place.'

'Irfon's a good bloke.'

She flailed her arms, laughing, then wiped her nose in her pinafore. 'He's good enough. Listen, you must bathe those bruises in salt water.'

Alone in Parc Villa, he doused his face in warm salty water. He slept until dark on the couch. Nine o'clock in the Legion Club bar.

'Sorry about the Missis, Dewi.'

'Aye, bad news don't come by itself. You fall down, boy?'

'Tripped over my feet,' he said.

'Nasty too.'

'Take it easy,' they said.

And, 'Well-well, look who the wind blew in.'

Ellis said, 'D'you see Julius Simmons?'

'Mollycoddled is he?'

'You're blind, Dewi. He's living tally, bungalow in Clyne Vale, him and the Sandra girl. Sick man, Julius is. Diabetic.'

'Two pints of Clyne Strong,' he said to the Club steward, union jack tattooed on his right forearm, arrowed heart above cursive *Ethel* on his left forearm.

'How you doing, Ellis?' inquired the Great War matlow.

'Pretty steady, Jakesy.'

'On me,' said Jakesy.

They saluted, 'Cheers.'

'Rule Britannia, boys,' and Jakesy Conybere (son of a Cornish father and Ogmore mother) added, 'Stick it, the Welsh.'

They passed through to the Side Lounge, Ellis whispering, 'I caught sight of two blokes yesterday morning, racing like mad to the old Quarry. Lost them up there in the big ditch. Too dark. Found one of our ewes outside the wall. Her feet were tied.'

'Borrow Mervyn's 12 bore. Riddle the bastards,' he said.

Beer slopping as he placed his glass on the table, Ellis hid his shaking hands between his thighs.

'Forget it,' Dewi said. 'I'll come with you after stop tap. We'll stay in the van.'

'This pint'll do me.'

'C'mon, Ellis, two or three pints and we'll be away.'

'You carry on,' said Ellis. 'I'll wait.'

Half-past ten when he parked the Rover outside Harris's barn. The farmer grimaced strong brown teeth. 'Nail the wicked buggers.'

The verged lane angled uphill under straggly hawthorns. Down below in the blacked-out town, muted grinding of tramcars. Roosting birds flurried like airgun slugs squirting through the thorned twigs. Ellis softly whistled a lifeless no-tune, then, 'Shh.'

Behind them, screaky yelps of a fox in the hanging wood above Tŷ-coed farm.

He said, 'Huh, creepy.'

Inside the G.W.R. van, he gave Ellis one of two mandrel shafts. 'Take the wall side. I'll walk up Bluebell Woods fence. Go slow. Bags of time. Shout if you see anybody. I'll be right there.'

'Afraid, Dewi?'

'Nuh. You?'

Ellis lobbed the mandrel shaft from hand to hand. 'See you inside the top wall.'

The 150 sleeping ewes were scattered. They snorted. Some lurched upright, rocked away on the big field. Returning to the van, the two men quartered ground to selected landmarks.

Thereafter the night dragged. He slept for an hour on a wooden settee, a Dinmel Terrace home-made ousted by Edwin Fowkes. He allowed Ellis three hours. The paraffin stove stank. He opened a window.

5 a.m.: 'Ellis, here we go, butty.'

'Same as last time.'

'Aye.'

He heard before seeing. Muffled. Exclamatory. Muffled. Running easy, hickory shaft at arm's length, he saw their shapes ambling, stooped like primates. Space between them, the first smitch of morning light.

Sprinting out wide to head them off, he lay in a shallow hollow behind a tree stump felled before steam coal. At the moment of charging, the flashed image of Spanish Elsie behind his eyes. Without a word he swung the shaft, missed a slant stroke, kept its round-arm parabola, WHACK across Sammy Samuels' kneecap. The man choked screams.

Now he had to chase, run, shout, 'Ellis!', the other sheep stealer lost, hoping to sight him again as he neared the wall.

'Dewi!'

'Top wall!'

Luckily Ellis came crosswise, shoulder-clouting Tal Lowry

(Benny Lowry the Whistler's brother) as Tal leapt for the drystone wall.

Dewi hit him on the head. 'Fucken stay there.'

Sammy Samuel hissed, groaned, writhing over his broken kneecap.

'No more,' cautioned Ellis.

But he struck Sammy a clinical glancing blow behind the ear. 'He won't move. Fetch the coppers. I'll see to Lowry, tie his hands and feet with my belt.'

'We'd better find the ewe.'

She was lashed upside down on a length of stick.

'Fetch the coppers, Ellis.'

'You're a hard bugger, Dewi.'

He released the ewe. 'Us or them,' he said. 'Sammy Sam went three rounds with Dixie Parfitt when Scarrett's booth came to the fair ground behind Dewinton Halt.'

* * * *

They giggled and squawked restrained bedlam, escaping the bulging, damp plaster-flaking ceiling of the snug for a corner of the MEN ONLY bar in the Legion Club, Jakesy saying, 'Bloody pipe busted up above there. I've sent for the plumber. No cause for flap, ladies. Make yourselves at home. Nice to have your company.'

They were a Moel Exchange ♀ sounding board, deprived yet incapable of despair, whether blousy or crumpled-up, glad-ragged or slapdash, and they immediately returned to their topic in the snug.

'Everybody gets the same since rations,' says Ceinwen Hicks. 'The dirty wasters as they are.'

'Seven day wonder,' bleakly from Selina, widow of Elton Nixon.

'It'll outlast this effin' war, Selina. Chop their hands off, too true I would,' says Dorcas Llewellyn.

'If Elsie was alive she'd be in her element,' says Sally Mathias.

'Oh, she'd be up there in court!' declared Lettie Williams.

And Pearl James, 'No need at all, not like during the strikes.'

Says Marina Lloyd, 'Ye-es, we went through it, all of us.'
'Bloody parish, they'd watch you starve,' says Pearl.
'*Duw*, that Sammy Samuels,' vowed Mattie David.
'That Taliesin Lowry,' says Charlotte Petrie.
'Out and out rodneys,' they said.
Says Betty-Ann Houghton, '*Iesu mawr*, thick as thieves.'
Striding through the bar-room, he said. '*Shwmae* everybody.'
'Hullo, Dewi,' sang Sonia Eynon.
'*Shwd i chi*, Dewi?'
'Dewi Joshua!'
'Nice to see you, boy.'
He went up to the Concert Room.
Says Clarice Maggs, 'Sociable, like Theo was.'
Greta Picton's maternal great aunt pooh-poohed, 'Them as don't know any better can think what they like.'
They disagreed with Greta's Auntie Jennie Norris.
Eira Roach, silky in widowhood (her husband *spoke in tongues*—found dead in the bed of school cleaner Cranwen Thomas), 'Name names then, please, Jennie.'
'Left our Greta in the lurch, he did,' says Jennie.
'Never!' they said.
'Did!'
'Talking out of turn, you are,' they accused Jennie Norris.
Antipathies spluttered, comforting venom.
Says Cassie Greenaway, 'Six months they'll get for killing sheep.'
'Not near enough for Taliesin Lowry,' says Doris Petrie.
Equally vindictive Eleri Gammon, 'Deserve the birch they do.'
Flawless news-bringer Amy Pearce, 'Elsie herself, she went private to see Jacob Tanner the Council about things.'
'She it was paid for Dewi's sheep,' says Clarice.
'Their own business after all,' cautioned Lettie Williams, 'seeing as they're man and wife,' adding '*Was* man and wife.'
Says Amy, 'Bella Tanner's under Doctor Tibbs. All nerves since the German aeroplane.
Ceinwen Hicks cried out, 'Burnt to cinders, poor dabs!'
They clucked and repined for the unknown aircrew, for the downtrodden, for victims since the world began.

'Your Greta's still after Dewi Joshua,' insisted Sonia Eynon.
'Yes, she is, Jennie, for definite.'

Jennie Norris sighed '*Ych y fi.*'

Whereon Pearl Jones inspired a decorous sing-song: *Let me call you sweetheart*. Seemly too, Eira Roach launched *You always hurt the one you love*. The blue mood ballad quietened the men in the bar.

Jakesy came from behind the counter, 'Ladies, glasses of Mackeson's all round, paid for by Syl Rice'—Sylvanus, the club-footed eldest son of Iolo Rice (deceased), former Funeral Director and Monumental Mason, was playing dominoes with his comrade, Gus Marsh, leg-ironed from childhood, only son of Augustus Marsh (deceased), former Timber and Mortar Merchant.

Syl doffed his duckpond trilby to on-her-feet spokeswoman Dorcas Llewellyn.

'Thanks ever so, Mr. Rice. Awfully kind of you, I'm sure.'

Abashed as expected, '*Iechyd da i gyd*, ladies.'

They smiled and clamoured, 'Same to you and all the best!'

Up in the Concert Room, Dewi confided to Gabe and Deborah Coles what they already suspected, the signed deal with Ellis, giving Ellis the sheep while Dewi rented Bluebell Field.

'Because I want a job, Deb. Can't think straight. All I want is a job.'

'Reserved occupation, here in Moel Exchange!'

'Yeh, I'll stay put.'

'Undo what you've done,' she said.

Ex-cashier Gabe smoothed the paunch of his retirement. 'Rescind, boy. Withdraw your agreement with Ellis Rhys. Goodwill remains. Quite frankly, with upward of eighteen thousand capital, I would consider venturing into property.'

'Speak plain, Gabe.'

Exasperated Deborah, 'Exactly, please.'

Gabe went, 'Huh, God forbid speculating in this day and age, but quite logically there must be a boom when the war is over. We saw it after '14-'18.'

'Depend on my husband,' she said. 'He's always right.'

Harrowed in his heart, Dewi said, 'I want a job.'

The Sunday night concert chairman clapped several times.

'Ladies and gentlemen, at this juncture, please show your appreciation for our great local artiste, Madame Olwen Jones!'

Deborah's mouth within an inch of Gabe's wiry-haired earhole, 'Tch–tch–tch, she's well past it.'

'Hush now, my dear.'

Olwen Jones, Penderyn Villa, projected herself as evergreen despite a gourmand's hangbelly and the underarm flab of dotage. Erfyl Boon accompanied her rendition of *Rose of Tralee*, Olwen's swansong as it happened. She fainted backstage. Ambrose Adams (Care Hire . Weddings . Funerals) took her to Moel Ward.

'Thanks anyhow,' he said to Gabe. 'Someday I'll transfer the sheep back to my name, leave the shepherding to Ellis, pay him proper dues too. Cheerio, I'm away now.'

Deborah suggested, 'Lock up, Dewi, give yourself a break, take a holiday.'

'I would not recommend running anywhere,' advised Gabe. 'Sooner the devil you know.'

'What?'

'He's always right,' repeated Deborah.

The ex-cashier's fingers pianoed his half glass of Guiness. 'You are registered as self employed, and a new employer will require your insurance card, consequently you will be nabbed by the authorities.'

The chairman announced, 'Information as regards Madame Olwen, ladies and gentlemen, to the effect she's out of danger. Olwen will be sent home tomorrow. I suggest we continue the concert after the interval. Much obliged to you one and all.'

Dewi went to the Comrade's Club.

X

A Salvation Army giantess was selling *War Cry* in the Long Back Room. He put two pennies in her collection box but refused the paper.

Greta gave him thumbs up. 'Heard all about you and Ellis Rhys. Funny thing. I never took you for a tough nut. But there again, seems like you always get what you want. Right, *cariad*?'

A grainy negative of Elsie while ambushed by the *cariad*.

'Just come in, Dewi?'

He said, 'Aye. What you drinking, Greta?'

'Clyne Strong shandy.' She turned to a jaundice-faced munitions worker. 'Dewi and me used to knock about together from when we were kids, before I went up to West Ealing.'

'Seven years back,' he said. 'Same for you?' he asked the woman—fortyish, freaky looking, bouffant hair yellowed like her face and hands.

'Okay, ta, boy. Shift up, Greta, plenty of room for him.'

He brought two glasses of shandy and topped up his own pint with a bottle of Clyne Extra.

'God Almighty, I could do with a day off,' prayed the woman. Tartar slotted her teeth in shy smiling. 'Terrible about your Elsie. My gran was in the Pavilion that night, lost one of her shoes.'

'I was in work,' said Greta.

'Lucky you! On dispatch since you came home to Victoria Street.'

Said Greta, 'This is Nesta Lougher from Railway Terrace.' Greta side-flicked her head. 'Dewi Joshua's in the Villas.'

'Course I know tha-at! How's things in general, love?'

Hang on, he thought, saying, 'Nesta, there used to be a few Loughers in Pencaer, steady grafters in the face.'

'Drummed into them from early on. Work or starve.'

'True enough too,' he said.

A resigned tripartite pause. Cigarette held to her wide mouth, Greta mused about her ambition, 'I'm glad I came back to Moel Exchange. My experience in service is over and done with, thank you very much. After the war, nice clean job in a shop until I settle down.'

Staring without seeing her, he said, 'I'm looking for a job.'

Nesta eyed him across her nose. 'They won't take you in the Arsenal, only disabled and over age for call-up.'

'Oh?'

'Bad or compo cases,' said Nesta.

I'm bumped, he thought, but it doesn't show.

When Leyshon Lougher and his wife came into the Long Back Room, Nesta retreated. 'Seeing as you found company Gret, I'll have a chat with my sister-in-law.'

He said, 'I've no idea where to start.'

Greta crossed her elegant mannequin legs, showing gleaming scallops of parachute silk petticoat. 'It's the ache inside. Yes, yes, I know. Elsie did good for you. I mean you came nowhere in school, same as me. Now you've passed the fireman's exam, and there's that smart Villa place. Sooner than later, boy, you'll have to come out of your shell. See poor Nesta, three kids in school and Shosh Lougher gone lost without trace in France. She can't *cwtch* away indoors day after day. There's her kids to think about. Glad I didn't have any.'

'Hear from him these days?'

'Markie married a Land Army girl. He's better off. Old Mrs. Rowley, she's gone. As I know from when his father died, there's no real fight in Markie.'

He explained quietly, 'I saw Elsie dying.'

Strangely diffident, 'My mother won't last much longer either.'

Up in the Comrades' Concert Room they were cheering *Blue birds over the white cliffs of Dover*, a tenor/baritone duet.

Greta recrossed her legs. 'My house y'know. I'll create ructions if Glyn thinks he can bring his wife and kids into my home.'

'Where's he living, your brother?'

'Wern Row behind All Saints Place, her family included, packed in like rabbits. Glyn's still on compo, riding it since he was squashed between two drams on top pit. *Ych*, their kids drink tea out of jampots.'

'So what? I came from Dinmel Terrace.'

'Why put on? You don't respect anybody at all, go your own way no matter what. I'll pay this round. Gin and tonic for a change.'

'Shove it back in your purse,' he said.
'Left you money, did she?'
'You can say that agen.' Then he lied formally, sliding the drink to her hand, 'I promised to meet Ellis at ha'-past nine.'
'Not walking me home then.'
'I'd be a right shit.'
Cynically monotone, Greta chanted, '*Tell me the old, old story.*'
Awareness struck him: I managed great in the field when we downed Samuels and Lowry. That's my answer. Action. Keep busy. Do, aye, DO.
'Hey, girl,' he said, 'I don't want to brag, but who broke you in?'
Rubbing her diaphragm, pawky as a crone, 'More'n you can say for Elsie Kitchener, boy.'
Grinning his upslanted feral eyes, 'We're evens. So-long for now.'
Once outside the Comrades' Club, he began laughing. Safe in the black-out, laughter yowled, purged from him down to thoughtless hiccups as he walked to Parc Villa.

*   *   *   *

Taliesin Lowry and Sam Samuels were each fined £20 and sentenced to six months in Swansea prison. The magistrate praised Dewi and Ellis. Zena kept a cutting from the *Exchange and District Leader* in her handbag, to show workmates in the Arsenal canteen.
Christmas came and went as if struck off the calendar. And the American ack-ack unit disappeared from Cape Cefn. He remained self employed, paying Ellis £4 a week to winter feed and shepherd his sheep. Elsie's money from Lloyds Bank. Sometimes he laboured for small builders in town, mixing concrete, trenching, hod-carrying. He drove the AMBROSE ADAMS saloon bus, transporting Moel Boys' Club soccer team, the depleted Male Voice Choir, occasionally the Women's Guild. On call for odd jobs, he dug allotments, repaired walls, cleared blocked ditches, and he sheared the never-cut hedge around Moel Ward.

He felt quieter in his mind, onset of recovery, another Dewi Joshua emerging tempered by heartbreak.

But Ellis Rhys, he remained flawed from humility and suffering. Ellis rejoicing while late night listening to Lord Haw Haw. Vengeful Ellis, 'Smash the bastards, smash the bastards.' Faithful Ellis, less grateful to Dewi than simply loyal, the dumb ewes relieving his alienation.

The day before Germany surrendered on 7th May 1945, Dewi went to Lloyds Bank in High Street.

'Between you and me, Mr. Clarke.'

'Why the secrecy?'—Mrs. Joan Clarke had a secret place, their youngest son's bedroom in Golau Villa: Signalman Colin Clarke, killed in the battle of Alamein, September 1942.

He said, 'This is between you and me, man, that's all.'

'Twenty pounds to every street party in Moel Exchange?'

'Correct.'

Prototype money-minder, Bertram Clarke crackled a knuckle in his left hand. 'Mystification isn't healthy. You're dealing with capital as ah, a public benefactor.'

'Elsie would love the idea,' he said.

'The anonymity?'

'No, my idea.'

'Which implies you are doing this for her, a charitable gesture to local children. Ah'm, a good deed done by stealth as recommended by Jesus Christ.'

'Didn't know about that,' he said.

Life-time C. of E., Bertram Clarke declared. 'So be it.'

'They'll remember, won't they? Kids'll remember their street party. No favourites. Everybody equal.'

Mr. Clarke quivered his mouth.

When Moel Exchange revelled on 7th May, Dewi turned off the dearth valued Roman road to the sunken medieval ruins, circular corrals diminished by unrecorded centuries, stones carted away for boundary walls, pigsties, byres. Skylark and wheatear song at the campfire site where they cooked sausages, potatoes and runner beans in the Bijou Camp Kit.

Last time, he thought. Never again.

Cool wafts sliding down the tiered morrain whiffled abstract symmetries on Pwllmelyn pond. Fattening tadpoles writhed the shallows.

Never again.

He flung a screestone skidding across the water, saw it spurting a dusted whiff of mud on the far bank.

Never.

As if he inhabited time out of mind.

Eight o'clock when Ellis came to Parc Villa. Ellis wearing a new double breasted light grey utility suit, his first since 1938.

'War's over! I'm free as a bird!'

He said, 'Where we bound for?'

'Legion, for Chrissake!'

'I'm with you,' he said.

Sylvanus Rice was half-singing half-reciting 'Dinah' in the Legion Club bar: *'Every night, why do I shake with fright, because my Dinah might change her mind about me. O Dinah, is there anyone finer in the state of Carolina, if there is then show her to me. Dinah, with her gypsy eyes blazing, let me come and sit and gaze in, into the eyes of Dinah Lee.'*

'Your turn, Gus,' they said.

Gus Marsh sloped upright, walking stick smacking his leg iron.

'Order, boys!' called Jakesy.

Gus sang *Old Faithful*.

Dewi heard his mother in the Side Lounge, Zena singing *When the blue of the night meets the gold of the day*. Later, peeking his head around the door jamb, they were singing *Alexander's Ragtime Band*, Edwin Fowkes playing two spoons on the thigh of his stiff leg, Zena gazing at him, singing, her shoulders jigging the beat, entranced as a girl.

'Share the joke, butty,' said Ellis.

'Miracle in there. My old lady and Edwin Fowkes performing.'

'Live and let live.'

He said, 'Bound to. Let's try the Comrades' Club. We might run into Irfon Tŷ-isaf.'

'By the Christ, old Tŷ-isaf from down the Four Deep.'

A Great War veteran was retching in the gutter outside the Comrades' Club: Meirion Dutfield, main line haulier by night in Pencaer until the pit closed. They helped him back into the bar.

'What he win his medal for, Ellis?'

'Brought ammo up to the trenches when the shit was flying on the Western Front.'

'You feel sorry for Meirion?'

'Well-aye.'

'Not much left in him, I mean he couldn't work a holt of *pwcins*.'

'Quiet! Fuck all to do with it.'

'Irfon should be here,' he said. 'Somewhere.'

'Long Back Room, I suggest.'

They found Irfon and Hetty celebrating with neighbours from Heol Cerrig. Staccato and legato on harmonica, a tousled Dewinton Grammar School youth played *The Woodpecker's Song*. The shrunken little Saturday night pianist plinked occasional phrases.

Irfon whispered, 'The very man I want to see, C'mon to the pisshouse. More private.'

Hetty invited Ellis, 'Chair for you by here.'

They were in the Gents, Irfon saying, 'You're after a regular job? I've found you a bloody job. Make some big *dwsh* if we go about it the right way.' He licked a gargoyle grin. 'I know for the three-foot-six Cantrebach housecoal seam. Safe to work. Solid rock top, about a yard of bottom muck. In fact, butty, if we wanted we could make a fortune.'

He said, 'Steady there. Ystrad and Talbot Mining Company own everything in Moel Exchange.'

'Not at all! Jessop owned Cantrebach housecoal when a big jump knocked it out seventy or more years back, the time my Grancha moved into Tŷ-isaf. Get my point? There isn't a bloody Jessop left in Moel Exchange.'

'Jessop's Brewery?'

'Aye, dee-fucken-funct. So we lay claim.'

'How?'

'Christ knows. We'll find out.'

'Where is it, Ive?'

'You'd never guess.' Irfon spun a knees-up jig on the slippery terrazzo. 'Know where you turned the water from the old airway on Glas Tump? Well, boy, the flood-out did us a favour. See, the water made a gutter, five feet deep in parts. Got that? And there's a little waterfall no taller than me'—flat palm on his head. '*Behind* the bloody waterfall, the Cantrebach three-foot-six seam. It's the Cantrebach def-in-it-lee!'

He thought, Show Irfon you're all for it, but '*Iesu*' crawled from his mouth.

'Here's the griff. We go straight across Glas Tump, twenty, say thirty yards, stay well clear of the Cwmffrwd water. Then we drive in level. There's miles of coal on in front. Miles!'

'What about the muck?'

'Dram the fucken stuff over the Tump.'

Leaving the urinal, he said, 'What d'you say we talk it over with Gabe Coles?'

'There's a fucken Ystrad and Talbot shark inside Gabe.'

'Who else then?'

'Somebody as we can rely on to keep his trap shut.'

'Who?'

'Dewi, you're asking me!'

A woman's hand plucked, gripped the hem of his jacket.

Irfon shook his head, warning, 'Don't be long, boy.'

'Bella Tanner from Brynhyfryd Place. We spent it on chocolate eclairs, nut clusters, lovely cakes, trifles, blancmange, coconut ice, jellies, wafers and cornets, flagons of pop, oh-and-we-sent-away! Mementoes! brooches for the girls, badges for the boys!'

He said, 'Oh aye.'

Feigned admiration haunting her dark violet eyes, 'Elsie would be proud of you, Dewi Joshua.'

'No idea what you're on about, Missis.'

'Jacob made out the list for Mr. Clarke the bank manager.'

'Sorry, Missis, wrong bloke.'

'Please . . .'

Lightly thumbing her shoulder, 'Pull the other one, Missis.'

'Ow sorry! Sorry! I forgot!' Her eyelids fluttered as if governed by static. 'That Bertie Clarke, he's a proper swine.'

Sitting beside Ellis, he shrugged at Irfon, 'Silly old bag.'

Said Irfon, 'There's your pint.'

Hetty chinned her palm, 'Pestering you, was she?'

He said, 'She's missing upstairs.'

The Dewinton Grammar School youth tapped spittle from his mouth organ. He blew a sharp top C tongue-rattle. 'I was eighteen last week. They'll have me in the forces before I go to Uni. Think I'll join the R.A.F.'

Ellis mumbled inoffensive curses. 'I can't put a name to you, mate?'

'I know *you*. Ellis Rhys. Family nickname, Mabon.'

'Coslett,' Dewi said. 'Rhidian your old man?'

Another forced *brrrt* before, 'Shadrach Coslett.'

Irfon acknowledged, 'No flies on Rhidian.'

Hetty smiled, 'Shad's mother comes from Riverside Lane where I used to live.'

'The long-haired few,' quoted Shadrach, 'have swept the Hun from the skies above this Land of my Fathers.' He grinned to mock cringing, '"Scuse me, pleez.'

'Hoo-fucken-ray,' muttered Irfon.

'Lots of brave ones's like to jump out of their graves,' said Hetty.

Prompting Irfon, hands in prayer, 'Bai Christ awbleddy maighty.'

Earnest Ellis advising, 'Watch out for propaganda, Shad. Go to university. They'll back-stab you with propaganda.'

Dewi said, 'Everybody empty?'

Rounding the Long Back Room to avoid Bella Tanner, he met Dai Greg at the counter.

'Out of bounds, Dai?'

Flourishing his wallet, 'Affiliate member, years and years. How's tricks, boy?' Dai tipped up the brim of his hat—his third pearl grey slouch since baldness threatened. 'Fuck 'em all,' he said miserably. 'Whoa now, I'm paying.'

'I'm with Irfon and Hetty and Ellis and Rhidian Coslett's son.'

Day swayed jubilant, 'Bloody great!'

His toecaps clipped Dewi's heels.

'Watch it, Dai.'

'Carry on, boy.'

Lowering the tray, Dai held himself rigidly aslant.

Hetty supervised, 'Chair for Dai next to Irfon.'

Happy-ending generosity uproared the Long Back Room. Renewals, bonds of hearths, pavements, workplaces. Feuds and grudges absolved, instinctive opposites reconciled. Dai Greg's head drooping, tears glinting, plop after plop into his beer.

'Oh, *Duw-Duw*, man,' sympathised Hetty.

Wiser than most, Irfon said, 'Tend to the poor bugger for a minute.'

Unlike dratting old Mrs. Greg in Druid Uplands, Hetty pulled Dai's head into her shoulder, held him in close rock-a-bye, her hand stroking his nape.

Ellis Rhys Mabon talked, wondering to himself, 'Never seen the likes before.'

The Club chairman waved his arms for order: 'Comrades and friends, the committee have just decided a few seconds ago! Free beer 'til stop tap! Spirits half price! Thank you, comrades.'

They were reviving Wales on a slow arm-in-arm meander towards massed singing on Moel Square. Among them ordinary patriots, neer-do-wells, the fearful, obedient, time-servers and skivers, the short-memoried and intractable, shoppies, the self-appointed town *crachach*, a distinct middle class, Council employees (all grades), orphans and lodgers, Arsenal and factory workers, housebound escapees, dole-men, Sick Benefit quietists, committee-men and women, Dewinton Grammar School scholars and drop-outs, G.W.R. workers, Moel Male Voice, school teachers, contract labourers, chapel members, leather-faced farmers, Home Guard, A.R.P., fire-fighters, four policemen, two Specials, one sergeant, one inspector with the wary bonhomie of a guard dog. Children were 'taking advantage', approved by Hetty, who, with Irfon, embraced cheek to cheek, singing to each other: *Ar hyd y nos, Calon lân, Home sweet home, Drink to me only, Sweet Adeline, Keep the home fires burning, Swing low, sweet chariot, Old man river, Keep smiling through.*

Finally *Mae Hen Wlad Fy Nhadau*, repeated, fading in spurts, winding away to terraces, streets, lanes, crescents, rows, the neat pebbledashed complex of Druid Uplands and the old, oldest, police-stationed Labour Ward 1 of Rheola All Saints Place.

For the first and only time in Parc Villa, Dai Greg ate dried egg scrambled on toast. He slept on the couch.

And Moel Exchange shrugged itself back to come-day go-day

norms of work, food, sex, leisure, governed by habits and circumstances, the freedom of immeasurable bits and pieces.

Wives, mothers, brothers and sisters of men in Japanese P.O.W. camps kept vigil unto themselves.

★ ★ ★ ★

Dewi left the Rover parked behind the pithead stables on Pencaer, crossed the polluted bog to the parish track and set off as if casually roaming. Glas Tump billowed standstill green and scree charcoal-grey. Homing pigeons careered low as if funnelled, exploded across the double-humped summit, swept down and out, bee-size, high above the giant's spread hand of feeder streams into Nantglas.

He scanned Glas Tump. Perhaps Irfon's wrong. Could be a rider seam. But Pencaer and Cwmffrwd are far, far deep down. Down deep. Can't be a rider.

Legendary Cantrebach. They were all gone who worked the housecoal seam by candlelight. Shanks' pony days. More Welsh than *Sais* until they found steam coal.

Subterranean water frothed a three foot deep gully in gravelly clay across the parish track, so he climbed, searching for stepping stones. Leaping zigzags on outcrop rocks, he crossed below the man-high waterfall. Like bubble-grained glass the water flailed virginal white on invisible scree. Spillage of gleaming shale underneath the outer edges of the falls, ocherous concaved clay behind, streaked with scaly shale. Contained by impulse he sat on dry turf to watch Cwmffrwd water gushing down the flank of Glas Tump, scouring roots of relict oaks, isolated hawthorns and pooling alders where it joined Nantglas half a mile away. He stared at the waterfall, comforted by stupor until, 'Get a move on,' he said, stripping off to his underpants.

Downpour pounding on his rump, he stood braced, had to, arms and legs straddled, brilliant coal touching his nose, blunt rock jutting over his head. He dug with his fingers. Coal mushed in his left hand. He leapt out with a lump in his right hand.

'*Iesu Grist!*'

Wringing his underpants, he yammered defence against glacial cold at his flesh and bones. His stretch-mouthed face the pallor of shell, he towelled himself with his pullover, hauled into his trousers, singlet, shirt and jacket, stamped and flung about until his arm sockets and knee joints numbed heat. Shining on the grass, a flaky sample of Cantrebach housecoal, which he carefully bundled in his underpants. Now he counted fifty paces from the little waterfall. Here, Glas Tump ended, converged with steep bracken and scree mountain-side. Yet higher ground beyond, rising to Pen Fawr a mile away, dark scarp curving west on the horizon. Ice age bog above the skyline, source of Nantglas.

He swung his head. Cuckoos were bubbling and calling in the hawthorns. His fingers cupped the wrapped coal in his pocket:

'Irfon, we need some advice.'

XI

Long forefinger and middle finger signalling victory, Julius Simmons sang his genteel, 'San-dra, two teas, please. Now then, Dewi, excellent progress to hand. First, you *have* re-located the Moelfrehebog Vein, commonly known as Cantrebach. Furthermore, my inquiries indicate James Ackroyd Jessop went to Bristol in 1932. From Bristol he sailed to America.'

'Any family left behind?'

'Without issue,' smiled Simmons.

'No kids?'

'Quite. Of greater significance, there are no probate records of a James Ackroyd Jessop estate. Consequently, in brief, you and your friend Mr. Francis may exploit and sell Cantrebach bituminous coal.'

'Good,' he said, as if inevitable. 'When?'

'Under licence of course.'

Sandra tinkled a spoon on the sugar bowl. 'Two sugars?'

He said, 'Ta. How soon, Mr. Simmons?'

The solicitor tapped a desk calendar with his fountain pen. 'We are dealing with the Ministry of Fuel and Power. Ah'm, several weeks I should say. Early August. You appreciate this enterprise comes under the Mines Inspectorate.'

'Fact is,' he said, 'I'm a qualified deputy.'

'Splendid.'

Sandra turned from the inner office door. 'Congratulations, Mr. Joshua.'

Julius Simmons intoned certainty, 'Our first local coal owner in modern times.'

'Thanks. There'll be a few other items. Permission for a dramroad up Glas Tump. Tippler and chute down on the parish track so's we can send out loads by horse and cart, lorry later on, I reckon. And we'll need one of those big iron scales like they use in the railway goods yard.'

Simmons made a note. '*Avery* platform scales. I shall arrange delivery when you are ready.'

'And widen the track down to Upper Road.'

Frowning as if distracted by gnats, 'With regards to the parish footpath, it's common land.'

'What about the dramroad?'

'Formal application to Britannia Quarries Estate. My advice, Dewi, simply go ahead.'

'Hey, I like that.'

Simmons crossed to a wall cupboard for a decanter of sherry and glasses on a pewter tray. 'Allow me,' he began, filling the glasses, 'May I wish you the success you deserve.'

Sweetness gorging his gullet: *Iesu*, we're living in different worlds. 'It's what I want to do,' he said. 'Be my own boss filling out coal.'

'Absolutely I'm sure.' Stalking clockwise around his desk, the solicitor paused. His heels clicked as if echoing resolve. 'Dewi, would you consider a partner? Financial partner?'

'Done. You're on. We're definitely short of a man to sort out the paper work.'

'San-dra!'

They tippled sweet sherry again, Sandra gushing polite excitement.

★   ★   ★   ★

He scouted Glas Tump for a safe gradient for the tramroad. His conscience insisted: my responsibility. Elsie's money. All down to me. Dramroad, tippler, loading bay. Christ, Elsie-girl, miss you now. Once we're into the coal, we'll work it right. Just two of us. Half size peggy drams. Start off small. Build up trade, as they say. Lamps? Order carbide every week. No fire-damp, thank Christ. No electric. No blast bags to drag up and down the faces either. One face. Me and Irfon working Cantrebach. Rails? Sleepers? Posts? Flats? Pills and dets? We'll haven to blow bottom in there. Break a man's arms digging through bottom muck with a heavy mandrel. Bloke like Julius Simmons, he'll be worth his weight.

Questions and answers while pacing fifty yards from the waterfall. Why not? Smoother ground around here. Any case, we must cross the flood-out water. Culvert? Bridge. Girders and concrete. Horse and cart? There goes a packet of her Wills Woodbines money. Wish me luck, Elsie. He kneeled. First of all find the coal, both hands tugging out green stalks of summer bracken. Compelled to backtrack, he jogged until he saw the waterfall. How make sure we strike the seam? 'Surveyor's job,' he said. Tap Jacob Tanner.

Who responded, 'Rest assured, this authority will encourage your business in every way short of investment.' He picked up the phone. 'One moment, Dewi, one moment.'

The only surveyor in Moel Exchange refused his offer to carry the theodolite. Surveyor and his assistant, they were terse, secretive, hidebound, two of a kind marching around the breast of Glas Tump. Warm July day, Dewi, thumbs-in-his-belt spectator, thinking, Big fish in the Council pisspot.

The assistant hammered a pointed length of 2 inch x 2 inch into the ground.

'For services rendered,' the surveyor handing him a bill on plain notepaper.

He glanced at the spot where torn, sappy ferns were shrivelling. I was five-six yards out of line. Bloody guesswork.

'Ten quid, Mr. Mundy. Okay, bring you a cheque.'

Left eyebrow cocked, 'Cash in this instance, Mr. Joshua.'

'Right, favour for a favour. I'll leave the *dwsh* in your office.'

He gave the £10 to Jacob Tanner, who complained, 'How greedy. Employees working in Council time. Are you surprised?'

'Mr. Mundy's worth remembering.'

'It won't happen again.'

'I'm learning, Mr. Tanner.'

'So petty,' said Jacob. 'I assume you'll be keen to join the Chamber of Commerce, won't you? Why don't we have a drink in the Con Club tonight? Say nine o'clock in the Lounge.'

'See you there, Mr. Tanner.'

'Jacob!' rumbled the chief executive.

'Sure thing, Jacob.'

Polio right shank and foot sliding forward, retracted in sleek distort, the chief executive preceded him to the door. 'Have you met my wife, Dewi?'

'Yeh, once.'

'Rather a *faux pas* on V.E. night in the Comrades' Club. No harm done I'm sure.'

'Nine o'clock in the Con,' he said.

Strolling outside the Council offices, he dry-spat as if de-misting a mirror close to his face. 'Joshua-boy, you're a bloody scraper already.'

* * * *

'*Extract*,' laughed Irfon. 'Nice that. Jot the date down. Never dreamt I'd live to see the day. Us two extracting coal from what's it called? Moelfrehebog Vein.'

'August the eighteenth, nineteen forty-five.' He threw a shovelful of turf. 'Here goes.' Then he hung his cap on the 2 inch x 2 inch peg. 'Let's not forget the flood-out from Pencaer airway return.'

Seven shifts a week into September, when they found shale. Clean coal by 10 a.m.

Licking his fingertips, Irfon stroked the three-foot-six. 'All ours, butty.'

'Right. Now leave it 'til we're ready.'

Eating Spam sandwiches on the sunny hillside above Nantglas, neither Dewi nor Irfon remarked the surrender of Japan in Tokyo Bay the previous day.

Disregarding the Council's civil engineer, he bridged Cwm-ffrwd's flood-out stream with ten G.W.R. rails boxed inside concrete, the shuttering devised by a former pit-head carpenter (maintenance handyman in the Arsenal) and two G.W.R. wagon repairers. Mervyn Harries's cart-horse dragged the rails along Upper Road from Pencaer sidings, G.W.R. rails stacked under gorse and brambles since Britannia Quarries Estate trucked out permanent way ballast. Rails from pioneering days, Moel Exchange burgeoning as navvies dynamited Gaer Cutting below Dinmel Terrace.

They worked on the tramroad incline. Sighting along nine marker posts, he scythed bracken while Irfon levelled hummocks and scree. Trundling coiled signal wire, they strung a line down from Cantrebach to the parish track. Ninety yards of paired tee-head tramrails indefinitely borrowed from Pencaer screens were cramp nailed on sleepers newly sawn from creosoted railway sleepers bought as firewood from the G.W.R. dump behind High Street station.

On top of the incline they built a lean-to shed, nine foot posts and corrugated sheets, brakehouse for a main and tail haulage, steel ropes and drum acquired by night from Garw colliery, closed in 1932. Likewise, seven rivetted sheet-iron peggy trams from a *cul de sac* alongside Pencaer blacksmith shop, *reliquiae* deemed as worthless. Three full peggy trams sent downhill hauled up four empties, the journeys braked to crawl, bypass on a midway double-parting.

A pick and shovel gang of partially disabled men widened the parish track for 6/- a day. Bribes, bartering and promises remained word of mouth. Bills for materials and labour went to Julius Simmons.

There was a first crimp of October frost when he drove the muddied Rover up the lane to Tŷ-coed farm.

'Can't guarantee positive,' said Mervyn. 'Should be they'll all drop around Easter-time. You'd go a long way to find better rams than mine. They'll be in your field next month.'

'I don't know what they're worth, Merv. That's why I've come to see you. What I do know, we're nearly set to deliver housecoal.'

Wrangling friendly, without humour, in the farmhouse kitchen until Harris agreed to market the ewes.

'I'm trusting you to buy me a good strong horse, Merv.'

'Cart as well.'

'Same principle, nothing patched up to look *spracho*. We'll split the difference. About my van up the lane, I'm putting it at the bottom of Cantrebach dramroad.'

'There's Ellis Rhys'—Mrs. Harris stanced above the table with a large brown teapot.

'I'll find a job for him.'

'Don't you go pushing Ellis beyond,' she said.

'God strike both of us dead.'

Mouth clenched, she poured tea. 'Bite that nasty tongue of yours, Dewi. Sugar and milk by there.'

They were out in the farmyard, Mervyn saying, 'You've altered since November last year. Want my suggestion? Find someone tidy to look after you in Parc Villa. There's more to life than nose to the grindstone.'

He said, 'Be seeing you. Listen, Merv, tell Mrs. Harries I'll watch out for Ellis Mabon.'

Ice-rimmed puddles marked Cantrebach's first sales: 1 ton Jacob Tanner. 2 tons British Legion Club. 1 ton (no charge) Mervyn Harris. 2 tons (3 due) Dewinton Grammar School.

Ellis was perched high on the shafts behind single-paced Gilbert the chocolate brown shire-horse. His sixteen year old helper sat on the back of the cart, legs dangling over bags of coal. Ellis pocketed a 1/- tip off Tanner, 1/- off Harris, and he shared half a dozen scones off the School caretaker's wife with the youth. Dark by now, Gilbert stabled in the railway van, Dewi holding up a storm lantern, watching Ellis watering and feeding the horse.

'How'd it go, Ellis?'

'I'll cope. I sent Teifi home. He's a good kid, done his whack.'

'Think you'll manage the job permanent?'

'Haven't let you down yet, have I?'

'Six loads on order for tomorrow.'

'I'd rather be in the level than 'round the streets.'

He said, 'Not on. You'll get half a quid a week extra, being responsible for looking after Gilbert. Sign off the Sick if I was you.'

'If. Everything's *if.*'

'Some bastard might shop you, that's all. Where's the takings?' He pushed the money into his rear pocket. 'Lock up then. See you in the morning.'

He felt stiff, heavy-legged climbing out of the car. After eating he dozed in his pit clothes. Tankful of cold water in the airing cupboard. *Iesu,* right mess here on my jack. Irfon and Ellis, they're bathed and in bed. I'm a mug to myself. Light the bloody fire, muggins. Wash the muck off, muggins.

Forgetting to remember Elsie, he waited for hot water, bathed and went to bed.

* * * *

His advertisement in the *Exchange and District Leader* brought Deborah Coles.

'It isn't a housekeeper you want, mister . . .'

He said, 'Don't call me that.'

'Wife, for God's sake! I'm referring to a wife!' Lanky Deborah caricatured pomposity. She delivered critical nagging, 'Quite shameless, young man such as yourself! Housekeeper indeed! As if you've got one foot in the grave! Where's your pride? Your self respect? Let me finish! I shan't stand by while you fetch some *didoreth* bitch to Parc Villa. I'd never forgive myself. Wait! I shall have my say regardless! The very idea, it's enough to make Elsie turn in her grave.'

'Leave be, Deb.'

Touching his lapel, 'Good luck with Cantrebach, Dewi.' Her long thin arms outflung, 'Hundreds of girls in this town are frantic for husbands! Scores of men are coming home! For goodness' sake, find yourself a wife! If you can't make up your mind, somebody else will do it for you, mark my words. And she'll put you through the hoop. But seriously, don't cripple yourself with work, work, work. Go out and about, socialise like you used to with Elsie.'

He said, 'I want the house kept clean and someone to cook my dinner.'

'No!'

'Yes.'

She stormed, 'I pity you! You'd sooner break your back than listen to common-sense! More fool you!'

Zena came, prompted by canteen gossip. She hated the *Exchange and District Leader* for the column inch alloted to Theo when he died.

'You're as bad as a nancy-boy too sloppy to fend for himself,' she said. 'Whyn't you find a woman of your own age?'

'Live tally, Mam?'

'What the eye doesn't see the heart won't grieve. Won't be the first time. Just be careful.'

'Oh aye, careful.'

'Stop acting as if you're stupid.'

Zena spent a Saturday and all Sunday shopping, washing, polishing and hoovering Parc Villa.

'Leave it to you now, son.'

'How you getting on with Edwin Fowkes?'

'We know where we are.'

'Thanks for everything, Mam.'

'Yes, well, one thing for certain, your father would never have been his own boss, not in a hundred years.'

'Makes a change,' he said.

'So long as it's for the good.' Zena's giggle exposed careless humour. '*Nos da*, boy.'

'I'll drive you home.'

'No reason to. I'm meeting Edwin outside the Empire. Harry Pollit the big Communist is there tonight.'

'We had a few on Pencaer Lodge. All the best, Mam.'

The following evening, smells of polish, Jeyes and Brasso in Parc Villa, he walked to the Legion Club, dampness underfoot, thawing mist seeping from the west.

Greta in the Side Lounge calling, 'He's upstairs.'

'Who?'

'Ellis Rhys.' She finished her glass of shandy, lunged full tilt alongside. 'Al'right'al'right, buy my own ticket.'
'Huh, there's no scrum,' he said.
'Monday night hop, Bobby Baker's band.'
'Ah.'
'Saw your advert in the *Leader*. Any luck?'
'None.'
Three half Jewish sisters were finger-touching, dancing in line: Rebecca, Rivella and Rachel David, daughters of Benjie and Irene David, Benjie's the only accredited pawn shop in Moel Exchange. Alone too, Benjie craved for news of his race in the bedlam of Europe. In prayer he blessed his exile, his sanctuary with Irene. Honouring their mother's sixtieth birthday, the black-haired trio swayed, veered, slow-swirled and pirouetted in blooded unison. Bobby Baker's plangent tenor crooned *Goodnight Irene*.

Dewi felt pleased in his gut, and grateful.
Greta was prudently envious, 'They've been practising.'
Friendly smiles *en masse* prior to clapping the sisters off the floor. Young men saying, 'The girls are on form.'
'Great. Can't fault 'em.'
'Where's Ginger bloody Rogers!'
And now patience dulled him like the ancient of days. Greta accepted a Wrigley tablet.
'Three *brammas*,' they said.
'Beauts, say what you like.'
'Where'd he come from, Benjie?'
'Wandering Jew.'
They said, 'Definitely.'
'Irene Kingdom came from Long Row,' said the bronchial M.C.
Chairs against the walls each side of the dancehall, Ellis half-way down, his brown hair a shaggy swatch like Johnny Weissmuller's.
'Hullo, Dewi. Say, how far you in?'
'About ten yards.'
'Good top?'
'You'd never believe. Another five yards we'll turn off a stall.'
'Big plans,' said Ellis.

'This fella'll take some beating,' Greta said. 'Married into money for a start.'

'Shut up, girl.'

'Ditto! Don't lay the law down to me.'

Leery of conflict, Ellis puffed out his cheeks.

'Who you with, Ellis?' Dewi asked him.

'Austin Viner, used to be in my class before I left Dewinton Grammar for the Four Deep. *Duw*, centuries ago.'

Greta walked away.

'She makes me tired,' he said. 'Howbe, Austin. Still working in the Arsenal.'

'M.O.D. inspector,' Viner's epicene fingers fluttering like a pastry cook shedding flour. 'Now it's all over I'll be on the dole unless I'm sent away to some engineering firm.'

Ellis hugged himself. 'Austin's exempt in any case.'

'C4, slow ticker. Ask my wife, she'll tell you it's a load of *caca*.'

'He's divorced,' said Ellis.

Viner threaded through couples towards Rivella David.

Ellis left his chair. 'Proper dog he is.'

Again pressured by sufferance, he watched Viner and Ellis waltzing with Rivella and Rebecca. The third sister's arms were around the neck of an R.A.F. corporal. Up on the stage, Bobby Baker combed his hair.

He looked for Greta, a fleeting cameo behind his eyes: Greta's red lips agape. She's twenty-six. Changed her name back to Picton from Rowley, the copper who took over his father's farm. Twenty-six. By thirty they're on the shelf. Greta, she's nowhere near desperate. She'll find what she's after. They go away and they come back to Moel Exchange. Me, I'm just starting. Without Elsie. Elsie's gone. Now I'm on the climb. I don't want any barney with Greta. Grievance over sod all. No way. Given time, I'll win back the stake I put in Cantrebach. Elsie's money, but I didn't marry her for money. Greta can shoot her mouth off until her teeth drop out.

More taunt than amiable inquiry, 'What's bothering you, boy?' she said. 'You look lost.'

'Used to be lost the time I worked with Llew Kitchener, when you and me went to the pictures with two-pennyworth of *losin dant*. Lost, aye, until I moved in with Elsie. Only then you came down from the Smoke, treating me like a whoormaster, and your own marriage was going bust. *Iesu*, as if your personal say-so mattered to any bugger. Honest, you're about as straight as corrugated bloody zinc.'

'Finished?'

'Aah, by the Christ . . .'

'Cheeky waster you.'

Laughter splurged to his throat.

Calmly exact, 'Grow up, boy.'

She'll go tit for tat with her last ounce of breath.

Greta's mouth hardened. 'Look, I'm sorry. *Sorry.* That do?'

Palms raised, 'Righto,' he said.

The M.C. was croaking, 'Ladies Choice,' when, from over her shoulder, 'Dewi!'

'Yeh?'

He part lip-read, 'Lend me a hundred quid?'

'Out with it,' he said.

'To start a business, that empty place on the corner as you turn into High Street from the station.'

'Sort of shop?'

Greta stood frozen as a huntress. 'Gwalia Embroideries, selling material, curtains, cushions, sewing stuff. I've met the Singer's agent, hand and treadle machines. Best of all there's no competition except the little market on Saturdays behind Dewinton Hall.'

Keepsake memory fragments steadied him. What's a hundred quid to me? Paper. I'd have chucked the lot away. Felt like chucking myself. I was round the bend. 'Greta,' he said, 'let me talk it over with Julius Simmons.'

'Why?'

'The man knows the ins and outs of contracts. Who's this agent bloke?'

'Damn, sorry again. He *was* a Singer's agent. They put him in the secret lab. on Rhos Estate. Brilliant he is, all brains. Stone deaf though.'

Guts beats brains, he decided, saying, 'You'd better come with me to see my solicitor.'

'Cut the bull, Dewi.'

'Serious. You won't get stung. Without Julius Simmons I'd be in the mire.'

'They clique together, always do,' she said, 'Different from us Welsh.'

'Yes or no? C'mon! I may be narrow but I'm not daft, neither am I stingy.'

I'll lose a day's pay.'

'For Jesus sake, you want to start up on your own?'

Stiff-necked Greta's head snapped affirmative down and back.

'I'll fix it.' What's she afraid of? 'Must point out one last thing. Elsie and me, we never argued about money. We were okay, we were all right.' He turned Greta's wrist to read her watch. 'Twenty-five past nine. Think I'll finish off in the Con. Quieter. Want to come?'

Verve unleashed, Greta outpaced him, foxtrotting to the exit door.

★   ★   ★   ★

Sotto voce Irfon, holing under the stank,
Christmas is coming, the goose is getting fat,
please put a penny in my old cocked hat,
if you haven't got a penny, ha'-penny will do,
if you haven't got a ha'-penny, God bless you.'

Whereon he upcurled to kneeling. 'That Greta Picton, she's coining profit in Gwalia Embroideries. Hetty says they're queuing up as if she's flogging silk stockings. Where's she getting the stuff from? Black market?'

'Maybe Greta's in the know.'

'She's open all hours like a *bracchi* shop.'

'Supply and demand, catering to the public, it's the law according to Julius. See this soft rashing over the top coal?'

'It'll come and go, boy.'

'Selling dirty housecoal won't do. Let's take five, butty.'

Irfon smoked. Dewi knocked out spent carbide from his cap lamp, recharged from a cocoa tin, spat on the fresh chips of carbide, re-screwed the pot, swept his palm across the reflector and a two inch flame plopped glaring from the flint spark.

Said Irfon, 'To think when I started we worked with bloody oil lamps.'

Dewi adjusted the drip-feed water. Troubled by his clandestine role, mistrusting the Chamber of Commerce snakepit to whom he owed formal allegiance, where tangled rumours bred more rumours, he decided once and for all, tell it and let go: 'I put up the money for Greta Picton's shop. She wanted hundred, took twice that to settle everything, rent, repairs, supplies etcetera.'

'Et-fucken-cetra! Fella, the way you go about things!'

Brusque, trying to absolve himself, 'It'll all come out in the fucken wash. Start filling. This dram's empty.'

Irfon arced his Woodbine stump. Surprise broke inaudibly, choked by growling.

Later, feeling guilty, he sought appeasement. They were on grub behind their fourth peggy tram.

'Looking forward to Christmas, Ive?'

'Least I'll have a couple of days off.'

'Bought things for the kids, ah?'

'You're not interested in my kids.'

'Give over,' he said.

'Look! My head's the same!'

'Mine's too big for my shoulders?'

'Want it straight? When you bought Cantrebach you didn't buy Irfon Francis.'

'I wouldn't try.'

'You paid for what I found. Luck? Course it was fucken luck. *Mine*. My luck.'

He said, 'I'm paying you well over the odds.'

'*Ask* decent,' warned Irfon. 'Ten or 'leven years back down the Four Deep, I never bullied you, never ordered you about like a fucken Nazi. There's plenty enough, always have been, colliers who treat their young butties like dirt. They're not men. Pig's bastards they are. Only one remedy and all, boot the shit back down their throats.'

'You took me wrong, Irfon.'

'Think so? *You* think so? Think I'm your fucken lackey?'

Put it true: 'I trust you more than Zena my mother.'

Chagrined, rubbing his mouth, his nose, his eyes, 'Seems every man must go his own road.'

'Sure to in the end,' he said.

'Only don't step on some other fucker's neck.'

'Right. I won't get your back up again, Irfon.'

'Real bloody Jonah you are. I've seen you knackered, weak as a baby pooping yellow, but there's fuck all going to touch what's left inside of you.'

Reasonably as before, 'Right,' he said.

Irfon exulted, his dauntless howling joy escaping Cantrebach level, sundered by hissing rain at the mouth.

Down below, secure within himself, Ellis Mabon at Gilbert's head was backing the cart to the loading bay. His third load since 7.30 a.m.

Graceful behind the counter in Gwalia Embroideries, Greta welcomed a new face: Mrs. Prudence Mackie.

Ystrad and Talbot Mining Company were re-opening Cwmffrwd Colliery.

XII

Lester Mackie had greyed to sad restraint.

'Pleased to meet you, Mr. Mackie. Been a long time.'

'Ha, the entrepreneur.'

'Come again, Mr. Mackie?'

'Captain of industry.'

'What does that make you then?' he said.

'Dogsbody bureaucrat.' The agent blinked queasiness from his eyes. 'I had no previous knowledge of the Moelfrehebog Vein.'

'Only two of us are filling out coal,' he said. 'Another mate of mine from Pencaer days, he's on deliveries.'

'High quality housecoal.'

'So far so good, aye.'

'We have lost our son.'

Reflex '*Iesu!*' echoed, worrying him. Too quickly he said, 'That's bloody wicked. Excuse me, I know how you feel.'

'Father and son, both murdered,' the agent's features anguished.

'I lost Elsie, seventeenth of November last year.'

'Are you reconciled?'

'It's not on, if I follow your meaning.'

'It's meaningless. We suffer like dumb animals for the rest of our lives.'

'Work's the best medicine.'

'Or faith. My wife has faith. Divine universe, the great design. Grin and bear it with faith. Phu, omit grin. Bear grief with faith.'

Connecting as to Irfon or Ellis, he gently pummelled the agent's shoulder. 'Come out for a pint, Mr. Mackie.'

'Booze in lieu of the unforgiveable.'

'Pipe down, man, you're heading for pain, the black hole.'

Wetting his lips, confessing, 'Hysteria, at the brink I suspect hysteria.'

'No matter for Christ's sake'—here's how Zena my old lady used to panic. 'See you in the Legion Club at eight o'clock.'

'Perhaps,' behind a squeaked keening spasm.

'We'll argue the toss. Let yourself go, okay, Mr. Mackie?'

First came Ellis.

Minutes later Irfon entered the Side Lounge. 'Give us the gen. Want me and Ellis to back you up, or we supposed to sit like dumbos while you pair tally prices like two bums?'

'We're all level pegging,' he said. 'Any topic you fancy bar playing betsies like some of the twats in the Council Offices. Say, Ive, d'you get wet when you found Cantrebach?'

'Soaked from the legs down. I borrowed my son's cycling cape. He rides with Clyne Clarion. Seventeen now, our Ceri, taking his CWB exam in the Junior Tech. next year. When I saw the old black diamonds behind the waterfall, I'm off down to the house for his cape and sou'wester.'

'You'd wriggle out of a straight jacket, butty.'

Ellis said, 'That makes two of you.'

'This bugger,' vowed Irfon, 'drop him in the pickies, he'll come out with *Toblerone* fucken chocolate. Look at him, Theo's one and only, spoilt since he was on the breast.'

Confidently acquitted, 'My old lady, she had more grouses than Llew Kitchener.'

'When you came to me the sun shone out of Llew's arse.'

'My ignorance,' he said. 'Hullo-hullo! *Shwmae*, Mr. Mackie. Meet our Cantrebach team: Irfon Francis and Ellis Rhys.'

'How d'you do,' said the agent.

'We're on Clyne Strong. What's yours?'

'Whisky and water if I may.'

Irfon advised, 'Fetch him a doubler else he'll be sip-sipping like a budgie all night. How's it going, Lester?'

'In particular,' now hopefully smiling at Ellis, 'I recall your Pencaer sobriquet taken from William Abrahams, *Mabon*, man of destiny in the history of Welsh coal-mining.'

'You mean bent as a butcher's fucken hook,' said Irfon. 'Ne'-mind though, water under the bridge.'

Said Ellis, 'Like Dunkirk by the time I'm on Old Age.'

Dewi at the small serving counter, demanding, 'What's the news about Cwmffrwd?'

Lester fingered the corners of his mouth. 'We shall concentrate on the Five Foot seam from North Main before opening up the Nine Foot West.'

Irfon raptured, 'Loving Christ, some big coal down the Nine Foot. Once, as a boy, I worked there from Sankey's heading. Coal! Am-maze-ing! And those bloody niners! I couldn't lift one end of those posts. Took six men to put up a pair of timbers. No steel flats in them days. Not so many *trychs* either, come to that. Tell you, it was quieter. You could hear what went on. Yard of clean top coal in the Nine Foot West. We worked it off dram-planks laid across oil drums.'

'Fascinating,' acknowledged the agent, raising his glass. 'I'm delighted to be back in Moel Exchange.'

'Cheers,' they said.

Lester again scratched the corners of his mouth. 'The signs are propitious for our industry.'

Irfon leered innocence over his beer, 'Prop-what?'

'Favourable,' Ellis reversing Churchill's vee sign.

Dewi said, 'Gabe Coles forecasted a boom.'

'Really?' inquired Lester.

'Round about the time we caught two sheep killers, Sammy Samuels and Taliesin Lowry. Not so long after Elsie's funeral.'

The agent sighed to down-eyed silence.

'C'mon, Lester,' urged Irfon, 'tell us the good signs.'

'Five of our six local collieries, possibly all six, are being considered. Cwmffrwd certainly, Pencaer probably, Garw probably, High Seven probably, Pontfedw probably. Triangle remains a doubtful proposition.'

Said Irfon to Ellis, 'He could write a fucken bible.'

'All because the war finished last summer?' Dewi said.

'Economic necessity.' The agent grimaced, 'After total war.'

Irfon drummed coal-grained fingernails on the table.

Lester continued mordant judgement, 'Total war when murder becomes virtuous, sanctified from every Christian pulpit in Europe, Africa, America, and what's left of Holy Russia.'

He felt Irfon's elbow nudge, heard the side-mouth mutter, 'Right fucken damper.'

Ellis gasped, 'Put him on a charge. At the double, left-right left-right left-right,' plunging from bombast to irony, 'Comedian you are, old cobber.'

'I lost my son.'

Ellis buffed his fingernails, world-weary, 'Bring on the dancing girls.'

'Hark at the sheik from Chapel Street. *Riff Song* next,' said Irfon.

The agent hid behind his handkerchief.

'Lester,' he said, 'where'll you find colliers to work five or six pits?'

Lester Mackie cleared his throat, stating, 'Build new homes by arrangement with your Council authority. Conveniently for Ystrad and Talbot, there are empty houses in Moel Exchange.' Fastidiously alert, Lester arranged their glasses on a tray. 'Mr. Tanner has provided a list of vacant properties.'

'Aye, fit for knocking down.'

'You are quite wrong, Irfon. My information says they can be repaired.'

Chortling fancy-dan short-arm left and right hooks, 'Take a gander, I was reared in a slum cottage, dragged up if you like.

165

Our health inspector's a bit of a prick, so's Jacob Tanner only he's craftier. He'd flog his mother's fanny. They're at it like stoats in our Council Offices.'

Ellis folded sideways. 'Don't dirty the nest, Ive.'

He remembered Dinmel Terrace, Zena complaining about stinking drains, damp walls, blackpats, cracked ceilings, rotten skirting boards, draughts whining through the house, broken firebricks in the grate under buckets of boiling water. Where Theo died, 9, Dinmel. Silicosis contracted in Cwmffrwd. Pencaer steam coal in the grate. Cwmffrwd silica dust stoning Theo's lungs. Ages since. Lost and gone.

'Take it easy on the man,' he said. Turning to Lester Mackie at the counter, 'Who's the new manager for Cwmffrwd?'

'Sidney Ginty will be responsible for Cwmffrwd.'

'Ta, cheers,' they said, the agent priestly in mien, the laden tray held low.

Ifron slapped the table, 'He was fair in his ways, Sid Ginty.'

'Elsie and myself, we had a few good times in Plasmarl.'

'Too right. Yes-boy, the way you went fat-arsing with the *crachach*, I was fucken green.'

'Envy?' inquired Lester.

'Christ aye! He's my butty, both of is sweating cobs trying to earn the min. down the Four Deep, until they brought the cutter in.'

'Longwall machine,' said Ellis. 'They put me nights shovelling duff, so I'm here tonight. As for Ginty, I'd paint a swastika on his forehead.'

Lester Mackie expelled air, 'Haaah' dying like a whimper, evoking unease, but he went on, 'You are most generous, you fellows, inviting me here this evening. I'm not responding very well, rather depressed these days, I mean thinking about the war. You'll have to excuse me,' tics snatching his mouth, 'inflicting my, this damned neurosis on you people.' His face lightened, insight glittering his eyes, 'Altogether strange! We all belong to the world of coal production. Private lives, certainly, each of us . . . each of us.'

Ellis wagging his shaggy head, hands alongside his ears, apishly scramming, 'Every man-jack on his tod when he's licked outright, nothing left.'

Forefinger and thumb scratching the corners of his mouth, Lester escaped to the Gents.

'Bit on the queer side,' suggested Irfon. 'Bad nerves?'

Wilfully stolid, 'There's no telling,' said Dewi. 'His old man was killed on the Somme. Now he's lost his son, navigator in the R.A.F.'

'Bloody cruel that, poor bugger.'

'Bad,' he said. 'What I want to know, will his Company put the screw on my business?'

'Naah!'

And, 'They won't bother,' said Ellis.

'Right, boys, knock it back. Tonight's my treat.'

By ten o'clock they were evenly fraternal, exchanging circumstances and credos, when the steward beckoned, 'Dewi, wanted in the lobby.'

'Who's there, Jakesy?'

'Luke Picton's daughter. She didn't want to disturb you gents.'

Greta said, 'It's Bella Tanner. I caught her thieving.'

'Oh?'

'Earrings. I'm selling jewelry. Small assortment. Best quality.'

Iesu, she'll branch out like Woolworths.

'They were in her handbag. Swear to God, she offered me eight quid!'

'It's either Jacob Tanner's office or the police station,' he said.

'But she's mental!'

'Look girl, what d'you expect? Nothing to do with me.'

Greta leaned from her square shouldered, cat-walk parading height, appealing, 'I'm trying to keep my good name in town. Help me settle it quiet. I mean you're well in with Jacob Tanner. He'll listen to you. This last favour, please come with me to explain to Mr. Tanner.' Closer still, her forehead against his eyebrows, 'Please,' eau de cologne wafting up to his beer-thickened sniffing, his itch-minded pull to the legend: girl. Girl. Girl signatured *Greta*.

Sighing into her neck, 'See you in the shop tomorrow.' Backing away: Christ, I'm on my own. The worst off.

Pursuing his Eros ache, soprano and alto, the snug regulars were ending, '*When you were sweet, when you were sweet sixteen.*'

'Al'right, butty?' asked Irfon.

'He's slewed.' said Ellis.

Lester Mackie had the smug enhancement of a tweed-suited, collar-and-tie buddha. 'Splendid evening, most enjoyable.'

Jakesy bawling, 'Tuh-ime pluh-ease! Time to go home, ladies and gents!'

The lights flicked off-on, off-on.

Gusty February night, shopsigns creaking, street gas lamps prupping as they grouped, saying, 'G'night then,' or 'now,' except the agent's, 'Goodnight, Dewi. Goodnight, Irfon. Goodnight, Ellis.'

In Parc Villa he banked up the kitchen fire with damp slack, pledged like fate to the 6 a.m. alarm bell next morning. For supper, cold steak and kidney pie from Pegler's Stores, mug of milk to hand.

★ ★ ★ ★

True to his promise, next day he parked the Rover outside Gwalia Embroideries.

'Dewi, how are you? We haven't seen you for weeks.'

Archly feline behind the counter, Greta saying, 'We were in school together; Dewi's awfully determined, he really is. Will that be all, Miss Ford?'

'So kind of you, Miss Picton. Bye-bye, Dewi.' Parcel under her arm, the solicitor's Sandra on spiked heels leaving Gwalia Embroideries.

Julius and Sandra from Clyne Vale. Him inside her. Only they don't intend making kids. I tabbed Julius wrong. 'Okay,' he said, 'we've got fifteen minutes before they lock up the Council Offices.'

And while the chief executive correctly invited them to side by side chairs away from the front of his desk, even as Jacob stanced himself against grey daylight at the window, he ready-witted himself for deceit.

'I must warn you at the outset, this is a very serious accusation . . .'

Butt in *now*: 'Straight forward, Mr. Tanner. Greta saw your wife putting the earrings in her handbag. What followed was meant as a bribe.'

Greta emerged into her own, striding to stiffly upright some distance from Jacob, courteous in the shoppy manner, 'Actually I feel sorry for Mrs. Tanner. Perhaps she's forgetful, you understand, due to, how can I put it, due to her time of life.'

Jacob powering dignity, 'Arabella has been under considerable strain for several weeks, indeed, months of ill health. Various tablets from the doctor, so on and so forth. Extremely difficult for a mere male to appreciate. Consequently I am pleased you—and Dewi—are here to discuss the matter. We are sensible individuals capable of resolving the problem.'

Crazy Bella, he thought, saying, 'Awkward though.'

'May I suggest compensation, Miss Picton? A suitable agreement, mutually satisfactory.'

Hastening towards Greta, rounding to her, disregarding the chief executive, 'Want me to leave?'

'I think so, yes, under the circumstances'—Jacob Tanner limned against sky and window bars, jigging off his polio leg.

Prompting in murmured aside, 'Relax, girl, nothing to worry about.'

'Wait in your car,' she said.

He slanted a statutory nod, 'Mr. Tanner, I've told Greta not to worry.'

Cajoling assumed from petulance, Jacob planted himself foursquare to shake hands. '*Bore da*, Dewi. Remind me to Mr. Mackie, won't you?'

More Chamber of Commerce guff; heads or tails it's scraping. He said, 'Aye-aye, Lester's the key man, bringing work to Moel Exchange, putting us back on the map all right.'

Jacob boomed, 'Mr. Mackie's professional.'

Slumped in the Rover, he watched employees leaving the Offices. Clean, tidy Dewinton Grammar people, safe from the cradle to the grave. Greta came running the lobby and forecourt, purse clutched to her thigh.

'Take it,' she said. 'Quarter of what I owe you.'

He refused the £50 cheque, 'We'll stick to our deal. You shove a tenner a month in Lloyds Bank.'

She pecked him on the cheek like a matron, 'Oh *Duw*, I'm shivering to pieces.'

'Know why, girl? There's more clout in old Jacob than all the Councillors piled together. Jacob runs the town.'

Fiercely grasping, shaking her knees like a sprinter, then tautening her whole body, 'He can't afford scandal. I signed a receipt for this cheque. Mr. Tanner called it a token of goodwill and not to be inquired into other than that. She's cracked. She doused paraffin over his supper last Sunday. He's sending her away for treatment, somewhere private. Said she'd be the death of him. Never to God, he's too smart.'

All grins, hugging the wheel. 'Back to the shop?'

'Please.'

'You're doing great.'

'Thanks to you, Dewi.'

Leaving the car, Greta turned, rapped the window. 'I'll be closing at nine. Come to Luigi's.'

'Slap-up nosh. Good idea. Hey, we've both been through the mill now and then.'

They had Luigi's Special Grill, fried egg, baconish rasher of ham, two sausages, two rounds of black pudding, tinned tomatoes, two slices of fried bread.

'For afters, icecream and chunks?'

'Hi-yi,' he said.

Two scoops of icecream splashed with raspberry sauce and ringed with pineapple chunks. Customers grumbled about rations in Luigi's. Futile. Money the only solution.

'It's a real drag, cooking,' he said.

Irritation creases puckering her lower lip, 'Cooking's for slaves.'

'The *crachach* style is coming strong since you took on Gwalia Embroideries.'

'You insulting me?'

'No way.'

'I lied to Mr. Tanner, told him there were other customers in the shop.'

'Without dropping names,' he said.

'Give me credit! I made out they *might* have seen Bella when she pinched the drop earrings.'

'Some nerve,' he said, thinking, to be a liar.

Obstinacy or adrenalin salivating her teeth, 'Who cares whether or not he believes me! That woman trying to say it was all a mistake on my part, how she's friendly with the police inspector since her father was on the Council. Never heard of Mog Mayhew, don't care a damn about him anyhow!'

He agreed, 'Before our time.'

'She's blah-blah-blah, forcing eight quid on me! Four times the price of the earrings!'

'Temper, love.'

Grimly tonguing a sliver of black pudding skin from behind her teeth, 'The stupid cow!'

'Cool head, love.'

'I'm not *your* love, mate.'

'Figure of speech,' he said. Two-faced Greta. Last night in the Legion I'm the Owain Glyndŵr of Moel Exchange. Here in Luigi's, as if I'm just a thick *sioni* unloading drams of muck.

She drooped tiredly, eyes hidden, elbows on the table. 'You turned me down, remember? When you had the motorbike.'

'I was living with Elsie.'

'I was engaged.'

'Ah?'

'That first time behind Plas Cistfaen, under the trees in the blackout.'

He said, 'Marvellous, your memory's like a gintrap.' Looking back now, there's me grafting twelve hour shifts in the stokehole. I was starved, dirty sweat freezing under my arms and up from my ankles. All of a sudden, who's stepping out into the road?'

'Throwing myself at you like a bag. Truth is, you're not the chap you used to be when we were snogging in the pictures. Huge difference. Your eyes look dangerous. Your mouth's different. You've changed altogether.'

'I went along, set you up in the shop for old time's sake.'

'I took a liberty,' she said.

'And that night outside Pencaer stables, Elsie was waiting for me in the house. How could I?'

'Old flame, me, Dewi Joshua's bit of skirt.'

Factual hinging on sullen, 'Only the once.'

Inscrutable Greta, 'What's on for us, boy?'

With impunity to spare, 'Start from scratch?'

'I've changed too, don't forget.'

Now, stealthy in his mind, he removed Spanish Elsie from the living room wall, turned her back to front inside his (Llew Kitchener's) wardrobe, purblind to subtlety, his motive honest, instinctive.

★ ★ ★ ★

Squashing cheese sandwiches in his tommy box, sheeting rain dehumanising the black morning (senseless complaining about the weather), he finally shouted up the stairwell, 'Greta, I'm off.'

Skelping down prancy as a gazelle in her white petticoat, avoiding his pit clothes, she angled kisses.

'Tonight?'

'Yeh, sure. So-long, girl.'

Climbing the incline with Irfon at ten to seven, workers' buses streamed like phosphorescence between street lights down below, and the slow, persistent dot-light of Ellis pushbiking up the parish track.

'Set your mind on it,' Irfon's wind-blown voice at his ear.

He said, 'Plenty of orders coming in.'

'Bound to, this weather. I keep reminding you, time we thought about a return airway.'

'Enough on my plate as it is.'

Once inside the mouth of Cantrebach, they stripped off oilskins and leggings. Irfon re-lit a stumped Woodbine from his carbide flame. 'What we'll do, face west where the wind mostly comes from.'

He said, 'Pen Mawr.'

'Exactly. Myself on the straight, I'm driving on at roughly a yard a week. You in the stall, same thing.' Grinning paternally ruffian, 'Say three months from now. Twelve yards. Right then.

Out there along the mountainside we take a bearing to come across until we knock through twelve yards on from where we're standing this very minute.'

'Deadwork.'

'Aye. Leave the pillar of coal for safety. See, boy, we've got to have a return somewhere out there. You and me, we don't want to fucken suffocate.'

'We'll build a fanhouse at the mouth next summer. Electric motor.'

'Best of all!' said Irfon. 'Give me a shout when you're full.'

He worked in reflective peace, hewing, sounding face slips, prising out ragged lumps, tumbling them into the tram, fluently swinging the size 5 square shovel, listening to faint creaks, roof pressure slowly crushing the lids on posts. He felt invulnerable, freed from his mother depriving herself to rear him, delivered from the legacy of his father. Safe, his cap lamp softly whuffing. Secure and steadfast. Whole among men. And the other life with Elsie. Elsie the beginning. Thinking about her rooted his mind, magicked his senses. Shade remained. Ghost, eidolon, icon to his gender.

And Greta. Greta. And her.

Irfon braked three trams down the incline at 10 o'clock. Within an hour they filled another two.

'We're piking it in today, butty.'

He said, 'Ive, what d'you reckon on this news about nationalising the pits?'

'Won't touch us. My old Cardi grancha used to gab after the Great War, up on his feet in meetings, preaching for nationalisation, his arms waving like he'd seen the Light. Oh, it'll come, it'll come with Clem Attlee. They've been running the pits on the cheap since Queen Victoria wore daps. Your mate Lester Mackie, he'll be wearing a fucken badge.'

'He's a thinker, Lester is. *Iesu*, cruel ideas steaming inside his nut. Bugger all the man can do.'

Said Irfon, 'Fellas from all over are signing on for Cwmffrwd, even fucken spivs I knew in the Arsenal. Colliers? Not a clue. They'd sell you fags, blades, Brylcream, Lovell's, lipstick, you name it, but they wouldn't raise sweat sticking it up Jean Harlow.'

'They might learn,' he said.

'Gerraway, boy,' denied Irfon. 'I'll bore first. Top of my road's bare as a badger's.'

They fired bottom holes simultaneously at twenty past two. Drizzle maze outside the level mouth, Moel Exchange buried in thick fog. Irfon was dah deh dah-ing *Peg o' my heart*, his pigeon toed gait reaching from sleeper to sleeper down the incline.

'Where's our boy Mabon? Wouldn't mind gambling he's knocking off the widow.'

'Who's this, Ive?'

'Nice lovely piece she is, Lois Gethin, used to be married to Stan Gethin who joined the Merchant Navy. All hands went lost for keeps on the Murmansk run.'

'Jumpy kid in school, Stan, but he filled out later. Same age as Ellis.'

They sat on bales of hay in the van until clopping Gilbert pulled the high-wheeled cart up the parish track.

Irfon went home.

'You too, Teifi, on your way,' he said. 'See you in the morning,' and, 'Any problems, Ellis?'

'Course not. I'm doing my job. I don't ask for trouble.'

'Want a lift to Chapel Street? Tie your bike on the rack.'

'With you in two shakes.'

'How's things with Lois Gethin?'

'I like the way you poke your nose in, boy.'

'Good luck anyhow,' he said.

Ellis handed him a baize string-pull-neck money bag. He opened a red hard-cover notebook. 'Three can't pay 'til Saturday.'

'Usual ones?'

'And Mrs. Gethin. I gave her two bags on the slate.'

'Until Saturday?'

'Next week when she draws her pension. She had to lash out on new outfits for her kids.'

'How many, Ellis?'

'Boy and a girl. They're seven and five.'

'Oh aye,'

'Any objections?'

He shook his head.

Ellis phewed, changing hands on a bucket of water. He poured it into Gilbert's galvanised manger. Then he scooped oats and bran into a cast-iron gruel pot and filled the hay rack.

'Tell Lois the two bags are a present,' he said. 'Only hush-up about it.'

Ellis staring at him above Gilbert's withers, 'Present?'

'Like Greta said a few nights ago, I want to keep my good name in town.'

'That's creepy bloody chapel Welsh, mate. Never show your feelings no matter if you're in fucken shreds. Stick close together, everybody afraid of the next bastard and the next and the next. It takes a skinful of beer to make us speak our minds.'

'Aye, Welshy Welsh. Us two though, we're not afraid.'

As Ellis climbed out of the car in Chapel Street, 'I'm marrying Lois.'

He said, 'I think Greta's moving into Parc Villa. Haven't asked her outright yet.'

'Christ, real brass neck on you, Dewi. They'll chatter like monkeys.'

He said, 'Talk is cheap.'

'Lois is three months in the way.'

'You're off to a good start, butty. Invite me to the wedding.'

* * * *

'Dewi!' through the letter box.

He opened the door.

Greta seized him in wordless excitement, fisted hands squeezing, knuckling down his spine.

She slept with her right palm on his chest, her right knee hooked up, her instep slack to his scrotum. Unseen in the night, swatches of brown hair stranded across her face.

Mystery Greta.

Absent Greta.

She comes out like the sun.

This isn't the girl who wouldn't let me touch her in the gods in the Rialto.

Woman Greta.

There's no finish now.
She's separate from Elsie.
No comparison.
Well, the worst is done with. Patiently he levered himself and her heavy limbs to sleep his head against her breast.
Until *Trringngng* went the alarm.
A milpuff blanket fog ushered in March.
'Next summer,' she said, her toes sliding his shins under the kitchen table, 'if we feel the same way about each other.'
'Deal,' he said. 'I'm glad for Ellis too. He's come through.'
'Think I'll make a good wife?'
'It's vice versa. You've got to live with me.'
'I won't bring you hurt.'
Pushing away from the table, 'I'll be late up the incline.'
Inside the front door, Greta's abrupt, 'Wait!' She flashed herself, goose-pimply reckless, 'With love from Gwalia Embroideries.'
'My life, girl, my life . . . lovely tits,' then he sprang, franticking himself like a man predestined for underground, jabbing the Yale door key, the ignition key, reversing the screeching Rover on choke like an Edward G. Robinson hoodlum, '*Iesu*' parroting witless from his mouth. Another world at his feet in the fogged morning. Song on his life in Cantrebach. Full opera.
'Saint David's Day,' said Irfon.
'Aye, right, leek day.'
Irfon threw sleepers into one of the empty trams. 'We'll be needing a few more after clearing our bottom holes. Leave word for Ellis.'
Message chalked on the van door, he added, GOOD ON YOU.
It was the day Sidney and Grace Ginty returned to Plasmarl. Lester and Prudence Mackie had moved into the empty Mechanic's House boxed inside jungly privet off a bridleway behind Exchange Manor ruins.

★   ★   ★   ★

Dewi remembered Luke's ashen face as Mrs. Picton's coffin lowered into the grave where his bones mouldered. Greta sprinkled dirt, rubbed her fingers, held her hands to her throat, tucked left thumb nervously turning her wedding ring.

He felt pity mishmashed with his own bearable ache, sighting Elsie's gravestone fifty yards away.

'She outlasted Luke,' said Irfon.

Two cock song thrushes vied for territories in Brynrhedyn, phrases repeated, inexplicably varied, repeated from bulging elms, distinct and vibrant above torpid dulciloquies of woodpigeons, above the oblivious (other then to raptors and chiffchaffs) onomatopoeia of chiffchaffs skulking, flick-flick-flick. Yellowhammers wheezed monotonous on gorsed slopes outside the cemetery wall, and from a shiver-throated starling on the chapel belltower, cutshort blackbird fluting and wheel-squeal mimicry.

Less than a dozen mourners sang *The old rugged Cross*. They turned away with measured homage towards the parked cars.

Irfon loosened his black tie. 'So Greta's renting the house to Glyn then?'

He said, 'Glyn's a Disabled Person, cleaner in the engine sheds.'

'Compulsory light jobs through the government, for the crocked and battered so long as their guts isn't spewing giblets.'

Irfon grinned, 'Picked by fucken office blokes you wouldn't trust to fill a sack of horseshit.'

'They think they're almighty,' he said. 'Anyhow, Ive, thanks for coming to the funeral.'

'Where's Ellis?'

'Delivering. I asked him to; it's no disrespect. Greta understands. Ellis is finding it tight these days.'

'She's full of life, boy, your Missis.'

'Yeh, we're made.'

'I won't come indoors. Remind her, y'know, from me and Hetty.'

They were alone long after the funeral, sharing moods in gloom behind drawn curtains, Greta saying, 'Bella Tanner's back in Moel Exchange.'

'Cules,' he said. 'Known as Bella Tanner while she lived with Jacob. Once upon a time she married Archie Cules.'

'She's looking dreadful, staying with her Auntie Sally Webber in Cross Harp Row behind the Mortar Mill.'
'Rollo Webber's widow, that's Mog Mayhew's sister.'
'Bella's been through the wringer, poor thing,' said Greta. 'She organised the concert.'
'Eh?'
'When Elsie was killed.'
Her long, swinging hair sizzled against despot chance.
Electric street lights flared motionless gleams inside the room.
'Old Elias Roberts, he passed away last week,' she said. 'And Mrs. Greg from Uplands.'
'Ike Houghton the week before. I worked with Ike. As for Dai Greg, he's well into his fifties but he'll make out, given time. He's no dope, Dai Greg's like the rock of ages.'
Greta flexed her ankles across his thighs. 'Things are improving. Councillor Ossie Ross brought a new customer. She's buying curtain material for right throughout Plasmarl.'
'Ah, Gracie Ginty, she's the boss in Plasmarl.'
'Prosperity has come!'
'We're in on it,' he said.
Greta walked around the room, isolating herself. For the second time in five days she succumbed, racked herself in tears, 'Oh Mam . . . Mam, oh Mam.'
'Bad times, love,' he said. 'There's no cure for cancer. She was beaten by pain.'
Early summer night over peace-time Wales, Greta's mourning canticle transposed from tenderness, the burn of her own life flaming wanton, unforgettable to his senses.
Greta seemed normal at breakfast.
'Stop staring, Dewi.'
'I'm seeing you fresh.'
She snaked the tip of her tongue through spread lips. 'Pick me up at five o'clock outside the Coop. Rations today.'
'Without grub, no coal,' he said.
Came the British rune: 'Thirteen ounces of meat, one and a half ounces of cheese, six ounces of butter and margarine, one ounce of cooking fat, eight ounces of sugar, two pints of milk, one egg each—per week.' She purred roguery, 'Heard this one?

Hugo Meredith's story about Churchill. Churchill said, "There but for the grace of God, goes God," referring to that miserable tyke Cripps.'

He told the story to Irfon at 11 o'clock, after sending five trams down to Ellis. Not a soul knew the whole about Hugo Meredith (abortionist chemist struck off in 1927, who owned the Arcade Newsagent/Tobacconist inside the entrance to High Street station), save Jacob Tanner. The chief executive sold his terrace houses to Hugo, while Bella's personality fractured under quackish treatment in a nursing home.

Lumping Bella's breakdown as evidence, Irfon said, 'You could fill a tramcar with all the head cases in Moel Exchange. Harmless they are, kept indoors, don't see daylight bar down the backyard to the lav. There's a couple in Heol Cerrig.'

Cold as a robot he said, 'Everybody makes out as best they can.'

Hefting two small newspaper bundles from his tommy box, 'Try a jam tart. Cooked last night.'

'My sweet tooth's dripping spit.'

'How's life in the house, boy?'

'Greta cried again.'

'Natural, aye. Don't let it get you down.'

He rinsed jam and pastry from his mouth. 'Working by myself in the stall, sometimes I don't even bloody think.'

'Dewi, we could use a collier-boy apiece, stock our extra coal down below ready for next winter.'

'It'll get pinched, man.'

'Fence it off, leave a big alsatian roaming 'round, bite the bastards' legs off.'

'I'm selling to order.'

'Suggestion,' explained Irfon. 'There won't be many kids looking for a start when they re-open Garw.'

'I tapped Lester. He's putting Wyndham Mabon banksman on top pit, afternoons.'

'You worked a lovely flanker there, Dewi. Don't fret, I won't even tell Hetty.' Irfon cleared his chest, parted his boots to discharge a gob of black-streaked phlegm. 'Housecoal will always be cheaper than steam coal. You'll undercut the buggers. Wait and see, they'll be begging for housecoal next winter.'

'I'll ask Julius Simmons to sort out the figures.'

'*You* know how much we can fill out from Cantrebach. Fuck Simmons, he's just another name on a brass plate.'

'Julius does what you and me can't fucken do. The books.'

Clapping his shoulder, 'Boy,—known you since you was a ragged-arsed *cwtyn*—your head's screwed on the right way.'

'Belt up, ah?' he said, grinning.

★   ★   ★   ★

Fattening like a eunuch, prematurely slowing without loss of dignity, checkweigher Ossie Ross delivered the invitation. July's last Sunday evening, Greta lolling on a deckchair, tanning herself between bouts of amateur gardening; Dewi cleaning the Rover spark plugs after drubbing the sheets of American oilcloth seat covers soiled by his pit clothes. Entertaining Greta, he broke out on, '*Marta, rambling rose of the wild wood, Marta, with your fragrance divine . . .*' thinking as Ossie hulloo-ed at the gate, Kerr-riste, the man with no balls at all.

'Ossie!' Greta up and swinging light-boned, animally lithe towards the gate.

'*I awake to the dawn,*' responded Councillor Ross, '*and I find you are gone!*' Composed with overlapped hands on his chest, 'Mr. and Mrs. Ginty request the pleasure of your company next Saturday evening. Their wedding anniversary. Thirty years!'

'Come inside, Oz. Tea or coffee?'

'Very kind of you. Busy, Dewi? Coffee, please.'

'I'll whip these boots and overalls off,' he said. Thank Christ for Greta, she can take this Ystrad and Talbot stooge without feeling sick. Actress Greta. Greta from Gwalia Embroideries. My godsend pusher. Hot Greta, she'd burn Clarke Gable's bloody tash.

'You're looking well,' she was saying. 'Where have you been keeping yourself, mister?'

'Loving Christ,' he muttered flatly, incapable of distress, yelling from the bathroom, 'What time's the party?'

'Seven o'clock, darling. Would you like a sandwich?'

'Doubler,' he said.

Chit-chat with the long bag of wind who backed off. Ossie versus Dai Greg. No contest. Cancel it.

'Should I wear my turquoise ankle length, Oz?'

'Entirely up to you, dear girl. I have made it known you have excellent taste.'

Yap-yap Ossie, he's bringing puke to my throat—*Iesu*, Llew Kitchener had a bump across the throat before his stroke. 'Lester and Prudence be there?' he said.

'Oh, most definitely.'

Find a quiet corner for Lester. Let him spout. He's lost. I used to be lost once.

They were charming each other like uncle and niece.

'I say, my old colleague Dai Greg has resigned. He's pumpsman by day in Pencaer.'

'Good,' he said. 'Nice doddle for Dai.'

'*And*, Gabe and Deborah are going to breed spaniels! De luxe kennels in their back garden.'

Said Greta, 'You bring us all the news, Oz.'

We're marching to Zion sounding muffled from Bethel chapel across Nantglas and the quiet bankside lane behind the Villas. Elderly congregations were magnifying the Lord all over Moel Exchange, compliant worshippers, while Ossie Ross crooked his little finger, drinking black market coffee brewed in Elsie's percolator. Between sipped swallows he munched banana sandwiches—the first bananas available since 1941. Greta's indirect perk from Barry Docks via the salesman employed by a Lancashire manufacturer of brocade silks.

Ossie mooted ostentatious nostalgia, 'Wonderful parties in Plasmarl before the war. Ever so smart, especially Easter, Whitsun and New Year's Eve. Fancy dress parties every Easter. Once I dressed up as a bullfighter. Wig, naturally, with a little pigtail. All the ladies fancied my outfit. D'you know, after the carnivals the gazooka bands used to come to Moel Square to play for the manager, round and round the Square playing *Marching to Georgia*, *Swanee River* and *Campdown Races*. To finish off, certain members of our Male Voice were invited in to entertain the guests.' Ossie stroked his white hair. 'I have been friendly with four managers altogether.'

'Ever bump into a coal owner in your day, Oz?'

'Not introduced personally. Mr. Aneirin Talbot at a distance in nineteen nineteen, say from here out to your motor car.'

Greta was glowering, pruning her lips.

You're yapping to a coal owner, he thought.

'Having served Ystrad and Talbot for thirty-eight years, I shall retire next February.' Piously, 'God willing.' Ossie flipped out and straightened his Dewinton Grammar School tie. 'Delicious, Greta.' Marching sedately, 'Mission accomplished.' Then proudly, 'Goodbye, goodbye.'

When Greta returned from the front door, he said, 'What a daft burk. I'd put him on a top hole with a square shovel and a blunt mandrel.'

'He's useful to Gwalia Embroideries. Oz can't help the way he is.'

'Same goes for every bastard under the sun.'

'Vicious thing,' she accused, clinking Elsie's cups, saucers and plates.

He said, 'I'm meeting Irfon in the Comrades' Club. Might get loaded tonight.'

'I'll make up the bed in the back room for you.'

'That's my clever bitch.'

'Dewi Joshua, lord and master.'

'Never,' he said.

From the Coles' garden wall he heard Deborah's '*We'll gather lilacs in the spring again* . . .' She waved, opening the window. 'Hullo, Dewi.'

Leashed spaniel at his feet, Gabe watched two men assembling the ship-lap kennel.

'Pitch pine, damned expensive,' said Gabe.

'The dearest is always best, Gabe. Going to Plasmarl Saturday night?'

'Yes,' harumphing as he bent over to scratch the spaniel's ears.

Deborah flung open the back door. 'You watch yourself, boy!'

'I'm easy, Deb.'

'No showing off. You seem to have a gift for upsetting people.'

Impassively, 'Hush now, my dear,' as Gabe waddled closer to the wall. 'How are you, Dewi?'

'My wife, she's under the 'fluence from Ossie too.'

'Nonsense,' scolded Deborah. 'Ossie Ross, he's like part of the furniture. Don't be so spiteful.'

Gabe tweaked the leash. 'There you have it, boy.'

He left them baby-talking the spaniel.

Pique disturbed him. Ballocking off Deb. Greta doing a fucken Mata Hari in Parc Villa. Early yet for Irfon. Crawl for an hour: Stag Arms, Royal Arms, Prince Hotel, Riverside Inn, Comrades' Club, Irfon saying, 'Last leg,' at the dart board.

Elbows wide-spread on a table, waiting, he brooded below a sepia photograph. Platoon of South Wales Borderers, Sergeant Mostyn Jones from Stuart Drive in the middle. Old Mostyn, killed in Pencaer before Zena bought my first working boots. *Bulla* chain snapped, flew back, split open Mostyn's skullbone. Big name in his time. Buried up the line from Elsie's grave. Won't be the same without Elsie in Plasmarl. Sid and Gracie tied for thirty years. Who's gaffer in bed? Greta thinks she's boss now and again.

Anyhow, we've licked the past.

'Shan't stay long, Dewi. Hetty's bad. Doctor Tibbs says it's bronchitis.'

'How old are you, Ive?'

'Fifty.'

'Look, don't hang about on my account.'

'Where you been?'

He said, 'Here and there.'

'I'd best bugger off. Go steady, boy. Your gut'll be like a dub come morning.'

Measuring clock-time, he drank a pint every twenty minutes. Out on the road, a sauntering group of schoolgirls sang *Keep smiling through*. They slowly faded.

Pulling beer, the bland, middle-aged stewardess encored, '*But I know we'll meet again some sunny day.*' Changing style and timbre, 'Last orders, please!'

Forgetful on the pavement, alcohol fuming his brain felled him to his knees beneath the steel-grilled window of Lloyds Bank. Footsteps paced around him. Hands gripped under his arms.

'It's me, Shad Coslett, Rhidian Coslett's son.'

'Obvious,' he said, stiff-tongued, his concentration awry.

'I'll help you home.'

'Most obvious man who ever carried a safety lamp on his belt, your father is.'

'I wouldn't know,' said Shad.

'He puts things obvious.'

'Hang on,' hooking Dewi's arm around his shoulder.

'Commonsense bloody things. Rhidian, your old man, Rhid, he'd make a good prince. Fucken Prince of Wales.'

'Let's keep moving.'

'How's it going, Shad-boy?'

'Fine.'

'Fuh-ine ah? Good, Shad, bloody great.'

Greta took over at the front door. She lugged him up to the back bedroom.

'Hey, gimme a call.'

At 6 a.m., Greta shaking him, he slurred like a zombie.

'Cantrebach!' she screamed, round-arm pillow swings once, twice, softly duffing his face. 'You'll be late for work! Bacon and egg in five minutes.'

'Right,' he said.

'What a man.'

'Be quiet.'

She turned away. 'I don't want to nag.'

Before breakfast he made himself drink three tumblers of water. After breakfast, two mugs of tea, Greta watching him change into pit clothes in the bathroom, saying, 'We mustn't quarrel. Are you all right? I'm worried about you.'

'First shift of the week,' he said. 'Sweat myself into shape by grubtime.'

She kissed his eyes. 'I'll make us a big dinner.'

XIII

He looked down at Pencaer from Glas Tump, scurries of pygmied men to and from the pit head, sunshine killing cap lamps as they left the cage. Men and boys, all faceless.

Before entering the level he squatted behind the brakehouse with half a page of *Exchange and District Leader*.

'Country shit, can't better it,' said Irfon.

'I put away too many last night.'

They sent nine trams down to Ellis. Three journeys. Saturday's coal.

Walking the straight heading, Irfon said, 'Don't trust it at all. Like a fucken bag from my left side road post, and still coming over the top coal. So watch your body.'

He slid the corrugated steel flat into the face. 'First of these flats ever put up since they started working this housecoal.'

'Now there's a thought, clever-boy!'

'Posts ready, Ive?'

'Beer made you fucken blind or what? By there under my dram. Cut to size.'

Sounding the alien, foxy grained roof, 'Let's hope this dies out.'

'Like Moses said to the fucken burning bush.' Irfon slanted his propped post. 'Me lift, or you?'

He balanced, trapped one end of the flat on Irfon's post, held up the weight on his bent-over shoulder, raising it higher as Irfon sledgehammered the post upright.

'Leave go, butty.'

Then, sloping his post under the opposite end of the flat, Irfon again hammered it firm to the roof.

'My belief, Dewi, we work as a pair until this bad ground is behind us in the gob.'

'Maybe.' He sat on his heels.

'After grub?'

'Righto, Ive.'

The shift wore away.

And four more shifts to Friday morning. Harsh conditions while building a cog of posts between the flat and the seam, Irfon pulling top coal, making space for two final cross timbers, Dewi chopping them to length in the roadway behind the tram.

Irfon crabbed fast out of the face. 'Leave it settle a minute. Bit of a squeeze. We'll master it.'

He said, 'Should.'

'Hark!'

Golden sap sprayed, globuled from the posts under the steel flat.

'We might have a fucken big *awmp* unless that flat holds.' Backing away, Irfon cursed absent-mindedly.

'Double up on those posts, Ive.'

Almost pensive, watchful, puffing a Woodbine, 'Not the way it's moving. Leave it settle.'

'We'll have to finish off the cog.'

'Wouldn't try if I was you.'

Grinding rock creaked, whispered insensate syntax older than life on earth. Imploding air echoed the heading, bluffing as burpy reverberations at the mouth of Cantrebach.

They sat in a manhole.

'Christ, it's coming down,' he said.

'She'll start easing away now.'

They walked on. Table-smooth rock hung tilted from the incomplete cog.

'Wait, Dewi. Listen.'

'Dribbling down below our cog. We'll stick posts up as we clear. Okay! Okay, I know . . .'

'Easier said than done.'

'Yeh, but what else?'

'No other way, posts behind our arses, posts next to our boots.'

Punishing, dangerous, loosening and manhandling jumbled stones. The slabbed rock cracked, pitched severally apart. A cross timber whanged off the cog.

Crouching on top of the road, breathing shallow, ready to sprint away, Irfon hissed through his teeth. They heard pressure lifting, thinly faltering within, high above the seam.

'Hey-yay-yay,' cheered Irfon.

His last words for forty minutes.

They were each side of the cog, temporary stayers and wedges raked against broken ground, shielding themselves with posts, calculating for head, knees, feet and arms, space to work, throw back stones, shovel debris, space to build a new gob wall nearer the coal.

In his mind, sneery humour at himself: rough crib, all *mine*, paid for with Elsie's money.

He heard the scratchy beginning preceding tinny chinks of shards striking the reflector of Irfon's cap lamp, saw him hooping up quickly off kneeling as roof and coal avalanched roaring, crashing down a post, chuting between the next two posts, Irfon breasting the hard wave, pounded backwards, trapped to his lower ribs, and a sprung stayer joggling, rolling away from beside his head.

He quashed fear in the way of madness never atoned. Grunting, heaving, mindless creature grunts—Irfon whoofing low groans, sensible: 'My right leg, boy.'

Dewi repeated, 'Right leg.' He's groping for handholds then powering the rockstone up his thighs, his loins, to his stomach. The jagged stone ripped his trousers. He half-circled, dropped the stone. 'Soon get you out, Ive,' working in blind faith, clearing roof rubble and coal. 'There,' he said, dragging Irfon to the top of the road.

'Fucken nasty, ah? You'd best shift down the incline. Send Teifi for the doctor.'

'Where is it, Ive?'

'Bumps and bloody grazes . . . my shinbone's busted.'

Running down the incline, he remembered Pencaer Four Deep. Twelve years ago.

★ ★ ★ ★

Friday night he cried out, convulsing in sleep, his collier's hands gripping flesh as enemy, Greta screeching, 'No! No!'

Guilt stupefied him.

'What is it, Dewi?'

'I was in Cantrebach.'

She mothered him, rueful, 'God, I thought you were attacking me. Go to sleep. It was a dream, that's all, only a dream.'

Wide-eyed in darkness, wetness crystalising on the wings of his nostrils: *Iesu*, lost control. Raving menace. Forget it, girl. Say nothing, girl.

She cued from the foot of the bed, nightgown swished aside from her buttock, 'See, fingermarks,' enacting feminine alarm, 'Brute! Dewi, the brute. What do you want for breakfast?'

'Boiled egg. Stay in bed, I'll make my own.'

'Why didn't you go with me last night?'

'I wasn't feeling so good.'

Greta lowered over him, hair and breasts hanging, her witchy seriousness firing inside him. 'My tough husband.'

He said, 'Clown more like.'

From crisis to gaiety, joy, folding themselves together, immune to the riving of Adam and Eve.

★ ★ ★ ★

Resolute Saturday shift in the straight heading. After finishing the cog he left a pillar of coal to support treacherous oncoming roof. As he explained to Ellis, who was locking the van door at 3 o'clock, 'I'll cut through from inside, open up the full stent. Take a week perhaps.'

'You're a winner for sure, comrade.'

'Look, Ellis, if we find a bloke to handle Gilbert on the rounds, you can work my stall. That do you?'

Replied Ellis, 'Too late now. I'll stick with my job.'

'I want a collier.'

'Not me. Lois wouldn't wear it either.'

'Lois?'

'Find another man, Dewi. Hope you don't mind.'

'Of course I fucken mind.' He tugged Ellis's jacket button. 'Born lucky. Stay where you are.'

'Thanks, butty.'

Curmudgeonly fellow-mate, 'Husht, for Christ's sake.'

He visited Irfon in Moel Ward before going to Plasmarl with Greta. Irfon's right leg was outside the blankets, plaster-cased from knee to ankle, squares of lint taped on lacerations across his lower belly and thighs.

'Dog's life in here from Blod Gethin. How's things?'
'I'm looking for a good collier.'
'Chris Prior's son, came home recent. Served with the Commandos. Danny Prior used to work in Pencaer.'
'Where's he living?'
'St. John's Terrace, apartments with Mrs. James. Glan James's widow, old Myra is. Glan did time in nineteen-thirteen for rioting. They pelted coppers locked inside the police station. Glan was ring-leader of the Boot Eleven gang. They had a den in Exchange Manor. Dirty bastards they were, the Boot Eleven.'
'They don't teach that in Dewinton Grammar,' he said.
'They'd rather believe fucken liars in *Exchange and District Leader*.'
'How's the leg?'
'Numb.'
'What's he like, Danny Prior?'
'Played centre-half for Moel Albion. Same type as Chris only not so *twp*. Danny was conscripted by Hore-Belisha the Jew before the war, so he copped the whole fucken *cabwsh*. Get to him sharpish or your laughing boy Lester Mackie might rope Danny in for Cwmffrwd.'
He put two packets of Woodbines and a bag of cream doughnuts in Irfon's locker. 'Greta and me, we're due in Plasmarl. Big night for Sid and Gracie, they walked down the aisle thirty years ago. I'll call in tomorrow.'
'By the Jesus Christ all-bloody mighty, still hob-nobbing with the spunk-faced lot. You'll be like Willie Bob Ochr, brown up to his elbow.' Irfon declared rugged pride, 'Dewi-boy, on my oath now, seven-eight weeks' time I'll be filling those peggy drams.'
'I'll wash your mouth out, Irfon Francis,' Blod *merch*-Gethin sweetly acid from pride in her vocational integrity.
Laughing boy Lester? He's all twisted up. Lester's in granny knots over his father and son. Pru can't be much help either, she's mean minded. Always the same if working class think they're middle class. There's no malice in Lester. Just bloody shattered.

★ ★ ★ ★

Her tucked-in blue eyes zeroed on him while Greta and Grace flattered each other, Sidney Ginty trailing behind them along the new, exotic-coloured balcony curtains. Sid had the nerveless dominance of power, his supremacy.

He said, 'How'd you do, Prudence. That's my wife with Grace. She's a career girl. You met her in Gwalia Embroideries.' Holding up his glass, 'Get you a drink, shall I? No? Settled yourselves in yet? For privacy there's nothing to touch the Mechanic's House, unless you live up in a farm somewhere. Everything al'right, Pru?'

'Certainly,' bobbing nods as if victimised.

'Where's Lester?'

'He's been called to London. I'm expecting him soon.'

'Things gone skew-whiff?'

'Really, young man!' her eyes quivering protest.

She's pitiful. I'm treating her like the Gestapo.

Dai Greg saved him from contrition. 'Well, Dewi, this is bad news from Cantrebach. You'll have to tighten up on safety.'

Mrs. Mackie squirmed around on her heels, a sideways escape. He called, 'Good to see you and Lester again, Prudence.' He looked at Dai, 'What do you know, man? Fuck all.'

'There you go, spitting fire like a *ddraig goch*, and me about to say how smart Greta looks in that long frock. She's like out of a catalogue.'

I'm rich both ways, he thought. 'How's the new job, Dai?'

Earnestly man-to-man, 'I have learned my lesson. Can't traipse up and down the faces any more. See, my back's gone. Some mornings I'm all seized up, can't move.'

'You're not the first,' he said. 'Come on, let's join the *gwt*.'

They crossed to the buffet table, Greta long-thighed in a modish hugger-mugger, slinking to the arrowing of her mind, this being the pulse of Moel Exchange influence/commerce, civic authority represented by two Councillors and chief executive Jacob Tanner.

'Dewi!'

Swallowing a humph of exult, he said, 'I'll catch up with you, Dai.'

'Mr. Ginty suggested we make a collection for Irfon Francis.' Searching her handbag, 'Lend me a pound.'

'Who's taking the cap around?'

'Grace and myself.' Greta kissed the £1 note. 'Shan't forget.'

Queueing with his plate, served by two women wearing waitress uniforms, he watched them, Grace Ginty late middle-aged, frizzed hair whitening, haloing her decisive face, and Greta swanning a dark green fruit bowl. Ahead in the queue, Dai Greg's jaw slackened to gawk. All around in the big room overlooking Moel Square, keeping up with the Joneses under the aegis of Grace and Greta.

Shocked Dai whispering, 'I'd say thirty quid in Irfon's pocket.'

'Or more,' he said. 'Look at Jacob. Look at Ossie. Tell me, Dai, what do you know about Danny Prior?'

Fingering flaky pastry off his elfin chin, 'Well, put it this way, there's not many who'd cross Danny. Mind, he's straight as a die.'

'I want him for Cantrebach.'

'Talk about bad luck. Danny was less than a month in his first stall when he had his call-up papers.' Ducking respect to the pit manager, 'Mr. Ginty, here's wishing all the best to you and Mrs. Ginty.'

Post-war, the same detached man, disciplined, narrow shouldered, hair thinning, waistline mysterious beneath his waistcoat, the same unreadable stone grey eyes.

'Thank you, Dai.' He spoke to Dewi, 'I understand Doctor Tibbs went into the face to attend to Irfon.'

'Top of the road in fact. Safe enough then, all the squeeze was down our left hand side. Bags of guts though, in Doctor Tibbs.'

'More guts than sense perhaps. Medicine seems a very taxing profession. When I'm ill I'm barely able to tolerate my own company.'

Vowed Dai, 'I've never known you to go down bad, Mr. Ginty.'

'Only saints in glass windows are exempt.' Sid Ginty went slow-stalking among his guests.

At nine o'clock Grace hauled back the balcony curtains. A four piece band arranged themselves. Mid Exchange Quartette plinked, blared, won key, shared nods with Idris Garfield the saxophonist, and *'You made me love you'* launched the first couples followed by others soon after. Volunteer M.C. Ossie Ross smiled cherubic high blood pressure in a purple bow tie.

'It's thirty-two pounds ten,' said Greta. She leaned slantwise to Jacob Tanner sitting beside Prudence Mackie, 'Hull-low, Mr. Tanner.' Softly sly beyond their hearing, 'Now *she's* awkward. Grace can't abide her. I've made loads of business tonight. Husband-*bach*, I'm enjoying myself.'

'Watch you stick to the rules,' he said.

'Yes, teacher.'

'You're throwing your bum about.'

'Jealous?'

'Yeh.'

Between *You made me love you* and *The very thought of you*, Sid Ginty beckoned him to his study.

'Lester Mackie will be along shortly. How do you stand regarding nationalisation?'

'Straight question, straight answer, Mr. Ginty. I shan't get big enough for this Labour government to take over Cantrebach.'

'Have a seat.' Ginty poured two whiskies. 'Good luck, Dewi.'

He felt solitary, centred, warm to himself. 'You too, Mr. Ginty.'

The manager opened and snapped shut his spectacles case. 'I shall become a cipher directed by planners and thimbleriggers, much the same as during the war. Unfortunately British coal owners are reaping what they have sown.'

He said, 'Agreed, only depends what it all amounts to.'

'Such matters are for historians to analyse. Historians moralise too, by the same token. History itself has no morals.'

'If you say so, Mr. Ginty.'

The manager's plucked smile invaded his eyes.

'Lester's a different case from you and me' ventured Dewi. 'Sometimes I wonder where he's bound for, I mean as a man.'

'Have you any further comments?'

'None at all. I'm taking on another collier to replace Irfon Tŷ Isaf. Once Irfon's back in work I'll be on the look-out for more customers.'

'We share little in common, Lester and myself.'

'That's life,' he said.-
'Reality,' countered the manager.
'Varies, Mr. Ginty . . .'
'Sidney,' minimal humour invisibly rippling. 'Sidney Horatio— my father's name.'
'Real one day, Sidney, changed the next day after. Say, how will nationalisation affect your jobs, both yourself and Lester Mackie?'

Open palms dismissed the query. 'Today is our pearl wedding anniversary.'

'Aye, good.'

'Stability in marriage has to be achieved.'

Like Darby and Joan, he thought. But lay off. Keep quiet. Why should I? This is face to face: 'Meaning after thirty years you won't be able to climb any higher, especially as they're nationalising the pits?'

Gutteral hacks came delayed by afterthought. 'I recognise the bite in your attitude. However, forewarned is forearmed. I may seek early retirement.'

'Not in Moel Exchange. Where to?' thrusting out his dimple-wedged chin. 'Hah, excuse me, I'm a cheeky bugger.'

Ginty decanted Johnny Walker. 'Have patience, fellow. We haven't even considered the issue.'

He toasted, 'Here's to you and Grace.'

Whereon, strident from the doorway, 'Dewi, your wife is looking for you,' and Grace stood behind her husband.

He thought, she's backed him for thirty years without let-up. 'Greta,' he said with ribald unction, 'she'd find me in the dark if I was a mile under.'

Eyes followed him leaving Ginty's sanctum, wordless inquiries from a melange of amiable curiosity, from civil regard and endless suspicion.

Greta was bantering with the band leader, Idris Garfield, hair-oiled son of the ironmonger in his Ystrad and Talbot blessed store in High Street. Rejected for military service, Idris walked out of Ely Sanitorium in slippers, pyjamas and overcoat. His sister drove him home in the family van reeking of paraffin. He went to a Spiritualist faith healer before curing himself, living alone for two and a half years in a custom-built cold water chalet on the thistle- and dock-infested home pasture of derelict Trefaen farm. Two older, married sisters supplied food, did his washing, brought books, music sheets, and never crossed the threshold. At forty-three Idris looked a decade younger. His married sisters became quiet grandmothers living in Clyne Vale.

'Miracle,' everyone said gratefully, time after time in the cavernous ironmongery store.

Old Len Garfield remained darkly sage, lugubrious, two generations of grimed ledgers stacked under the counter, precise records of trade: mandrels, shovels, boring machines, augers, curling boxes, cap lamps, carbide, toolbars, crowbars, sledge-hammers, hatchets, braces and bits, bradawls, chisels, files, gouges, hammers, mallets, pincers, handsaws, nails, screws and sundry domestic items.

Free from the *tubercle bacillus* bane, self-taught Idris became a dance band saxophonist.

Greta accusing him, 'Fibber,' as if they were children playing a schoolyard game.

'Word of honour, we're booked every weekend until November. *Shwd i chi*, Dewi?'

'Sid's whisky is doing the talking.' He winked at her. 'Seen Lester Mackie?'

Said Idris, 'Nice meeting you folks.'

Greta pointed, 'The man's over there.'

'Carry on the good work, love. I'll carry you home piggy-back.'

'I want to dance.'

'Give Ossie a thrill, bite his throat, see if there's any blood in him.'

'Sadist, you're in one of your moods. Don't apologise,' she said.

'Only kidding, girl.'

He walked Lester to a shelved alcove shrined with pot plants, the agent intoning, 'Poor Irfon Francis, he's a genuine rough diamond.'

'Maybe. What's the latest about nationalising the pits?'

'Don't you read newspapers, listen to the wireless? The Coal Industry Nationalisation Act became effective last month, twelfth of July. The National Coal Board was constituted a few days later. Meanwhile, Dewi, rumours proliferate. Hundred million pounds for assets. Hundred million pounds to royalty owners. Arbitrary figures at the moment, I assure you.'

'They're talking money like wedding confetti. When will they take over?'

'January the first, nineteen forty-seven.'

'Well, might be the beginning of the end,' he said. 'Same old story though, believing men we can't see. Hey, Sid and Grace got married during the Great War. They're like two old fogies in his study. Mind if I dance with Prudence?'

As they waltzed at arm's distance, she criticised, 'Why have you neglected Greta?'

'I'll make it up to her.'

'I should think so.'

'When we're under the sheets. Know what, Pru, if you and Lester settled down for good in the Mechanic's House . . .'

'Gosh no, you're rambling like a fool.'

'Come on, it's all right, Moel Exchange is a cushy little town. Once you're stepping out along the old Roman road you're in another country. Or, listen, you try up where Nantglas comes from. Two waterfalls up there, hidden from sight, nothing else except foxes and birds. Lester might come out of his dumps too. Lester's a worrier. He'll be at the beck and call of this Attlee government instead of Ystrad and Talbot, won't he?'

Contemptuously, 'Don't be silly.'

He said, 'It comes and goes.'

'Take your hands off me!'

Iesu, here we go again.

Following her, 'It's only a bit of bullshit, Mrs. Mackie.'

'How dare you!'

'Sorry!' This time I've pissed on my chips.

'You're vulgar.'

Affably, 'Aye, now and then. Please, Pru, shall we finish the dance?'

Her peasant features wrung on scorn, her spine jarred upright, 'Crude and vulgar,' gnashing from her as they broke apart. She left him clumsily, like a lame woman avoiding sludge underfoot.

He thought, she'd crease a better man than Lester.

★   ★   ★   ★

Monday morning in the heading with Danny Prior, a casual-seeming ex-soldier, lighter by two stones than his rugger forward father. At half-past two, hoarse from strained sinews and muscles, Danny said, 'I've gone soft since my de-mob.'

'So long as you don't jib on me,' he said.

'I won't jib if you keep your word.'

'Pick you up in St. John's Terrace at four o'clock. Wear a tie.'

He took him to Jacob Tanner's office. Tanner sent them to Hugo Meredith's shop in the brown-toned opulence of High Steet arcade.

'Rented properly with discretion to purchase outright,' says the struck-off chemist cum newsagent/tobacconist.

'My solicitor will tend to all that,' he said.

'He will?'

'Julius Simmons, Mr. Meredith.'

'Excellent! So you are Theophilus Joshua's son. Well-I-be-damned. Theo taught me the rudiments of fisticuffs before I went to university. I was being harrassed by erm, a rough element from Sinkers' Huts.' Hugo patted Danny's shoulder. 'Welcome home, my boy.' All-over grey (swept back collar-length hair, fluffy goatee, cardigan, pepper and salt check shirt with shot grey silk cravat, flannel trousers and soft suede shoes), Hugo said, 'Number twenty Druid Uplands. Beautiful situation. Panoramic view of old Exchange Manor, even Clyne Vale on a nice day.'

From closed years of soldiering, Danny quietly agreed, 'I'll take it.'

'Previous occupier rushed into St. Teilo's Infirmary three weeks ago. He's wasting away. There's no coming for him,' promised Hugo.

'Who, Mr. Meredith?'

'Gwili Tremain.'

'Aye, used to be repairer by night in Pencaer,' he said.

Across the road, a matronly group leaving Gwalia Embroideries,

Greta behind them, glamour girl swirling a flowered drindle waist skirt. She waited by the Rover.

Possession buoyed him, quelled to laconic, 'Love, this is Danny Prior. Danny, meet Greta. Danny's moving to Druid Uplands.'

Sobersides Danny, 'Pleased to meet you, Mrs. Joshua.'

Her smile emptied back to Dewi, urgent, 'I must have a telephone.'

'Okay, make it two, Parc Villa and the shop. Danny, tell your Missis to buy whatever stuff she wants for the new house from Greta.'

'My pleasure, Mr. Danny Prior.'

He said, 'Cost price. This man's on my books.'

She dipped theatrical curtsies, 'Anything you say, sir, yes, sir, yes, sir—like Hitler, isn't he?'

Danny clamped his teeth and mouth on sniggering.

But he foresaw stern graft working off coal, driving on inside the broken roof, opening up the face until Cantrebach returned to normal.

Which happened, came to pass while summer as always burned down to autumn, bitter-sweetening into winter, the town-folk generally heedless, a once wholly Welsh population conditioned by ages of soil and seasons, having inter-married immigrant workers from half a dozen English counties, along with Irish, Scots, expatriate Italians and Germans. Generations of hill farmers around Moel Exchange, but no landed gentry.

Shunting coal truck buffers clanged around the clock on three colliery sidings: Pencaer, Cwmffrwd and High Seven. Older Garw and Pontfedw were being reconnected to the G.W.R. Ariel ropeways carried skips of slag, extending pre-Great War mounds of pit-muck, where, from the streets, a few men with main line horses crawled Lilliputian. Busloads of workers roared the mornings, the town pell-melling into another heyday, steered and reined by N.U.M. committees in every institute.

December began with a cool injunction from Julius Simmons: 'We have to modernise.'

He sold Gilbert and the high-wheeled cart to Mervyn Harris. With a new lorry on H.P. from Ambrose Adams, he taught Ellis how to drive in 50 minutes. Negotiated by Simmons, another

Avery scales arrived on the loading bay. Ellis now had two youths helping him with the tram tippler, bagging and delivering housecoal. The weather-proof tarred railway van became Cantrebach office, stores and canteen. In the coal face, working arrangements were proposed, bargained, agreed, fixed: Dewi in the heading, Danny in the original stall, Irfon in a second stall turned off the straight.

Output increased, sales quadrupled. Once only, when Greta climbed to the attic with Spanish Elsie's framed photograph respectfully wrapped in brown paper, he thought: I'll be like Elsie's old man, big stack in Lloyds Bank by the time I retire. He rejected the prospect, rejected retirement, disregarded jealous blab circulating Moel Exchange, 'Coining up there in Cantrebach.'

He convinced himself: Money's for spending. From leaving school he avoided grown men serving behind shop counters. Shoppies were outsiders. Different talk. Men *worked*. Different and all, the women who married shoppies. Fussy. Secretive. Tidy. *Bopa* women for *bopa* men. Greta might turn out to be a *bopa* in about forty years.

Before winter's solstices the severest, long-lasting snowfall in living memory set in. Winter weather to endure as best known how, for want of condemning, disproving this act of God. After Christmas the incline vanished under arctic whitescape. the D. JOSHUA lorry stood bonnet-deep outside Ellis's house. They cleared the tramroad, stockpiled coal down below for four days. Meanwhile Council lorries snowploughed Upper Road. More snow boiled down. Leeward snow steepened to bedroom windows, to eaves by mid-February. Street life diminished. Schools closed. Trains and tramcars ceased running. Snow level-filled Gaer Cutting. Pit ponies hauled bread and groceries to out-lying terraces, on sledges of bent corrugated sheets nailed to wooden frames. Officials, safety men, boilermen, selected tradesmen and idle office staffs manned Pencaer, Cwmffrwd and High Seven. Contract workers at Garw and Pontfedw signed on for dole money.

Cantrebach stockpiled platforms of coal outside the mouth. Doggedly prophetic Irfon, as if hand in glove with Alpha and Omega, spitting on fresh carbide in his cap lamp, a smaller token disgust spit from a whiff of acetylene, 'You'll see, they'll be coming up the parish road with barrows and *carabwnjies* for our coal.'

'Says you,' he said—Irfon scarfed to his eyes like a Siberian mujick, joining them at grubtime in Danny's stall.

'Worst I can remember,' admitted Irfon. 'Men laid off right throughout. Few nights back, Gabe Coles was in the Comrades' Club with Sid Ginty. Sid looked like he didn't know whether he wanted a shit or a haircut. Already in Pencaer, it's bobby's jobs for the boys, useless buggers you wouldn't ask to put coal on the fire—they'd spill it over the mat. The beer ran out in the Club before stop tap. End of the fucken world then. Like days gone by it was, old Gabe discussing with Sid. Pick-picking Gabe's brains, I daresay. Gabe's fly, by Christ he's fly.'

'Dai Greg's afraid to shift from indoors,' said Danny. 'I helped him cut a path from his front door out to the road.'

He said, 'Lester Mackie's moving away again.'

Irfon offered boiled sweets, rattling them in the lid of his tommy box. 'Fucken cleckerbox shop, that Gwalia Embroideries.'

'Lester's going down west Wales.'

Ellis (temporarily working with Danny) unwrapped tissue paper from a slice of jam roll.

'Anybody smell jam?' smirked Irfon. 'Lois, she's looking after you, Ellis.' Serenely waving his hands, 'Innit fucken lovely, flags on all the pits and no coal coming up!'

'I'm not selling any either,' he said. 'They're asking Greta, "How much longer before Ellis comes 'round with coal?" Some people are chopping up their furniture.'

'Listen,' argued Irfon, 'there's only one Father Christmas and he's a blackleg. We can't do what no other fucker in Wales is doing, let alone Lord Hyndley, and where in the name of Christ did he come from, ah?'

Danny turned his cap lamp perched on the gob wall behind his shoulder. Shadowed, he said, 'We could try a sledge same as they're bringing us grub to Druid Uplands. The big shops are borrowing nags from Pencaer and Cwmffrwd.'

He said, 'Hundredweight bags are heavier than groceries.'

'Experiment.'

'Another fucken Jonah here,' said Irfon.

'Trial and error,' Danny refusing to haggle, patient, tried and tested for deeds and consequences.

'You and Irfon,' Dewi said, 'make us a sledge. Ellis, you come with me to Pencaer office. I'll bend Sid's arm to lend us a pony from the top pit stables.'

Irfon whaowed freakish, 'Dewi *Sant* fucken Joshua! There's no stopping him! Righto, Danny-boy, let's see your Commando tactics!'

★ ★ ★ ★

Glacial winter thawed, Nantglas raging clay-brown, sometimes offering the rare sight of bloated ewes rolling in flood or bobbling, trapped in backwaters. Storm thrushes clarioned Spring, fluting from gnarled oaks below Cantrebach.

Proudly secretive Greta in Gwalia Embroideries ticked off days from the ide of March. She paraded herself in the tall, grandiose shop mirror, fingers widespread over her tummy: 'Ours,' preceding unspoken, *Dewi Joshua's baby. Mine and Dewi's*, then again, 'Ours'.

Contained in the first-time proven miracle of herself until Sunday morning, Dewi downstairs, coal bucket in hand, feeding small lumps on the crackling, criss-crossed kindling. Blue-grey smoked purled, hissed from the bituminous coal, quickly winnowing to yellow flame, flame to thrown heat of binding redness. *News of the World* and *The People* slithered through the letter-box. The hinge-rusted flap creaked. Dewi listened at the foot of the stairs.

'Greta, fire's lit!' Turning away to the pantry for their indulgent Sunday bacon and eggs, marmalade on toast, sweet coffee and cream breakfast, 'Fire's lit!'

She tried a strange imperious voice, posed dignified, almost sacramental, 'Dewi.'

'Yeh?'

And flung out her arms to cruciform, unleashing nape-tingling joy, triumph belling from her throat to feline shriek. 'Dewi, I'm two months pregnant!'

'*Iesu*, this is the best.'

'C'mon, c'mon, man, quick!'

They went back to bed.

The arcane mystery of *another* cooped inside Greta's belly. Himself and Greta on earth. Cause and effect. Tryst without end, bright early afternoon livening Sunday-quiet Moel Exchange, strollers meeting, gossiping, shouldering into clubs (pubs and institutes were closed), cafes, children into chapels, a muttering gang of gamblers playing Pitch and Toss inside the ruined walls of Exchange Manor, scratch soccer teams prepared to run and kick until evening, men whistling in pigeons, women visiting relatives, men busy in allotments, handfuls of National Coal Board surface workers on Cwmffrwd, Pencaer and High Seven, youths with ratting terriers trespassing across railway lines to the Council ashtip, tramcars every hour, wireless sets broadcasting a safe, all-things-familiar B.B.C. universe.

'What do you want, boy or girl?' she said.

'I can't choose, love, pointless trying.'

'I want a baby.'

'With your Gwalia nerve and the way I bash on whole hog once I've decided something, *Duw*, this place will be too small to hold him.'

Greta placed his palm on her ovoid belly. 'Good too!'

Timeless peace.

'Dewi, I must have a strip-wash before dinner.'

'Aye, let's eat.' He rolled his forehead on her belly. 'Trust your mother, boy. She'll look after you.'

★   ★   ★   ★

Monday in Cantrebach, hewing and filling out coal, sending trams down the incline, eating with Irfon and Danny at 11 o'clock, Irfon quizzing properly casual, 'Awful quiet today, sonny-boy. How's everything then, al'right?'

I'm supposed to feel excited, he thought. Supposed to be normal. Aye, normal. Here goes then,

'We're having a kid, Ive. Nobody knows except Greta and me.'

Irfon bellowed, 'Fucken marv'llous, man! By Christ, she's a

one-off, that young Missis of yours. Seen her stepping out to the Villas like she's got Moel Exchange in her fist.'

Danny Prior stretched out his leg, clacked his pit boot against Dewi's. 'Good luck to you both.'

He said, 'I'll tell my old lady on the way home.'

'Hetty'll be over the moon.' Irfon raised his water jack, 'Good on you, butty.'

'Thanks, Ive.'

Danny reached across to shake his hand.

So he called in Dinmel Street at quarter to three, Zena routinely digging her backyard plot, her unconscious undertone hymnal sweetly wailing, '*We're here because we're here because we're here because we're here, We're here because we're here because we're here because we're here*' when he called from the gate, 'Hey, where'd you learn that lot, Mam?'

She blinked from far-away absence to present, 'My father when he came back from the Army in 1918.'

Taking her spade, he jabbed it in the soil. 'What's it feel like to be a gran, ah? Aye, Greta's having a baby next October.'

Zena's quivering mouth cried, 'Oh God alive, there's lovely, oh God, oh God alive . . . Dewi!' And she hung her head.

'Great news for us,' he said. 'Great news, Mam.'

She smiled tears while filling the kettle.

'Sit,' ordered Edwin Fowkes. 'I'll brew some tea,' lunging off his sound leg to clutch Dewi's arm. 'All the best, boy. As you can see, your mother's proud of you.'

Then he drove to Parc Villa, bathed, changed into day clothes, drank another cup of tea with a slice of sponge cake, and slept until Greta came home from Gwalia Embroideries, the same archetypal collapse into resurgence of the collier-boy in Dinmel Terrace. Boy inseparable from man in his time, in his place.

Glossary

Glossary of words and phrases used in the text which are derived from the Welsh language.

Annibynnwr	Independent/Congregationalist
bach	lit. small, an endearment
bethingalw	whatchamacallit
bore da	good morning
dwl	daft
dwsh (from English 'dosh')	money
caca	excrement
cam	step
cariad	darling, lover
cawl	broth
clecs	gossip
crachach	upper classes, snobs
crots (from *croten*, girl)	young girls
crwtyn	boy
cwar	(lit. quarry) a lump of stone
cwat (from *cwato*)	to hide
cwlff	chunk
cwmp (from *cwymp*)	a fall
cwpla	to finish
cwtsh (from *cwts/cwtsio*)	n. recess ('snug' in a bar)
	v. hug. protect
	v. crouch
cwtch dan stâr	cupboard under the stairs
cythral (from *cythraul*)	devil
didoreth	slovenly
diolch	thanks
Duw	God
dwt (from *twt*, small)	little one
glo	coal
gwddog (from *gwddwg*)	throat
gwli	back lane
gwt (from *cwt*, tail)	the back (of the queue)
Gymanfa	hymn-singing festival
Hen Wlad (from *Mae Hen Wlad fy Nhadau*)	the Welsh National anthem
hiraeth	longing for home
hwyl	fervour, high spirits
Iesu Grist	Jesus Christ

204

lorch (from *llawr*, ground?)	to laze on the ground
mawr	big, great
merch	daughter, girl
milgi	greyhound
mum-glo	mothering coal
nos da	good night
rhonc	out-and-out
scraching (from *sgrechain*, to scream)	screaming
shiggling (from *siglo*, to shake)	shaking
shwmae (from *sut mae*)	a greeting, equivalent to 'hello'
sioni/sioni-hoy	a witless Johnnie
teisen lap	currant cake
trych (from *trachwantus*, greedy)	a mean, greedy man
twp	stupid
Iechyd da i gyd	'Good health to all'
manno manno shenko	the equivalent of 'six of one, half a dozen of the other'
pwcins (from English 'poking')	'Cutting pwcins' refers to a tramtrack risen due to geological pressure. Sleepers and rails are dismantled and have to be relaid.
Shwmae'n mynd? (from *Sut mae'n mynd?*)	'How's it going?'
Shwd i chi? (from *Sut ydych chi?*)	'How are you?'
Y Pencaer ew y gora (from *Pencaer yw y gorau*)	'Pencaer is the best.'
Yma 'thrawes	'Here, teacher.'
Ych y fi	expression of distaste